Boundary Road

Also by Ami Rao

Centaur (memoir co-written)
David and Ameena
Almost, a novella

Praise for *Centaur*

Winner of the *General Outstanding Sports Book of the Year Award 2018* and Shortlisted for the *William Hill Sports Book of the Year 2017*

'Emotional and honest, *Centaur* is an unflinching look at how Murphy "came back from the dead" and the heavy price extracted for doing so. *Centaur* is a book haunted by ghosts: lost careers, lost memories, lost friendships and, most devastatingly of all, lost love... Not only a certain candidate for the William Hill sports book of the year but also sure to be on many non-sports fans' end-of-year lists.'   *Observer*

'A magnificent piece of work: never less than enthralling... a thing of dramatic beauty.'   *Mail on Sunday*

'Deeply powerful, [told with] grace and poetry... an entirely gripping drama.'   *Sunday Express*

'Brilliant, bold, at times brutal.'   *Sunday Telegraph*

'Heart-rending... a page-turner.'   *The Times*

Boundary Road

Ami Rao

Published in the UK, 2023 by Everything with Words Limited
Fifth Floor, 30–31 Furnival Street, London, EC4A 1JQ

www.everythingwithwords.com

Text copyright © Ami Rao 2023
Cover © Holly Ovenden 2023

Ami Rao has asserted her right under the Copyright, Design and Patents Act
1988 to be identified as the author of this work.

A CIP catalogue record for this book is available from the British Library.

ISBN: 978-1-911427-35-3

Printed and bound in Great Britain by CPI Group (UK) Ltd, Croydon CRO 4YY

I long to go through the crowded streets of your mighty London, to be in the midst of the whirl and rush of humanity, to share its life, its change, its death, and all that makes it what it is.

Bram Stoker, *Dracula*

For Sid

ARON

ONE

He is walking on air!

Oh yeah! Aron thinks, looking down at the gigantic shoes accessorising his feet, bright orange mostly, some streaks of blue, a touch of lime green, the whole look completed by the shiny white swoosh. So snazzy. So swank. Nike Air. Shit. So appropriately named. Of course, the ones on his feet aren't *exactly* Nike, but that doesn't really matter all that much. He is the only one who knows. He and the Jamaican brother who sold them to him, mate's mate, who assured him they were so close to genuine, even Phil Knight wouldn't be able to tell them apart. Who's Phil Knight? Aron asked. The brother performed a double facepalm in a gesture of extreme incredulity. The runner bloke who founded the company yo, with his coach Bill whatshisname. Okay, Aron replied, cool. You got these sweet boys in an 11?

He'd bought them specially to interview for the new job, the first day of which he has only – minutes ago – successfully concluded, which is the whole reason he is walking on air.

Nearly 6pm and still light. Above him, the sky is bright blue, the pavement is almost white. Extraordinary the things the sun does, turn grey to white like that, like a kind of magic paintbrush.

Little miracles of nature do not go unnoticed by Aron; he's always been like this, attentive, interested, the kind of person who takes the time to smell the roses. Been like this since when he was a boy. Unchanged still, at twenty-three. Although there's no roses here this minute in the bang centre of central London, none that he can see, but man, there's other things of beauty. Oh yeah. Of course there is – it's August! It's an inspired month, August, he's always thought, an inspired month that on a yearly basis reliably brings about some truly inspired behaviour. Take London for example. *London*, usually so cheerless and self-serious becomes in August a seaside town, sky like sea, pavement like sand, people walking around the streets like it could be a beach, clad in tiny pieces of cloth that conceal nothing at all, like swimwear, really. What could be better than that? The spectators are happy, the naked people are happy, everybody is happy – actually! – everyone smiling and greeting strangers with nods and waves and whatnots. What one would call a win-win proposition. It's good. Good! He is walking on air!

The job – just concluded – is at a suit shop. Or, as he has been instructed to refer to his place of work only that same morning, a 'bespoke tailoring house for gentlemen'. A miracle the whole thing. How it had all transpired, that is. Interviewed four days ago. Referred to by a mate's sister's friend's boyfriend who had worked his way up from nothing to the esteemed position of Head Cutter. Five years ago, the brother had wished upon a star and applied under the apprenticeship program. Five years later, there he was, Head Cutter. Faith – in the system, the stars, life – thus formed and cemented by his own incredible personal success, he had recommended (via his girlfriend's friend's brother) that Aron do the same. And so, Aron – always open to possibility – had done exactly that. Filled out an online form that enquired after his qualifications and previous relevant work experience and all that kind of thing. Done it and forgotten about it. Didn't think it would amount to anything given that he had none of anything they were asking for. No qualifications as such and no previous relevant work experience either, lots of previous work experience, but the requirement for these being 'relevant' had tripped him up. He had gone through a brief period of indecision in which he wondered if he should put everything down or nothing at all, both options being somewhat of a risk to the whole proposition. On a whim, he put everything down and pressed the button to send and then seconds later, after the thing had vanished into cyberspace, he realised he had made a big mistake owing to the irrelevance of his answer, but by then it had been sent and it was too late to fix. He felt bad about it for a while. And then in order to stop feeling bad about it, he made himself forget about it. He was good at doing that – making himself forget what was better forgotten – a talent he'd discovered when he was little and nurtured ever since. Then when he least expected it, he heard from his mate (via his mate's sister's friend) that they wanted to meet him. Amazed, he'd gone, shown up bright and early and exactly on time to the store on Victoria Street, just by Victoria station. Fixed his hair, flossed his teeth, dressed smartly in jeans and a clean shirt and his new Nike shoes and shown up, just exactly like they asked. In the store, they looked him up and down. And then down and up. They, meaning two white guys wearing suits. No sign of the superstar Head Cutter. Maybe he was away cutting, wherever they did the cutting. So, only him and the two white blokes. After the staring thing, they shook his hand, one at a time. Then one white guy – the dark, bearded one with shifty eyes – disappeared into the back room to answer the phone that started to ring. The other white guy, very tall and very tanned with a shock of brown curls, made him change into a suit. Just handed him one – steel grey with light-blue pinstripes – and directed him to the changing room. When, after getting into the suit, Aron looked at himself in the mirror, he couldn't believe his own reflection. Seems they couldn't believe it either. The shifty bloke was out again. The tanned one dropped his jaw. Both looked him up and down and down and up a second time. Wide open eyes. Asked him nothing. Made him the offer right then and there.

To say he had been surprised would be an understatement. His mate had warned him about all these questions they would ask when they met him. Such as? Aron wanted to know. Questions to catch you out man, to give them a *reason* not to give you the job. But why, enquired Aron, would they want to meet me if they wanted *not* to give me the job? Dunno, said the friend, it's the way it is innit, with white people. Okay, replied Aron, but what *kind* of questions? Not sure, the friend replied. Alls I know is that they gonna quiz you, but if you asking me what the *topic* of the quiz gonna be, I ain't got no clue, that's white person shit man, how am I supposed to know? But they gonna quiz you, that much I know. So, Aron had gone prepared to be quizzed.

Well, guess what, no quiz. Instead, he had been made to dress all fancy, his hand shaken vigorously by two white guys who asked him to come back in four days. For what, Aron asked, come back in four days for what? The tall white guy seemed genuinely baffled by the question. To start the job? If you don't have any other competing offers, that is? Then, looking at Aron expectantly, a shadow of concern passing over his face, darkening that already insane tan. Now, *that* had given Aron the jokes. Competing offers! Nah, nah, he said, laughing and shaking his head. This offer beats all my other offers, man – ain't no competition, really. The tall one looked mighty pleased by that and nodded and grinned a good many times. Aron turned to leave then, totally forgetting that he

6

was wearing something that didn't belong to him and probably cost more money all his other clothes put together, but then the other white guy with the beard reminded him, not saying anything, just clearing his throat politely and looking pointedly at where Aron's own shirt and jeans lay draped over a chair. Ah sorry, Aron said, laughing and fingering the lapel, forgot about these threads, didn't I? The tall white guy laughed as well, not a problem, not a problem, he said, clapping Aron jovially on the back, you can have it again when you come back Monday. For you to wear on the job, I mean. Actually, maybe after the first week or so, after you get acclimatised, we'll loan you a few. Plus, shirts and ties.

Sweet, Aron said grinning as he re-entered the changing room. Nice changing room. Not big exactly but not tight. Plenty of space to move around. Heavy curtains. Velvet or something. Old-fashioned mirror with side panels. Having bagged a job he had no expectations of procuring the last time he was in here, and being therefore in a more relaxed frame of mind, he took a good while to check himself out. Front view and side view and back view too. Mirrors don't lie. Shit, he looked sharp.

We think, the shifty one said when Aron re-emerged, that you're going to do a great job. Actually, we don't think – we *know*!

Aron sighed internally. But *do* you know? he thought.

The thing was, in Aron's experience, people *didn't* know. No, they didn't quite know what to make of him when they saw him. That was the crux of it. His story was History. Going back to before he was even born. Before, before, before all that…

All the way back to his mum and dad. Carol and Joe. Love at first sight. Married immediately. Married precisely nine months before the first kid came. That was Jordan. C'mon came at the end. Him in the middle. Except not that straightforward, this story, not a simple plot line at all although it started normally and ended normally, and that could fool a simple mind into believing the whole thing was normal. But nah. Neither minds nor families are ever that simple. In the middle, somewhere between Jordan and C'mon, Carol one day upped and left. Came back home, by and by, after a brief separation. But that was when it happened, *during* the brief separation. A certain mysterious event Aron doesn't fully understand, and no one wants to talk about, a strategy that seems to work out okay for the others, but not really for him, because the result of the mysterious event was him.

Is him.

The outward manifestation of said mysterious event is that while Aron has skin just like his siblings, same shade of dark, same kind of smooth, his eyes are a very startling blue, which unusual combination is the reason that people don't quite know what to make of him when they see him. Aron understood this about himself very early on in his life when he was not more than five or six years old, understood that there was something unusual about the way he looked, and understood also the practical lesson that came out of it. Or two practical lessons, really. One: the whole 'don't judge a book by its cover' was some kind of crazy bullshit, 'cause *everyone* judged *everything* by their covers. And two: if you happened to look like something people do not straightaway expect, it could go one of two ways – either they found you extremely beautiful or they found you extremely frightening.

In the suit shop, they had quite clearly been taken by his beauty. Meaning, it had gone the first way.

It's very simple, the shifty-eyed white guy explained with a very serious facial expression just as Aron was leaving, the nature of your job. You just need to watch the door. That's it. He pointed two fingers at his own eyes, then at the door, then back at his eyes. Watch.

The. Door. Got that? Amazing! So that would be the first part of your job. The second part is this: as soon as someone comes in, you go up to them, not too close, not too far, just the right distance, and you greet them. Good morning, you say, or good afternoon or good evening, depending on whether it's morning, afternoon or evening. As charming as you can. Nice, big smile. Shoulders relaxed. Legs slightly apart, not too much. Then you ask them how you can help them. How can I help you, you say, just like that. Then you hear them out, smiling and nodding the whole time, and when they're done talking – doesn't matter what they say really – you tell them you're going to fetch just the person to help them. Then you call one of us, Richard or myself. I'm Richard too, by the way, Richard or Richard, couldn't get easier! And that's it, really. That's part two. You still with me?

That had been four days ago. This Monday gone. Now, having just successfully completed Day 1 of the job – he had watched the door like a hawk from 9am to 5:30pm; no one had come in, a bit anticlimactic the whole thing, but still – Aron is walking on air!

He walks down Buckingham Palace Road to the Victoria station bus stop, gliding, like he owns the road. It's a bit of an act to be honest, a mini show of bravado. Truth is he's unfamiliar with this part of London and it strikes him in that moment how different it is from his ends, almost like a different country. People walk different here, and talk different, *look* different. (Read: *No one knows him here; no one knows his name.*)

He walks past a café. August's inspiration on display! For the café too has expanded in the heat, its capacity easily doubled by the addition of tables and chairs outside that are arranged in a Parisian style, chairs lined up close together, facing the street under a huge green awning that says Café le Monde. A blackboard on the sidewalk advertises the plat du jour, Sole Meuniere, priced at £34.

Jesus. That must be some special sole he thinks. With a special soul. To be worth thirty-four-bleeding-quid. He knows something about food himself. Used to be a chef once. Well, not *exactly* a chef, but close enough. Thirty-four quid. *Man.*

On a table that's placed so far out on the pavement it's almost sitting on the road, a striking blonde in a white summer dress and bright red lipstick is smoking a cigarette. In her other hand she holds a champagne flute. Her head is thrown back, she is laughing. Next to her is a handsome, well-dressed man wearing the expression of someone who has said something that has caused the woman to laugh. Another couple is with them on the adjoining table that's touching theirs. They are also beautiful, also laughing.

The blonde notices Aron as he approaches; she stares. He has become somewhat of an expert on the anatomy of a stare. He knows the stares of admiration from the ones of unease. This one is the first kind. She is staring unabashedly. Big, round hazel eyes. But why wouldn't she stare, after all he is walking on air! So, he grins. She casts her eyes down slightly, purses her lips, smiles coyly. The man on her left says something, then his hand is on her arm, and she is distracted by it. She looks up again searchingly, eyes wide open, lips slightly apart, but by then he's chipped.

It's busier now, rush hour proper, the traffic is a continuous stream of moving lights, red one side, white another. Going to take him a while to get home, he thinks. Took him an hour in the morning, but it hadn't been this busy. Now, it would be more like ninety minutes. To be fair, he is as far from home as it gets, needs to traipse literally all the way across town, ride the bus nearly to the end of the route. It had been his one reservation with this job, but the money was good and the job itself entailed watching the door and reminding people of the time of day. I mean, how could he possibly turn down being paid that kind of serious dosh to do something his five-year-old nephew could do? Plus, he gets to look all posh in those posh clothes and all for nothing. Plus – very important – he's been needing to get himself properly out of the shit he foolishly got himself into not long ago, some bad shit with some bad people he now wishes he had stayed well away from. Only a conventional nine-to-five job would reliably extricate him from that 'situation'. This Aron believes to be true. Normal is as normal does, as they say. He had to take the job, of course he did. Pros and cons. At the end of the day, everything, all life's choices, Aron feels, are about weighing up those pros and cons. If one is smart, that is. He had been a fool. No more! Ninety minutes is a trek though. He hasn't eaten since lunchtime. The tall Richard had watched the door while he sprinted across the street to get a sandwich which he then ate while returning to his post and resuming watching the door. He's still laughing about how both those guys are called Richard. White folks, he thinks, have such little imagination sometimes. Anyway, that was six hours ago. Long time to go without a little extra sustenance. There are coins in his front pocket, leftover change, he can feel their weight. He pops into a corner shop on a whim, whips out the change, buys a Coke and a bag of crisps. Salt and vinegar. Finishes both before he reaches the next street, bins the empties diligently into the separate compartments of the recycling bin.

He has no reason to realise that he's left his wallet in the store. Why would he? Both it and its contents are forgettable. Polyurethane, worth ten quid on the internet. Inside it, a fiver spent on lunch, an expired driver's license flashing the only photograph of Aron in existence in which he isn't smiling, an ATM card connected to an account in overdraft. The wallet is still in the jacket pocket of his borrowed suit, forgotten in the heat of the moment, the fake leather resting against the genuine silk lining.

Looming ahead in front of him is the vast canopy of Victoria bus station. A crush of red London buses parked one behind the other along three parallel rows of bus stops. He starts at one end and begins to walk down the line. He stops when he sees the sign for the number 13. The bus is already there, waiting.

TWO

The benefit, Aron thinks, of getting on at Victoria is that, with a bit of luck, you could walk on to an empty bus. Meaning, more relevantly, you could get to have your pick of seats. Which was important to Aron. He liked having his pick of seats. Some people are not choosy about such things, some people care only about the destination, getting from A to B; the question of *how* you get there – the journey, so to speak – is of no consequence to them. Not Aron, nah. Aron cared. To Aron, the journey was important. The journey mattered. In fact, it almost mattered more than the destination. The *destination* in his mind was a moving target, for that too – to have a constantly moving destination – was the whole point of this life, wasn't it? To keep on moving. Moving, moving. As long as it was in the right direction of course. No point moving backwards – like certain other members of his family – the idea was to move forwards, but to move was the important thing. Keeping on moving. Enjoying the ride.

Aron walks into the empty bus with a wide grin that showed, if you were curious about these sorts of things, some fairly impressive metalwork – two gold and one silver – football related, all three knocked teeth. He is grinning because he is happy, and he is happy because the bus is empty. In fact, the bus is so empty that even the driver is nowhere to be seen. Tea break, Aron thinks. Or pee break. He laughs out loud then, slapping his thigh and laughing raucously, his own humour striking him as very funny. But after the funniness of the situation has dissipated, gravity resumes. For now, the immediate question confronting Aron poses for him somewhat of a moral dilemma. Not new this one. He's faced it before many times, not only in the same situation (public transport), but in other comparable situations too (bar, restaurant, crowded shop, supermarket). Summed up nicely by that proverbial wisdom about cats and mice. Whip out the bank card and lose £1.50 or turn a blind eye and up the stairs he goes? Yup, same conundrum every time, only presenting itself differently. A continuous renewal of an ancient dilemma.

But the dilemma is an even deeper one for Aron – and equally ancient – because he knows from time, from experience, that even if he paid, even if he heeded the calls of his conscience and did the right thing, the driver, when he eventually showed up after his tea break or his pee break or both, would conclude the opposite. Yeah, that's what always happened. Ten times out of ten. Aron knows the routine like the back of his hand. First the driver would walk up and down the whole bus to find him, no matter how long it took, even if it delayed the entire bus schedule, who cares, wink, shrug, someone else's problem. From there would commence the usual drama, in the usual order. Peering at him as if he had six eyes or ears growing from the top of his head or something, then asking him if he'd paid, then asking him if he was sure, not believing him either the first time or the second, because of course he had already made up his mind about that just by *looking* at Aron on the camera.

For a second Aron is stuck. Literally stuck at the door, not knowing what to do, paralysed in his current precarious position of taut moral ambiguity.

Then just as quickly, he unsticks himself. Fuck it, Aron thinks, angry suddenly at himself for his own indecision. Why should *he* be respecting the system if the system weren't bothered to be respecting *him*? £1.50 was £1.50. £1.50 was a coffee at the shop down the road from the estate, weren't it? Where that nice girl from Bucharest (or Budapest, he always got those two cities mixed up) worked so hard every day keeping the shop open twenty-four hours for other people's convenience. In his mind, he visualises her face; narrow, pale, ridden with the most persistent kind of acne. He visualises the driver who he still hasn't seen but whose face is not hard for Aron to imagine. Who should his money go to? She or he? Put this way, the answer is easy. Nice girl. More deserving. Speaks in a peculiar accent, can't follow a single word she says, if he's being honest. But who cares about all this, Queen's English and all this, not like she was about to go serving the Queen now, innit? The coffee was not bad, that was the important thing. Hot and strong, not bitter and nasty, like in those big shops where it cost someone three times as much for a cup the same size. How they managed to get away with that, Aron doesn't know. He's thought about it deeply many times. Hasn't come up with any decent answers, except that there must be loads of gullible people in the world to be duped like that, just 'cause someplace has some fancy sofas and table lamps with dim lighting and shit. Like they're selling atmosphere instead of coffee and all these people buying it too! Not him, tho. Not swayed by marketing. He is smarter than that. And with that final confirmatory thought, the last flicker of doubt dissipates into the evening air.

Decision thus made, Aron bypasses the machine, grabs the metal railing, swings himself nimbly up the first five steps and runs up the rest, two at a time. Once on the deserted upper deck, he makes his way right to the front and sits on the window seat on the left side which to him is the best seat in the house.

Front view. Side view. Stair view. Score.

THREE

Five minutes later, and he's fully in character, doing what he does best, standing on an imaginary stage, performing in front of an imaginary audience. Except this time, it's real! The stage is the northbound number 13, and his only audience is the large, smiling, round-faced woman on the seat next to him. But for Aron, that will do.

But it ain't about what you do *now*, he is saying, I'm talking about, you have to ask yourself where that can take you, what it means for your life, your goals, what you want from this life, from your own future, it's all about all that, innit? The big picture, you can say.

The woman next to him is American. From Texas, she said, when he asked amiably where she was from. He had guessed she was a tourist straight up. Outfit gave it away. Baggy jeans, plain black trainers, white T-shirt that said 'Hakuna Matata' in maroon print that stretched across her ample chest area. No one dressed like that in London. Or at least, he thought, allowing for a bit of generosity towards the American lady, not in August. Got on the bus at Victoria too, just minutes after him, old-fashioned camera slung round her neck. Who doesn't take pictures on their phone

17

these days? Aron wondered curiously. Who traipses about town lugging big heavy cameras around their necks? Woooof, she said as she sat down, woooof, wiping her brow with the back of her hand, it's hot. I didn't think London got so hot, it's almost as hot as home here. Of course, that was the point in the conversation where Aron felt obliged to ask where 'home' was. Texas, she said. Which he knew was down somewhere at the bottom of America. Ain't that down somewhere at the bottom of America? he asked. She seemed to find that very funny. Yes, she said, yes, right at the very bottom. Bordering Mexico. In fact, our one state shares a border with four Mexican states, that's how big we are. Texas on the United States side, and on the Mexican side, you've got Chihuahua, Coahuila, Nuevo León and Tamaulipas.

Sounds like names of dogs, Aron noted.

This remark too, struck the woman as very funny. Her head rolled back and then flung itself forward, the camera hitting her chest with a thump that made Aron wonder how it didn't hurt but clearly it didn't because she was at it a long while, just smacking her big thighs and laughing extremely loudly.

You are very funny, she said finally, wiping the tears from her small brown eyes. I had heard about the famous British humour, they told me all about it before I came here. They weren't wrong, oh no, they weren't wrong at all! You are funny, very funny.

They did? Aron said, bemused by this new knowledge. Our funniness is famous in Texas?

Oh yeah, the woman said. The British are known for their humour.

Hunh! remarked Aron, hunh! Now who would have thought that! Thought we was known for the Queen and winning the war and things.

Oh yeah, the woman said exuberantly. Yeah, that too. Winston Churchill and the Queen! In fact, I've spent the entire day walking around the whole of Buckingham Palace. I watched the changing of the guard this morning. Boy, was it *awesome*! Like woah! I mean the way they are so coordinated and that red uniform and those huge furry hats like it's a real live animal crouching on their heads and so serious their faces, absolutely no expression at all, even though people were trying to make them laugh you know, like deliberately clowning around and stuff, but no, nothing, not even a teeny-weeny smile. Talk about a poker face! I mean, *just* the most awesome thing I've ever seen!

I never seen that, Aron confessed. Born and bred in London and ain't never seen this thing, this guard-changing business.

She turned towards him in a sudden motion and clutched his skinny forearm with both her hands. Noooooo she said, her narrow cat-like eyes as wide as they could possibly grow.

Serious, Aron replied, unfazed by the clutching and the surprise and all of it – Aron wasn't easily fazed, no, it took a lot to faze him. Ain't never been nowhere near the Palace really, if I'm being honest with you.

But you *should*! the lady gushed, still holding on to his arm. The Palace is awesome! Seriously, I'm not kidding you, it's like totally awesome! She sighed loudly. I guess I'm just a sucker for tradition. And you've got so much of it. England obviously, I mean, not *you* personally. And the Palace kind of symbolises all that stuff, you know. Tradition and ceremony and history. It all comes together in that one building. That's why it's so awesome. It's not just the structure, it's like what it *stands* for, you know what I mean? She nodded. Yup, I must have taken like five hundred pictures of it, all from different angles and in different light and stuff. That's why I've been there all day. I wanted to capture it first thing in the morning, then in the afternoon and then now, at sunset. I wanted to stay longer, and capture it at night, but I'm meeting a friend for dinner...

Finally, she let go of his arm and opened out her hands in a gesture that he interpreted as denoting her lack of choice in the matter.

... so gotta head back to the hotel and shower and get changed out of these awful, sweaty clothes into something nice. A dress or something. I hope I packed something appropriate; I can't even remember anymore. I didn't expect London to be so hot. He lives here. My friend I mean, the one I'm meeting for dinner. He's a tennis journalist. I met him at the US Open last year, in the line for food actually, it was so long you won't believe it... they're always so *slow* at these events and things. Anyway, he was in front of me, and we got talking and well you know how it goes. She winked. At least something good came out of all that waiting. Well, he's taking me to some fish and chips place he said, but I can't for the life of me remember the name right now, I wrote it down somewhere, but he said it was very famous, had to book like a whole month in advance. But the Palace! What a place! So royal! And enormous! Amazing how the Queen doesn't get lost in there 'cause she's really only a little old lady, isn't she? How old is she now? Ninety-two?

Aron shrugged. Something like that, he said noncommittally.

And the King, he's ninety-nine, isn't he? *Ninety-nine!* she repeated, shaking her head in disbelief at the fact she had just uttered.

Now it was Aron's turn to find humour in random utterances. Nah, nah, he laughed, he ain't the *King*! Queen's husband ain't called King. It's a respect thing, you know, for the Queen, respecting her and women and girls and... all the ladies, and everyone, basically, who is not a man. Feminism! he said triumphant at having found the suitable word finally. Nah, good old Philip is a Duke. Duke of E-din-bu-ruh to be 'zact.

The woman clapped her hands together gleefully like a child. Oh right, of course he is! The Dook! I knew that! The Queen and the Dook! Then her expression grew suddenly serious. But I understand, she said nodding. I understand the significance of what you're saying. It's the same reason we call The First Lady, The First Lady, not Mrs President. Although, she said, cocking her head slightly, now that I think about it, it's not exactly the same thing, is it?

Nah, agreed Aron. Is the opposite.

Gosh, the woman remarked. I wonder *what* we'd call the President's husband if the President was a woman. Though that's never like actually happened in the history of the United States, but if it ever happened, I mean. She nodded her head vigorously. Your comments have been very thought-provoking, I never thought about it this way. I mean, your monarchy is obviously very progressive. So many Queens. How many Queens vs. Kings?

Aron shrugged heavily. Aw, that's a very technical question now, innit? I ain't no expert on the monarchy, as *such*. But progressive, definitely, possibly, yeah. I mean, it couldn't have *survived* this long, you know, without being, as you say, *progressive*. Life, I feel, is all about progressiveness. Forward progressiveness especially. That is the secret, innit. Aron brought his one fist to his other palm. Bam! Without progressiveness, ain't no point in nothing, yeah? I mean if you don't *progress*, you ain't got nowhere to go, if you think about it. So, in those respects, our monarchy is good, man, it's good. I read somewhere on a poster or something that there is only forty-four of them monarchies left in the world.

Is that right?

Yeah, it's what I read, innit.

The woman nodded thoughtfully. How interesting, she said. Well, this has certainly been a very interesting conversation. Very educational. Are you a teacher by any chance?

Hahaha, Hohoho, Aron laughed, sliding off the seat, as if the very idea of that was so funny, it could not be contained on the chair. Me? A teacher? Hahaha, Hohoho. The very edge of his backside was balanced on the very edge of the seat, the rest of him lay somewhere between the seat and the floor. Me! A teacher! Just imagine that! Nah, nah. I ain't no *ejucated* brother. Ain't got no degree or nothing. Barely finished school myself, to be honest with you. Wanted to be a footballer. I was good weren't I! Got myself into an academy. Category one, too. Man, those were the days. I was only sixteen, believe! Sixteen and flying. Then I go and get injured. Tore my ligament, didn't I. Part that connects your thigh to your shin. That was it. Messed with my head. Couldn't play no more. Academy dropped me. But even before that, even back at school, the teachers and them, I think they were all a bit… unsure of me, you know, like they didn't know what to do with me 'zackly. Headmistress too. White lady like yourself. Could barely look me in the eye. Could never figure out why. Like she afraid of me or something. Start stuttering every time she sees me and shit. Just the look of me, innit, didn't have to do nothing or say nothing to provoke her. He pushed off the ground with his feet and slid his frame firmly back into the seat. But nah. I work in a bespoke tailoring house for gentlemen. Suits and things.

Oh, the woman remarked, raising her eyebrows, like Savile Row?

Eesh, Aron said, now you really making me feel bad. How you know so much about us! I don't know nothing about Texas really. Except the stuff you just tell me. About the Chihuahua and that. But yeah, yeah, exactly like Savile Row, only the shop's in Victoria, innit.

I knew it! the woman said, smacking her thigh. I *knew* you were either a teacher or in fashion. You're looking at me like how would *she* know, but easy! Trust me! Just from the way you're dressed! I mean, like look at your shoes! They're so cute! So, what do you do at the suit shop?

You like my creps? Aron said, smiling enormously. Aww, thanks, that's nice of you to say now, innit. Brand new too, just got 'em the other day, didn't I? But, about the bespoke tailoring house for gentlemen… you was saying…?

Oh, I was wondering what you did for the suit shop. If you were like a designer or something?

Aron nodded thoughtfully. Yeah. Kinda. Kind of a designer, you could say. Yeah. But it ain't about what you do *now*, he starts to say, I'm talking about, you have to ask yourself…

He sees her then. On the street standing at the bus stop. He sees her even before the bus slows down to stop. He sees her out of the corner of his eye, even while he's in mid-conversation. She's craning her neck with an anxious look on her face. He doesn't understand why people do that. They do that with the tube too, as if the thing were to appear if it knew you were looking for it.

She's not particularly special to look at or anything; just a white girl, young, in her twenties maybe, blonde hair tied in a knot, nice long neck, a bit pale though, face too, very pale, dark brown eyes. Unremarkable, really. She's dressed like a maid. It is this peculiarity that makes him notice her, even before the bus has stopped. He cannot explain it, but he cannot help himself, the outfit opens up a certain curiosity in him. His eyes follow her into the bus and when she's on top of the stairs, he's already looking.

She sees him looking, they lock eyes, but he doesn't feel the need to look away. She's looking at him too, he can see that, but there's no mutual acknowledgement, no nod, no smile. At the next red light she steadies herself, holds on to the railing and makes her way to a free seat next to an old man with no hair. She's wearing black court shoes on her stockinged feet. She has nice legs, he thinks, slim and shapely, nice ass too, for a white girl.

Maybe she *is* a maid, he thinks, at one of them fancy hotels that stretch along Park Lane, the Hilton or the Dorchester. Sufficiently convinced thus by his own explanation for the girl's peculiar choice of outfit, he turns back to the woman on his right.

… I'm talking about, you have to ask yourself where that can take you, what it means for your life, your goals, what you want from this life, from your own future, it's all about all that, innit? The big picture, you can say.

FOUR

There are people sitting on the ground at Marble Arch. Not exactly sitting. More like squatting. It's a veritable campsite really, the small grassy patches littered with blankets, mattresses, cardboard boxes, tents, bin bags, suitcases. Whole makeshift houses set up in that iconic central London location. The people are migrants. It's been on the news, Aron saw it himself on the telly the other day, all about how the store owners on Oxford Street were complaining about these people encroaching on their businesses, their mere presence enough to drive potential customers away. Eastern European, they said on the news, from Bulgaria and Romania, some have travelled more than two thousand kilometres. Amazing, Aron thought upon hearing this – all that way over land and sea just to come to Marble Arch and sit on the ground. With nothing, the reporter continued, they come with nothing, no home, no job, no people, not a word of English.

It's impossible to ignore the sight even from the window of the bus as it makes the wide turn on the roundabout connecting SW1 to W1. Man, Aron thinks looking out, there's so many of them. He had felt sorry even watching the situation on the telly. Now seeing them like this in real life makes him feel even worse. Not like he lives anywhere fancy himself, only a tiny council flat with a roof that just does not seem to want to stop leaking, but mouldy or not, at least he has a roof, four walls, a proper bed to sleep on. But these people.

Just watching them makes him go all philosophical. A bit like his brother Jordan. Who has been philosophical from the age of ten. Why am I here? he asked their mother once while she was chopping onions in the kitchen, what am I here to do? Carol rubbed her eyes where the onions were making her cry and said, hmm… I don't know baby, to help your mama fix lunch, maybe? Peel the potatoes for this brown stew chicken? No Mama! Jordan said impatiently, pushing his glasses all the way up his nose, that's not what I mean at all. I mean, why am I *here*, on this earth. Why'd God put me here? Carol stopped chopping, looked at her son in amazement and said, Jordan baby, you here for one reason only, you here to be loved, and don't you forget that. You here on this earth just to be loved. Aron, aged seven, sitting on the floor playing with his toy car – broken and repaired so many times it was virtually sheathed in Sellotape – had been struck by that conversation. It had made him want to laugh and cry all at the same time. Much later he would learn that beautiful things tended to do that to a person, to make them want to laugh and cry all at once. It was the power of beautiful things.

He himself wasn't much of a deep-thinking person as such, not like Jordan, but sometimes things he saw or heard or read about made him a bit like that. Played around in his head. Like watching these people right now. There's whole, entire families here, he can see them, tiny little kids all huddled together on that small patch of grass. How hard, Aron thinks, must their lives have been in Bulgaria and Romania if sleeping on a cardboard box in Marble Arch was, for them, progress. It strikes him then that none of us really knows how truly bad things are until we have the misfortune of experiencing them. It's only then that we realise that what might have seemed insufferable to us at one time is in fact not so terrible after all. The only good part, Aron believes, is that most of us go through life without the terrible thing ever happening, but the bad part, therefore, is that we are naturally predisposed to view even the smallest setback as some sort of catastrophe.

Wonder what happens to them eventually, Aron thinks, as the bus rounds the corner onto Oxford Street, do they get sent back home or do they get to stay, get some assistance to try and make a new life? His father got here from someplace else too, across a different ocean, and not as dangerous, not risking life and limb, like what these people had to face, but still. He made a life for himself, didn't he, his old man? Not without complications, but in the end, he was alright. That these people come with nothing, he muses, ain't exactly true. They come with hope, surely. They must come with hope, or they wouldn't be here. Hopefully then, he thinks, it is all worth it for them in the end. *They* must believe that, at the very least. For what, after all, is life without hope, without optimism?

He too has only recently discovered this in a deeply personal way. Just in the last week, he has found himself filled with new optimism, this sense that his life so far has been a sort of dress rehearsal, a prelude for his real life, which hasn't yet begun.

Maybe, he thinks, it has to do with this new job, something proper finally, something relatable, something he could tell people about and they would understand. Unlike the other jobs, which had needed, on his part, a great deal of explanation just in conveying the nature of his involvement. Which to be fair may have been, in many cases, unusual, but not – surely – to the extent to which he had needed to explain things before people stopped staring at him with blank faces.

27

His first ever job, for example, had entailed being an unpacker, unpacking boxes for people who moved house. That had required a lot of explaining because people immediately assumed he worked for a moving company in the capacity of a professional packer. Nah, he would tell them, shaking his head vigorously to make extra clear not to overstate his capabilities, for that in Aron's mind, was deceitful – lying about you could do this and that, when you could really only do this but not that. So, he made sure he always told the truth when people asked. Nah man, he would explain, I'm just involved in the unpacking bit, innit, not the packing, that bit ain't really my *expertise*...

The truth was Aron had no interest in packing, this business of just putting things into boxes. Nothing mentally or emotionally stimulating about that. But *unpacking* – taking things *out* of the boxes, transporting them to their new places in their new homes – that part he liked, found unusually satisfying. Like he was fulfilling a kind of destiny on behalf of the concerned objects. So yes, definitely, he had enjoyed that aspect of the job. He also liked the part that came after, collapsing the cardboard boxes, flattening them out, selling them, mostly to the liquor store on Kilburn High Road, that part of the job he'd liked too. Although that was for a different reason entirely. That was less spiritual and more practical. In the sense that all that cardboard fetched him between £0.50 and £1 per box. Given that an average move for a three-bedroom house used up something like 25–30 medium boxes, 15–25 large boxes and 10–12 extra-large boxes, it all added up to a tidy sum. Aron had found from his experience that there were always far too many boxes for the items they contained. This, he concluded, was because people were, for the most part, inefficient packers. How often had he come across a massive box that carried a single glass vase the size of his hand? Enveloped of course in layers and layers of bubble wrap to fill up the space. Anyway, it weren't his place to point this out – what people did, people did. Plus, it benefitted him, truth be told. More boxes, less unpacking. *And.* More boxes, more money. So not just win-win but win-win-win. The people who moved didn't want the money for the boxes; no, they just wanted the boxes out. In fact, whenever he offered to take the empty boxes away, they would look at him with expressions of pure childlike delight like he was doing them some kind of enormous favour or something. If he'd been smarter, he realised later, he'd have charged them extra to get the boxes out, but he hadn't had those business instincts at that time, he'd only been young. Still, he got to keep the money from the boxes, plus what people paid him for the unpacking. Meaning, for his time. That too had been an epiphany, this realisation that time had value. Before this job, he had thought of time as something that happened, like clock hands moving or seasons changing or birthdays and such, not something that had a price, something you could charge money for. Good money too. So, that was all fine, but for Aron it wasn't just about that. He had needed something else, something more; whatever it was, he hadn't found it, there'd been that something missing. In any case, unpacking wasn't exactly a permanent job if you thought about it from a long-term perspective; hardly what one could call a *career* as such.

The thing that had done it for him in the end, though, was the people. Money is money, but there's limits to money, he realised: how much it can buy, how much of yourself and your morals you're willing to give up for it. That's where the people came in. The *people* in this line of work, he discovered, showed a side of themselves one never usually saw. For example, he'd broken this thing once – once in the *whole* three months he'd been in the unpacking business – in a house in W1, some kind of statue of a naked woman carrying a bird on top of her head, and the client, the owner of the thing

– who had been so nice and smiley before, that was the shocking thing – had gotten all nasty on him, sent him packing immediately, didn't even pay nothing for his time. He'd apologised too, he had genuinely been sorry, that was the truth, but it's like she weren't even listening, just yelling and asking him to get out. Such an ugly side to her, he would have never even seen it if not for the naked woman breaking in half. It had hit him hard, this transformation in her personality, how it could change so abruptly like that, how there were sides to people that remained dormant, like sleeping giants, until circumstances roused them. And then, well. It all came out in the open, didn't it?

Another similar thing had happened another time in SW10 when something had gone missing and he was never told what it was, but the lady of the house – French, she was – made it out to be his fault, just barely stopping short of accusing him of stealing it. Imagine! When she wouldn't even afford him the courtesy of telling him what 'it' was. Put him properly in his place didn't she, first offering him a coffee and some tiny French-sounding cake-thing, then literally kicking him out of her house without even saying why. To Aron, it had come as a shock and a disappointment, as stark and categorical a realisation as any that he was a mere factotum for these people, and that too, in the most mundane moments of their lives. So, there was that.

Then there was the matter of the things themselves, the possessions, and what they *revealed* about the people. Like you would not believe the stories he could tell you about the stuff he had unpacked over those three months. People, he discovered, had all *kinds* of strange things they carried round with them. One time he'd unpacked a whole box of sex toys: dolls and dicks and blindfolds and nipple chains and whatnot kinky shit for a couple in Earl's Court. Rich folk too. Smart folk. Worked in Canary Wharf,

30

dressed in suits and high heels and shit. Highfalutin'. That had shook him up real good. Just the weirdness of it.

After the unpacking job, he'd had a great many other jobs. Grocery delivery, barber's assistant, running instructor (different from personal trainer – that one had required some lengthy explanations), short-order cook, lawn mower... Now this one too had needed explanations. Are you a gardener? people had asked him. That Aron had found very funny. He had never lived anywhere in his whole life that had a garden, he didn't know anyone who did; come to think of it, he didn't know anyone who owned as much as a flower, except some old ladies on the estate who kept a few potted plants on the balcony and tended to them daily, watering them and feeding them and conversing with them with all the love and care he would expect them to give their grandchildren or something. Anyway, the point was, he knew nothing about plants and flowers and things. Lawn mower, he replied firmly when they asked. *Not* gardening. *Just* lawn mowing. But, his own father had said, squinting at him with his small grey eyes upon being informed of this line of work, why would folks pay you 'stead of a real gardener? 'Cause I'm cheaper, innit, he had replied as if it was the most obvious thing in the world. But, don't you see, Joe had persisted, why they'd be paying you *separate* from the other fella, who'd do it all anyway? In the end, of course, Joe had been right – and this was the part Aron hated the most, his father being right when they disagreed. But how was *he* to know that rich folk were so stupid sometimes that when he *said* he was a lawn mower they *still* chose to believe that he possessed some special ability to arrange petunias in little concentric circles? When they realised, eventually, that all that arranging and beautification business was not part of his repertoire – out the side gate he went, as quickly as he had come in. Still. That had been a good life lesson. The habits of white folk had always held a particular interest for Aron. Especially if they were rich. That combination, he had realised, was a thing unto itself, capable of eliciting the most astonishing kind of strange behaviour. He couldn't for the life of him get his head around it.

So, there'd been that. There'd been some other stuff after that. None had lasted very long. Mostly because, if he was being honest with himself, none had delivered the satisfaction – that inner contentment – he felt was vital if one was to dedicate oneself to something for the long haul.

The only time he had felt he was truly onto something, meaning something *worthwhile*, had been a year ago. The job... well not really a job, more a business idea, an *entrepreneurial venture* you could say... had entailed inventing waterproof wallets for swim shorts. The idea had come when he'd gone with his mate Trevor to the seaside in Brighton. They hadn't been able to find parking for Trevor's car anywhere close to the beach, so they'd parked on a double yellow on a nearby street. Together they had evaluated the situation carefully: it was six in the evening on a Thursday, not even peak summer, and they was only going for a short swim now, wasn't they? The potential risks thus logically mitigated, they left their wallets and phones and everything else in the car and sauntered off, clad only in their swim trunks and flipflops, a towel each around their shoulders. When they came back after their swim, in just the mood for some hot wings and cold beers, they realised to their horror that the car had been towed, with all their things in it! No money to even get to the impoundment lot. That's when the business idea had struck. Like a blessing from God above! 'Tis always de way – Yvonne, Aron's grandmother had once told him – when someting real good hatches out of someting real bad, is always de Lord Jesus doing his godly ting. Spurred on then by Yvonne's

32

rendition of divine destiny, he had gone into business with that same friend, put in five hundred pounds of his own money, brimming with an enthusiasm only topped by the enthusiasm of the friend who had put in double that stake. Together they manufactured two thousand wallets with plans to sell them at seaside towns first in the UK (stage 1), then in Europe (stage 2), and then in due course all over the world (stage 3). Sadly, they never even got to completing the first stage. The wallets were cut too small in an error which was caught too late – the result of the faulty design was that the tops of the currency notes stuck out from the top of the wallets, rendering the whole concept useless. Of course, all this had happened when everyone was still using paper notes. Not even a year had passed when the government brought out the new waterproof notes. But by then of course the one thousand nine hundred unsold wallets had been thrown away – in a ceremony that resembled a funeral in its sobriety – at the recycling centre in Willesden where Trevor lived.

Aron sighs deeply now, thinking of Trevor. Deeply and with real feeling. If there was anything Aron prided himself on, it was the ability to reinvent himself over and over again without any loss of enthusiasm. But Trevor? Not so much. Poor Trevor. Nearly killed him, not just the one-grand loss, but the loss of spirit, the insensible loss of *soul* from the failure of the thing. Never forgave himself. Became a different man. Got a job delivering Papa John's, married a girl he didn't love – and who, it was rumoured, scratched his bare arms with her fake fingernails every time he displeased her – had three kids in three years, and went to church every Sunday without fail. And yet, none of that brought the mojo back into him. They still saw each other from time to time, him and Trevor, but it was tough. Trevor had become a shell of his previous self. A shell with scratch marks on his arms from the cat-woman. Aron shakes his head at the thought. Failure, man, failure was tough. Tough, tough, tough. Tough enough to take the soul out of a man.

Again Aron sighs and adjusts his backside on the seat. Yup, it was a sad story, but as always there was a lesson to learn. In this case, the lesson was timing. Timing, timing, timing. Timing was everything! Aron had learned this lesson well and good. Timing was the difference between making it and not making it. Whatever it was that one was making. That part was less important. What was important was the timing of the thing.

And that, to go all the way back to where he had started this whole line of thinking, was the really exciting thing, because Aron believed that *this* was his time! Now! His time was now!

The number 13 slows down as it approaches the first of many traffic lights on this busy stretch of prime shopping real estate. Aron pulls his ear buds out of his jeans' pocket and puts them on slowly, one by one. Oxford Street bores him. It's a good time, he thinks, to listen to his music.

A white man in a light brown linen blazer slides into the seat next to his. He's got a book in his hands which he places on his lap with the back cover facing upwards.

FIVE

Aron nods in greeting. Listening to anyone good? the man asks. Aron patiently reverses the action from just moments ago, removing his ear buds meticulously, one at a time. Leans his head towards his neighbour. You speakin' to me, mate? Sorry couldn't hear what you was saying. He points to his ears. Listening to my music, innit.

Ah yes, the man says.

He's tall and slightly overweight with a full head of hair, greying at the sides. Aron reckons he must be in his fifties, though it is hard to tell with white people he's always felt, look old when they young and old when they old. Still. Early fifties, he reckons, maybe late forties. He wears rimless glasses and a brown leather watch with an enormous dial on his left wrist. His blazer – which Aron notices now that he is in the business and should, he thinks, be noticing these things – is beige and made of cotton or linen or one of those materials that crumple easily. Also, it is way too big for him, so Aron concludes that either the man was larger when he bought it, or he must have the peculiar habit some people have of buying the wrong size clothes.

As a matter of fact, the man is saying, that's what I was enquiring about. The music. If you were listening to anyone good.

Oh! Aron remarks, surprised at the question, like it is not the kind of question that he necessarily expects from someone who looks like the man. Yeah, yeah, mate. Listening to my man Bruza, innit.

The white man shakes his head. No, he says. I have to confess I'm not familiar with that artist. What style of music does he play?

Aron looks stunned. Bruza, bruv! You ain't heard of Shaun Barker? Chigga D? All the same man, mind. But *he* the man, bruv. *He* the man. 'Get Me,' that's the track. It's a banger, innit. You ain't heard it? Aron shakes his head many times. Oh man, where you been living all this time?

Yes, the man says apologetically. My students keep asking me the same thing, I'm afraid. Would he – this gentleman, Bruza – would he be in the style of hip-hop then?

Aron bursts into a fit of laughter, his whole body involved in the action of laughing. Aw man, he says, wiping his eyes, 'this gentleman Bruza,' I ain't never heard no one refer to him like that. 'This gentleman Bruza!' I like it, I like it. But sorry, you was saying something about the style of music?

Yes, the man says. I was wondering if it was hip-hop that he specialised in.

Yeah, bruv. Hip-hop. And lemme tell you something – blud's a genius. Changed the way we speak, didn't he. Everyone's speaking like Bruza now, innit. White people, posh people, ejucated people, people who been to college and shit. Sorry, I mean people who been to college.

I see, I see, the man nods, so Bruza is somewhat of a linguistic innovator. Fascinating stuff, really. It's true, I barely understand a word that comes out of the mouth of young Londoners these days.

It's not only a different language, it's a different rhythm. The history of spoken English you see, comes all the way from Shakespeare – Te tum te tum te tum. Beware the Ides of March. You hear it? Te tum te tum te tum? What linguists call a stress-timed rhythm, the stresses occur at equal intervals of time. But this new way of speaking is different, it's a syllable-timed rhythm you see, in which each syllable as it is spoken is given the same amount of time and stress. Anyway, too technical, my apologies. He takes out a large handkerchief from the inside pocket of his blazer and mops his brow. I get carried away sometimes. My students accuse me of that too. They're right of course, there's no defence for being old-fashioned when one is old. They don't mean it in a bad way naturally, they're a well-meaning bunch, my students. Slightly theatrical, but all young people these days seem that way inclined, don't you think? Life is a tragedy; everything is a crisis.

You got students, Aron remarks – it is the only part of the conversation he can get his head around. You some kinda speech teacher or something?

Haha, the man laughs awkwardly. Speech teacher! Now, that's a novel idea. Useful too. Speech these days does seem in dire need of being taught. But me, well, not exactly, but in some sense, I can't dispute the *j'accuse* either. He throws his hands up in the air. I am very interested in speech, yes, I can't deny that, but really, I'm only a Professor of English. I specialise in the Romantics.

The Romantics, repeats Aron, yeah, can't say that I know of them as such.

Well, the man replies. They wrote… well I suppose the name says it all… they wrote about love. Poetry and novels of great passion. All dead now of course. The Romantics I mean, not the poems and novels. Those, I would hope, are very much alive. For the sake of my own livelihood, that is. No, the Romantics are all dead. Wordsworth, Shelley, Keats, Byron. Not very diverse, I'm afraid. Mostly men. Some women. Mostly English. Mostly white. Oh dear, I'm not making this terribly compelling for you, am I?

Yeah, nah, Aron says kindly. It's your work, innit. Is what it is. If they all dead white mandem, not your fault, innit. So they all dead, so what? We all got to die one day anyway, so may as well they already be dead. And that other stuff, the mandem and the fact of them all being white, is the system, yeah? The *system*. The struggle. Black people, the ladies, the system weren't *designed* to give them equal ejucation. And a brother or a sista need ejucation to write proper. That's a fact. But that's why Bruza *the man*! And Dizzee Rascal and Lethal B and all them brothers. They not ejucated see, but they express with their music. Don't need no grammar to express with music, innit.

Indeed, the man says. Music is the language of the masses. How true that is. Do you sing yourself? Or play an instrument, perhaps?

Aron stares at the man. Aw man! he remarks, that is deep, bruv! Like you gone reading my mind and shit! See, I always wanted to learn an instrument my whole life. Always imagined in my head how it would be to just walk up to an instrument and make music, easy, just like that. But we didn't have no instruments at home when I was a kid. To practise and shit. Sorry, to practise, I mean. But my lil sister, C'mon? She was always musical. She sing like a bird. Since she were a baby, she singing and singing. Real good too. Close your eyes and sometimes, you can't tell it ain't Ella. That's the beauty with singing now, innit, you either born with it or you ain't, don't need no money to buy no instruments and music lessons and none of that bullshit. Oh man, I keep sayin' that word though I keep trynna stop myself, bad habit innit.

Don't worry, the man says with a little laugh. It's a very versatile little word, isn't it? Sometimes it's the only word that works, to express how it really is. So, you were saying your sister sings. Sang. Sings? Does she still sing?

Nah, Aron says. She gone and messed up her life, didn't she. Got involved with a whole lotta wastemen. Those guys, *man*! He shakes his head. Chirpsing girls, acting all nice and innocent like they real gents, and then getting them pregnant. They all run off in the end innit, all of them, don't take no responsibility for their actions. My sister, she nah learn. Keep thinking it's gonna be different the next time, the next man. She got so many children, she ain't got no time to sing. Nah, she got bare things to do innit, all those children needing her day and night.

Well, the man says, lowering his voice and looking around to make sure no one is listening. I understand perfectly, because it happened to me.

You get someone pregnant and run off? Aron asks, trying not to look shocked, though he's quite sure he looks shocked. Never was any good at hiding emotions.

No, no, quite the opposite, the man says firmly. I married her. We were classmates at Oxford. She was Irish Catholic, came from a very religious family, and not having the baby was simply not an option. Her father would have killed her. I don't mean that flippantly. He really would have. He would have killed her and who knows, perhaps he would have killed me too, just for good measure. In a horribly violent way probably. He shudders. Awful man. So, I did the honourable thing I suppose, I married her. We were both nineteen when our son was born.

Shit, Aron thinks, happens to everyone. He nods his head; his face is serious. Woah, that's deep, bruv. You still married?

No, the man says, shaking his head, unfortunately not. My wife – ex-wife now – fell in love with someone else a couple of years later. He shrugs. It's not surprising really, we were only a pair of kids. What did we know of life! Or love! He smiles, a small, sad smile.

For a short while, nothing follows. Aron doesn't know if the man's concluded the story and he is meant to say something in response, or if he's not concluded and he's meant to wait for more to come. Tricky sometimes to figure this out about people. He decides to wait. After all, he thinks, the man can't possibly end the story there, dangling in the air like that, a story like this – so many directions it could go!

The number 13 is making its slow, wheezy progress into the heart of Oxford Street, one of Europe's busiest and most famous shopping streets. A great throng of people stand ready to cross the road in front of the bus, so many that even the crossing isn't wide enough. Two skinny girls carrying yellow Selfridges bags on their arms stride across casually, so close to the bus, it feels to Aron like they are under it. He feels almost a sense of relief when he sees them emerge safely on the Primark side. One of the girls is dressed in a bikini top and ripped denim shorts and carries a transparent takeaway cup filled with a green liquid. Aron has often wondered about the contents of this drink, popping up with such amazing frequency these days, although he's noticed the price, outrageous at seven or eight quid; he could get two wholesome meals – lunch and dinner sorted – with that kind of dosh. Still, whatever the spendy green stuff is, the skinny girls seem to like them, they the only ones he's ever seen consuming them.

The man next to him says, great city London. There are a few great cities in the world. London. Paris. New York. Rome. Calcutta, perhaps. Rio. Lisbon. Something about them you know, real character, real soul. Do you know, he says suddenly, my wife at the time and I graduated university together and I took up a teaching post in Paris straight after, just for her? She was terribly distressed you see, after the baby, way too young of course to have a child, only a child herself, couldn't cope, almost dropped out of college, but somehow she got through it and I give her a lot of credit for not giving up, but she cried all the time, hated herself, hated the baby, never said it in those words, but I knew, I could see, one would have to be blind not to see. I mean, she would leave it to cry for hours in the bedroom and sit in the living room with the TV on full volume to drown out the sound. So, when I was looking for jobs, I found this one in France. It paid absolutely nothing – the French you see have no use for English teachers – but I thought the change of scene would do her good. I thought while I went to work during the day, she'd get a chance to explore the city with the baby, discover new things, take it in. It was springtime too. Springtime is glorious in Paris – have you been?

Aron shakes his head. So many places, he thinks, he hasn't been. So many things, he hasn't done. Never mind, he thinks. He has his whole life.

Flowers everywhere, the man continues, his face foggy with nostalgia. The entire city is in bloom, an exploding prism of colour and light and love. I thought she'd have a good time you know, enjoy walking the city, sitting at the cafés, do a little shopping maybe, just letting go and living life finally. Like she deserved to, you know, like she would have, if things had happened differently. But I was wrong! She *hated* Paris. She was miserable. Didn't know anyone, didn't speak the language, hardly anyone knew any English, she said, and if they did, they pretended like they didn't. She complained that she couldn't even read the newspaper or understand a thing on the television. Parisians, she said, were rude. The women especially. Also, unnatural. I'm sitting at the café, she would tell me, and I'm the only one ever eating anything. Everyone else, she said, smoked like a chimney and drank like a fish and ate like a bird. And I'm not, she lamented, either a chimney, or a fish, or a bird.

At this point he stops and looks out of the window. A group of five or six people are being shooed out of a souvenir shop by a policeman. It doesn't take more than a glance to know they are part of the same group of people gathered at Marble Arch. Torn clothes and long hair, bare feet. The English professor leans forward across Aron and taps the window with the knuckle of his index finger. I wonder when they're going to do something about these refugees, he intones. It's a proper bloody crisis.

What happens then? Aron says, intrigued.

Well, they send them back of course, to Poland or wherever they're from.

Nah man, I mean in your story.

Oh, the man remarks, oh. I didn't realise I was telling a story. But perhaps I was. Well, what happened next was that Claire – that's my ex-wife, *wife* at the time mind you, that's the irony of it, well, she went and fell in love with a Frenchman. Wonder what the Irish Catholic Church would think of that! An artist she'd met at one of those cafés. Ran off with him. Left me a letter saying she'd fallen in love, she hadn't planned on it, it had just happened, she was very sorry. A letter! On the kitchen counter, under the kettle where she knew I'd find it first thing in the morning. He shakes his head. She knew my habits, that much I'll give her. I did find it first thing in the morning.

Aw man, that's tough.

Oh yes. Yes, it was tough, I'll admit that. Especially in the first few months, I didn't know what to do with myself, I was a lost soul. Always think it's funny that the woman who used to make fun of the Romantics for their exaggerated versions of love ran off with a man who told her he couldn't stop thinking about the shape of her ankle. *The shape of her ankle*, can you believe it? Apparently, he would deliberately drop his napkin on the floor just to catch sight of it. Can you believe how little originality some people have? It was all in the letter, you see, that's how I know.

And the baby? Aron asks. He is intrigued suddenly, curious about the love child. He wants to know what happened to the love child. It's a stranger's story, but it seems intimate to him, like a movie he's watched before but never finished, so he knows how it starts, but not how it will end. The characters, they are familiar too. The professor... his father. The wife... his mother. The love child... yes, he wants to know how this movie ends, what happens to the love child, what happens to... him?

The baby? the man says. Oh, you mean Rupert! Left him with me of course.

Aron covers his eyes with his hands. Nah, he says in disbelief.

I'm afraid so, the man says sadly. Wasn't exactly a baby anymore. He was four. Lovely age, you know, full of curiosity and questions. She never came back, not even once. He tried to contact her a few times when he was older, wrote her all these letters, but either she never got them, or she was determined not to write back. I told him to forget about it. I'm not sure he ever did. Maybe it's an unfair expectation. It's hard, you see, to accept that one's parent is out there somewhere and has no interest in them. Can affect one deeply. He was always a quiet child. I worried about him constantly. He's thirty-five now. Married a nice girl. They live in the Midlands, that's where my daughter-in-law is from. Two kids. Dog. Walks in the countryside. Barbeques in the garden. All that. A simple life. They're happy.

Happy. Aron likes that word. He's always liked that word, considered it the definitive measure of a good life. Everyone, surely, deserved happiness. Right up there with clean water and affordable medicine. It's a state he tries to be in, as much as he can, as much as his life allows him, and even within those constraints, he's eager, always eager, always looking, always trying to find ways to find his happiness.

And you, mate? he asks generously, wanting nothing more than to spread it out, happiness like melting butter on toast, to everyone, even to strangers on a bus.

Me?

Yeah, you, Aron says, you happy?

The man's face changes suddenly and in a very dramatic way, like he has been touched profoundly by the question. For a moment, Aron is worried he is going to cry. He sits up somewhat anxiously, but thankfully, it doesn't happen. Do you know, the man says instead, his voice thick with incredulity, that it's been nearly thirty years since anyone asked me that? Maybe more. My mother used to ask me that sometimes. Giles, she used to say, are you happy? He brings his hands together in a gesture of prayer, and the movement causes the book on his lap to slide off it and onto the floor. Before he has a chance to pick it up, Aron has already retrieved it for him. The book is called *Rabbit is Rich* by someone called John Updike. Aron's never heard of the writer, he assumes it's a writer of children's books, he does find it strange that a grown man would read children's books about rich rabbits. Still, it's not his place to judge. Oh, thank you the man says, taking the book from him, you're very kind.

No problem, bruv, Aron says, smiling widely, showing all his impressive metalwork. You was saying about your son.

I was? the man says. Very well, so I was. Yes, well, Rupert is a forensic psychologist. Works with criminals. Analysing their minds, rehabilitating them, things like that.

Aron emits a low whistle. Serious? Like real live criminals?

You got it! The worst kind too. Serial killers, rapists. This one time, he told me, this fellow he was interviewing – he'd killed four women, this man, murdered them brutally, then cut up their bodies and thrown them away piecemeal for easy disposal. Yes, yes, it's true, every word. Anyway, so he was sitting across from Rupert in the interrogation room, you know, and Rupert had a glass of water on the table in front of him. Well, this guy, this murderer, turns out he had a glass eye, and all of a sudden, he pops it out and it goes plop straight into Rupert's glass of water.

Aron snickers. Woah man, that's a good one. Extremely funny.

It wasn't meant to be, the man says gravely. Scared the living daylights out of Rupert.

Oh, Aron says, stopping mid laugh. Is it. Well, yeah, I can see how it could do that, yeah sure. By funny I mean more like crazy. Popped his eye into a glass of water! Imagine you about to drink it and someone's eyeball floating about inside looking up at you! Man, that's some kinda crazy shit! Wanting attention, innit. Wanting to get a rise. But so long as no one drank that water, tho, it's all good, innit?

You know, the man says, peering intently at Aron through his rimless glasses, my son says that although there's no scientific way to prove it, he thinks that all people are born good and it's society that turns some of us bad. Do you believe that?

Aron frowns. Metapsychology in general is profound business. It needs time to think, space. But metapsychology on a London bus! Well, he says after a long pause, I ain't no *mind*-doctor or nothing, but some people just ain't right in the head. He shakes his own head vigorously. But if they born that way or not, man, I don't know, that's deep, bruv, that's deep.

The man sighs. Well, yes. It's almost a religious question, isn't it? The sin of Adam and all that. Not easily answered. Anyhow, this happens to be my stop next, so I must be pressing the button. He raises his arm to reach the red STOP button on the pole and Aron notices the large, expanding sweat blotch under his armpit. It's what prompts him to segue – with sufficient elegance, he hopes – into the next question.

Before you go, bruv, I just happened to be noticing your style and you wouldn't be needing some new garms anytime soon, would you?

Garms?

Yeah, like the garms you got on. Blazers and things? I work at a bespoke tailoring house for gentlemen, don't I, we sell blazers and suits and all nature of things like the kind a professor like yourself would wear.

Aha, the man says, grinning broadly. A bespoke tailoring house for gentlemen, you say! Well, actually, as it happens, I would be *delighted* to update my wardrobe. Would you happen to have a business card on you by any chance?

Aron throws back his head. Nah, I ain't got no card, man, this was my first day today at the store, innit. But why don't I write it down for you, mate? My name and the name of the store and the street it's on, all that info, so you won't get lost, innit and when you come, I'll sort you out, man, give you a discount won't I, friends and family rate, bargain price for some wicked stuff, make you look real sharp, believe!

What a genius idea, the man declares as he fumbles with his blazer. Jubilantly, he pulls out a pen from his inside pocket and hands it to Aron. Now let me see, he says, if I have a piece of paper. Always a challenge, finding a piece of paper when you need it. Ah, there's no paper. But wait, I too have the most genius idea... He reaches for the book on his lap, opens it out to the last page... aha! Blank like I expected. Updike to the rescue! Here you go!

Aron receives the book in both hands like he is accepting a gift – which if this works out, could well be one. Sticks his tongue out over his top lip in concentration, a childhood habit that had endeared him to his teachers when he was a little boy of nine or ten, when little black boys are still considered cute, before the years, that is, when their own teachers started putting 'context' around them.

He begins to write:

ARON WILSON, ASOSIATE
Suit Yourself
Victoria Street
Victoria SWIV IJU
London
England
UK

There, he says triumphantly when he's done, there's all of what you need, innit.

The man peers at it. Suit Yourself! he repeats gleefully. That is clever, very clever indeed! He stands up and shakes Aron's hand heartily. Say what, young man, how about we say Friday next week, round about 3pm?

Aron grins enormously. Deal, he says. Giles, is it? See you later, Giles my man, take it easy now!

Goodbye, the man calls as he goes down the stairs. Aron turns his body and waves. Catches the eye of the maid. Frowns. Something 'bout her.

Aron watches the man disappear from view and then appear again through the window, walking down the road with the slight hunch typical of tall men as they begin to age. He has to admit he's

47

rather chuffed with himself. Not even a day gone, and already he's wangled his first customer. The white guys at the suit shop? Richard and Richard? He can't wait to see their faces looking properly gobsmacked 'cause he's worked some magic, innit.

Pure. Black. Magic.

SIX

At the stop in front of Marks and Spencer a heavily pregnant woman squeezes gratefully into the newly vacated seat and plonks her handbag down carelessly on the floor area between them.

Lord, she says to no one in particular, they killing me before they even born.

There are some two hundred and fifty thousand Jamaicans in London, and yet, when one hears, from a total stranger, the familiar, pleasing cadence of one's own speech, one feels, if not a kinship, then at least a curiosity. Aron feels an unexpected rush of both.

She's somewhere in her mid-thirties, small and slight except for her stomach which is neither small nor slight. Beige shorts and a yellow sleeveless vest. Rubber slippers like she's going to the beach. The skin on her bare limbs is very dark with a particular sheen to it, what do they call it – pregnancy glow. She's wearing her hair in a big Afro puff, accessorised with a broad cloth headband in an African print that features blue and yellow sunflowers. The headband, Aron decides, makes her look younger than she is, like she's still a schoolgirl. Come to think of it, Aron thinks, even without the headband, she looks like one of them models in one of them pregnancy ads on telly, where they show a woman from the back, swaying her hips and sashaying forwards, and then they make her turn around, all dramatic, and that's when you realise the woman is pregnant. Meant to show how you can still look great when you're pregnant if only you used whatever product they were promoting. Funny, he remembers the ad but not what it's for, which makes him wonder if that makes the ad itself good or bad. In a *business* sense, that is. Personally, he's never understood the point of ads of that nature – only purpose they seem to serve is to make other women mad that they can't look like the woman on the screen. His sister, he remembers, used to get herself all kinds of worked up about it. This, as she tried to squeeze into clothes that were at least three sizes too small, rolling her eyes and yelling about how much those bitches been airbrushed and cropped and photoshopped 'cause ain't no woman on this planet who look like that in *real* life, believe! Anyway, the one sitting next to him, he thinks, isn't far off the kind of girl his sister would despise at sight.

Both her hands rest on the round of her stomach, fingers linked together. It's fantastically huge, he has to confess, almost unbelievable, like if you didn't actually see it with your own eyes, you wouldn't think it possible that a human stomach could stretch like that.

As if on cue, the pregnant lady turns her head towards Aron, catches his eye pointedly. Look at the size of me! she says. Twins if you wondering. She rolls her eyes. God gives us only what we can handle, they say.

Aron chuckles, how long more you got, he says.

Tirteen days. She shrugs. If it goes to plan.

It's nice, Aron replies, when things go to plan.

'Spose so, she says noncommittally. Those your real eyes? she asks.

Aron slaps the seat and throws his head back in a loud guffaw.

Yeah, he says, yeah. Sorry, I'm laughing 'cause you can't imagine how many times I get asked that.

But I *can* imagine, she says perfectly seriously.

Oh. Oh right. Is just that folks find it unexpected like…

Which one's white, Mum or Dad?

He shrugs. Dunno, he says.

She looks aghast. What kind of fool answer is that? she says.

Aron shrugs. Honest to God, he says. I don't know where they come fro…

They didn't even tell you?

The thing is *they* don't really…

Oh, they know, she says, nodding her head furiously up and down. Don't you go believing *that* foolishness.

Aron finds his interest piqued. How *you* know they know? he asks.

I know all about these tings, she says cryptically. *Seen* these tings. I'm experienced, you could say. Families, man! She emits a low whistle. Ask *me* about families. They all the same everyplace you go, built on a *foundation* of secrets and lies.

He's just begun to ponder the many significances of what she's just said when he feels the vibration coming from his back pocket. He raises one half of his backside to retrieve the phone, but it stops ringing before he can get to it. C'mon. His sister has this aggravating habit of hanging up if the person doesn't answer on the first ring. Instead, she calls someone else and then gets all hoity-toity when you try and ring her back. I'm busy right now, she says peevishly, should have answered when I belled, innit.

He shakes his head disapprovingly, pulls out his phone anyway – in case – and lowers his rear end back into place.

Why you gone and git yourself a phone fit for a teenage girl? the pregnant woman asks, looking at his mobile phone curiously.

Oh that, Aron says shrugging. Is only *temporary* innit. Broke my old phone didn't I, smashed to pieces, and then I get wind of a brother selling one for nothing, so I went for it. I mean, I know it's pink, but 'part from that, it works, innit. Actually, if I'm being honest, the colour helped me with *negotiating* the deal. I mean who's gonna purchase a pink phone from a brother, unless they buying a present for a girl. Got myself a deal, didn't I. But, only temporary, like I said. Till I got a few quid to spare.

It's sinful, she agrees, the cost of phones these days, and so delicate too, drop it once, and four hundred quid gone, just like that. Into thin air. Then the hassle to fix it and whatnot. She herself used an old Nokia, she said, which she'd never been so much as tempted to replace. Did the job and anyway she didn't trust the webs of the internets. World-wide too, these webs, their reach so vast and insidious.

True, Aron says, shit's scary. What they know about you and shit. Only the other day, he says, he was talking to a bruv about these creps he's got on – he lifts one leg in the air so she can see his shoes – next thing he knows is his phone's showing him all sorts of deals on orange Nikes. Serious! Makes you think, innit, like *who* are all these *people* listen…

Without warning, a parked black cab cuts right in front of them. The bus jerks violently to a halt.

Bumbo! the woman says, authentically Jamaican in her outrage, why dey always stop so sudden like dat. Like dey jus' looking for 'scuses to kill us off. Not nuff dey be chaining and murdering de lot of us for four hundred years. Gotta kill us off on de public bus too. Humph.

Aron nods in a gesture he believes is expected of him, expressing his solidarity with this assessment of the collective character of all London bus drivers and of the institution of slavery as a whole.

Yeah, for sure, he says, but ain't his fault this *one* time. Cabbie. I seen him do it. No signal. Total wasteman. But you good, sista? Babies good? Still jammin'? He shakes his head in empathy. Sudden movements like these ain't no good for someone in your condition, innit? Could have gone arse over kettle before you know it.

I'm hot, she says ignoring the concern and mopping her brow with the back of her hand. Only time I like it so warm is back in Kingston. In this town – shaking her head – this kinda heat is *nasty*. Makes folks *smell*. She dives for her bag, pulls it onto her lap and peers inside. Out comes a perfume bottle that looks like a pink present wrapped in a silver bow. Aron, who considers himself somewhat of an expert on designer knockoffs, knows that neither the container nor its contents are what they claim to be.

Yeah, is the sweat, innit, Aron says distractedly, as she fills the small space between them with the smell of roses and bergamot and pink pepper (fake roses, fake bergamot, fake pink pepper). A small part of him is still thinking about what she said before, that thing about families and secrets and lies. But the truth is he doesn't want to think about it. Serious matters of these kinds… who he is, where he came from, what it all means… the unresolved core and thrust of his existence, is delicate business to Aron.

Boys or girls or one of both? he asks. Strictly speaking it doesn't matter to him, he finds all babies cute. Wants some of his own one day. It's a useful question for the moment though when he needs to manoeuvre the conversation in another direction. He isn't about to let himself get drawn into serious matters. Not now.

She shrugs. Didn't bother finding out. All the same anyhow, boy or girl, not like one type is easier on you or anyting.

This strikes Aron as a particularly profound remark. Boys and girls being equally troublesome in the eyes of the parent. He wonders if Carol would agree with this assessment. Jordan, C'mon, he. *He* had been alright, as far as trouble was concerned, stayed away for the most part. Excepting the period when he was deep in it, could be no deeper really. Mercifully, just before that realisation, the realisation that he was slowly sinking – drowning – in trouble, he had somehow managed to come up for air and swim away. But that period of his life was secret business – his folks didn't know nothing about it. That was the way he intended to keep it. On that point, Aron was firm. Past is past. Present is all that matters. Leading to a future where he wanted to be happy. So, that was him. His brother Jordan had always been the good one, went the opposite direction of trouble, kept himself to himself, got A's at school, read books (read books!). It was C'mon who'd been trouble from the beginning, flunking out of school, fired from jobs for mouthing off to supervisors, high most of the time, pregnant the rest.

The woman next to him yawns. Lord, she says, I'm tired. All this traffic. Always on a Friday. Strange that. Not like working people ain't going home on the udder days. What's so special about Fridays?

Could be, Aron speculates, it's folks going away for the weekend. Takin' a break.

A female sound, like a cross between a cry and a sigh. Must be nice. To get a break I mean. She shifts her bum in the seat and turns towards him, knees together, collectively pointing in the direction of his own legs, which in contrast are spread as wide apart as the space will allow. She seems suddenly spirited, as if whatever she is going to say next has energised her even before she's said it out loud.

You know someting? Let me tell you a troot. This is the ting with kids. Kids, they want *all* of you *all* the time. Which means there ain't none of you left over at no time. Which, she says, wagging a finger didactically, is as good as sayin' they killing you to nourish

54

theirselfs… she drops her voice to a whisper… like parasites. There's a pause, for dramatic effect, then the voice resumes its normal volume. Know the best part? The best part is that we blatantly know this troot and still we keep popping out babies like they Smarties from a Smartie-tube! Now *you* explain to me why? Go on, try! See, you can't. It ain't logical. It just ain't. She shakes her head vigorously, the sunflowers on the headband dance psychedelically.

Is it? Aron asks, confused by all this talk of truth and logic. He looks down at her huge stomach. These ain't your first? he manages weakly.

But that's 'zackly what I'm saying is what I'm saying! she says, slapping her hand on the seat, making Aron jump. I got four already! And now deese two! Do you know, I went and got me a year's supply of pills? For nothing too, bless the National Health Service. I could have taken them. But I didn't. Too late now. I mean, *why* would I put myself through it *again*? Who's making me? No one. So why would I do it?

She looks at Aron expectantly as if he's ready to supply her with an answer. When she realises there isn't one forthcoming, she gives him a disappointed look and shifts her body back to the original position, knees still together, pointing out this time.

Aw, come on now, Aron says, it ain't that bad, is it? It's a miracle, really. You carrying new life an' all. *Two* new lives! *Two* miracles!

Can't sleep, can't walk, can't even tie my own laces.

Yeah, but it'll be over soon innit. Two weeks, you said, yeah? Two weeks be here before you know it!

She makes a petulant face like a child who's been told an untruth and knows it. The sleep ting? It ain't stopping then neither.

Aron shrugs, conceding the point. Time flies, he says. It seems the only thing to say.

Yeah, the woman says finally, 'zackly. Is all about time. That's the biggest difference between men and women, innit. Time. She passes an elegant hand – smooth skin, tiny wrist, long fingers – in front of Aron's form. In front of hers. Wags her index finger in the space between. Shakes her head. Once. Twice. Different for men than for women. Different *proposition*.

Like how you mean? Aron asks, sitting forward in his seat to convey his curiosity, which could not be more genuine. He has always considered himself a bit of a ladies' man, always a student when it comes to instruction on this nature of subject material.

Here, she says, lemme ask you someting. Tink time moves the same way for men and women? Equal? Nah. It only becomes equalised in the end. *The end.* The repetition of those two little words, duly emphasised, has its intended effect. Aron shrinks back. But, she continues, for most of our living lives, men are time-less. Time-free. Option ain't available to women. Look. She points two passionate fingers somewhere in the region between her stomach and her knees – you might tink of these women's parts as wombs. They actually clocks. You don't hear them, but yeah, they clocks, silently ticking away, getting ready for the big event. Preparing, constantly preparing. Month after month after month. Ain't the same for men. Then one day, she says theatrically, the clock stops ticking. Time's over. Ain't no chance of that big event *ever* happening again. 'Cause there's an even bigger event waiting down the road. That's when men and women become the same. When time becomes *equalised*. She sighs. Ask women 'bout time.

Aron nods, considering the matter, for it is worth considering. He hadn't thought about it this way before. To him, the differences between men and women were numerous and slightly less abstract. Women cared about my needs and your needs and listening and respect and those kind of things. Now he wonders if she's right. If this thing with wombs and timeclocks explains everything.

Explains women, basically. Meaning, my needs and your needs and listening and respect are actually a kind of superficial presentation of this far more interesting subtext. It's like an epiphany. He wants to grab both her hands in his and shake them in gratitude. But she's still going…

If you ask me, the woman continues, it's the single, only reason why women have babies. Scared of the clock, innit. Scared that if we don't have babies, we become the same like men, before our right time to become the same like men. That's the reason. No other reason. Why else would someone willingly put theirselfs in this position? As if they *wanting* to get disappointed. Nuttin' but a trap. Do you tink, she says suddenly, that it's wrong of me to be tinking these tings about my babies?

Nah, Aron says. Not really.

For how can Aron possibly sit in judgement? He knows that it's not wrong to feel disillusioned with the situations we find ourselves in, even though sometimes we are made to feel that it's wrong. Definitely, he's felt the disillusionment, deep and strong from his own parents, in the matter of his little sister, like everything she ever did or tried to do ended in disappointment, an endless series of disappointments that got amalgamated along the way, until her whole existence became for them one enormous disappointment. With Jordan it was different. Unlike C'mon, Jordan had somehow managed to successfully bridge the gap between expectations and reality. But even he, the whitest sheep of all, did not get to walk away scot-free. Even *Jordan* was not spared from judgement. As far as his parents were concerned, because their expectations of Jordan were as high as they were low for C'mon, any small slip-up turned into some great failure on his part to fulfil his destiny. It was a burden Aron had always pitied his brother for, because the situation seemed to him like a trap, impossible, no matter how much one tried, for anyone to escape from. No wonder Jordan had gone into that crazy depression a few years ago, scared the shit out of them all, trynna take his own life and shit. In this way and many others, Aron appreciates being in the middle. Middle child, middle of the road, not too hot, not too cold. Disappointing maybe, but just the right amount. Yeah, he thinks to himself now, listening to this pregnant lady talk, it's not unnatural for her to feel this way, for it seems the birth right of children to disappoint, and the birth right of parents to expect it, and if that is true, then what is the crime in pre-empting it all?

But Aron isn't sure how to express all these complicated ideas properly. It ain't wrong, he says finally.

She rubs one hand over her stomach. Most people don't tell you how it really is, she says. About kids. Somehow women feel more like women if they big these tings up. Love and marriage and motherhood and tings. Men like it too. Makes men feel those kind of women are *real* women. The other way, it scares them. They don't want women to be feeling the opposite tings. They don't want to hear it. They want to hear some other shit.

What about their dad? Aron asks, looking at the woman's stomach.

What about what about their dad? the woman says suspiciously. Told you already, didn't I? Men are men, aren't they?

Down on the street in front of them, they see a man in drag – stiletto heels, red tankini, blonde wig – crossing the road on a red light. The bus driver honks. Unperturbed, the man continues crossing, swinging his hips extravagantly. A crowd of Japanese tourists look on, holding their phones up in the air, taking photos of a man dressed like a woman crossing a street on a red light. So many things wrong with that; they would tell their friends back home over sake and sashimi: evidence, if one ever needed such a thing, of what the West has finally come to, I mean, Nakano-san, you just have to look at this photo to see… KY!

Oi! Look at that! the Jamaican woman exclaims. Anywhere near Oxford Street, always a circus, innit.

Is it, Aron says.

You ain't from these ends, she notes.

North London, Aron says proudly, born and bred.

She claps a hand on his thigh. A small square-shaped zirconia sparkles prettily from her finger. Bet white folk don't treat you like you half-white, she says, as if the thought has only just occurred to her. Wid any kind of half-respect I mean. Never does work that way round. But don't you let anyone be disrespecting you. You hold that handsome head of yours high in the sky. Anyway, I gotta get off here. Store I know in Marylebone got a fifty percent sale on. Baby tings. She rolls her eyes. Outgrow them in weeks, if you lucky that is. Less more likely. Then you gotta buy more. Money train never stops.

At this, Aron winces. Not the baby clothes bit, but the half-white bit. The truth was he couldn't remember the last time he had thought of himself as half-white. It had mattered once. It didn't matter anymore. There had been an instance, when Aron was twelve or thirteen – half a lifetime ago, literally – when he'd come home from a football game earlier than expected and seen his father sitting at the kitchen table drinking tea with a white woman with shockingly blue eyes. Her broad pale face, those round blue eyes, the sight had shaken him to the very core. Unable to stop himself, he'd walked into the kitchen, expecting… what? What had he been expecting? Neither of them noticed he was even there. He stood there silently for what seemed an eternity before his father suddenly seemed to register his presence. He stared at his son with a bemused look.

This is Irene, he said finally, from the council. That is our middle kid. He's called Aron.

The woman had failed to recognise Aron or done a good enough job pretending to fail, only given him a brief, uninterested smile and carried on talking – something about how teenage crime which had skyrocketed of late had no chance of going in the other direction unless they put more funding into education, not a magic bullet these things, takes time. Resources. Investment. Money. Need someone to care.

Oh man! It had hit him hard. Lethal like a death blow because he had been convinced instantly, at first sight, that the woman was his mother and if it was she who was responsible for his existence and she did not recognise him, then who was *he*?

After the woman left, he asked his father who she was.

Told you already, didn't I? his father said, surprised. Carol and I, we know her from *time*. From the council. Rehoused us all those years ago. If it weren't for her, we'd still be on the street, believe!

In a spontaneous burst of courage, Aron asked: Joe, is that my mother?

Incredibly, Joe started to laugh. Bent over, displaying his elaborate cornrows, laughing and repeating the question a long time, is that my mudder, he asks, is that my mudder! *Irene* from the council, is that his mudder! He had still been laughing when Aron left the room. Still laughing hours later. And then for days after that.

Aron remembers. Even now, he remembers. The memory is crystalline.

The next stop is Dorset Street, the bus announces, transposing Aron straight from his father's kitchen to Marylebone.

The pregnant woman stands up laboriously, grabbing the pole for support. Before she walks away, she places a soft hand on Aron's shoulder. In a lovely voice she says, everyone gotta know where dey come from. Helps figure out where you gonna go.

SEVEN

A throng of students are clustered around the entrance of Baker Street station, and watching them just in that split second, standing around with their backpacks, laughing and talking, makes Aron feel a sharp pang of envy. It is an unusual feeling for him, he is not by nature an envious boy, but he sees in these students what could have been his, a life he will now never have. He has accepted this. It is part of his story. His story. History. He thinks of it now like memory dulled by time, mostly devoid of emotion, of all that past pain. But pain, even if it is no longer present, leaves a few things in its wake. Shrapnel wounds, you can say. Shame. Hopelessness. Fear. And this, the worst of all, envy.

It is the same feeling he sometimes has when he sees Jordan and as soon as he feels it creep up on him, he crushes it. Quickly, very quickly, every time, atomises it and blows the particles away, like seeds when they are just burgeoning, before they have any chance of growing into a fully developed thing. This, Aron knows, is a matter of survival, crucial and necessary, for a fully developed thing with envy at its root is poisonous and it's one thing feeling it for a group of strangers and a totally different, more dangerous thing feeling it for your brother.

The irony of the whole situation of course is that just a few years ago, *he* was the one to be envious of. Every kid on the estate was envious of him, plus the kids in his class, in his school, on the football pitch. The adults too, his parents' friends, his parents' friends' friends. How could they possibly not be? He was Aron Wilson! The prodigy, the talent, England's future football star.

Things change though, how quickly things change. One second you've gone up the ladder and the next, you're sliding down a snake. It's savage. A mere roll of the dice. Although who, you may well ask, is rolling the dice?

But taking it back even further than that would not be overthinking the matter. The thing is he and Jordan had always been different people. Built different. Not that they weren't close, nah, the opposite really, they were thick as thieves, loyal as any two people could be, defending each other, loving each other not because they were meant to or because someone told them to, but just because. To question that love was never a matter of consideration for either of them, they just loved each other, that was all. Perhaps that is why one could take it back to the beginning. Perhaps doing so should not be dismissed as sentimental, for there were three years between them and for three years Jordan was all Aron knew, all Aron loved. Yet they had never shared the same interests even as children. Jordan was bookish and academic, reading, reading, always reading in his spare time, laying on his belly on the bed, on the floor, on the grass, anywhere, reading, reading, always reading, borrowing books from the library and never returning them – Aron would find them stashed under the bed, the first page stamped all over in faded purple, optimistically suggesting a return date somewhere way back in the past. Besides his books, Jordan had no interest in much else. Some small bit in music. None in sports. Aron had no interest in anything but sports. Jordan shone in class; teachers, pleasantly surprised, praised him to the high heavens. Imagine! they said among themselves, straight A's and a black kid too. Brother's a different matter though. Head shake, eye roll. Brother's bound to be trouble. At that time, Aron felt no resentment; what Jordan had, he did not begrudge, for what Jordan had, he did not want. He was dreaming a different dream.

On his third birthday, Aron received, among other things and without too much thought in the matter, Jordan's old football, which was as good as new because his brother hadn't touched it once. A week later, Aron and the football were inseparable. You was taking the football into your bed dear, his grandmother Yvonne told him later, like it was one of dem stuffed teddies. Your mudder none liked it, but I said to her, dere are many more peculiar tings out dere in de world to git all hot and bodered 'bout dis small matter of sleeping wid a football.

Aron first started to play with the other boys from the estate on their patch of community green. The raw natural talent was impossible to miss. He was quick and lithe and light on his feet. Or more relevantly, he was quicker and lither and lighter on his feet than anyone else, even boys two and three years older than him. And that, at the end of the day, this thing about the way he played, that no matter how good everyone else was, he was better – that alchemy is what set him incontestably apart.

It was on Jordan's insistence that Joe took him one day to the youth football pitches and it was here – at the age of seven – that Aron himself began to understand his own talent. The pitch was poor with bits of discarded chewing gum and cigarette stubs mixed in with stones and glass and mud, but it made no difference to the quality of Aron's game. He just wanted to play. He'd seen others do certain tricks and flicks on TV a million times and now he was actually – finally – getting to do them himself. So really, to Aron, it didn't matter *where* he was playing, it mattered only that he was playing.

A few times an ex-pro footballer often seen hanging around the pitch sat on a broken wooden bench and watched Aron. Aron knew some of the other boys made fun of the man behind his back, calling him all sorts, but Aron knew about the man, knew that when he was good, he was real good. Sometimes Aron noticed him sitting on the bench, a half-smile on his face, and despite what everyone else said, Aron thought of him as having a highly suave and debonair manner.

You're good, the man said to him one day.

Is it, Aron replied.

You're the best I've seen here in fifteen years, he said.

Is it, Aron replied.

Let me see you play again, he said.

Aron played.

Finchley United, the man said. Got a spliff?

Nah man, Aron said, putting his hands in his pockets and turning them inside out.

The man shrugged. Nothing ventured, he said cryptically. Up the road and to your right, he said.

Is it, Aron replied. I'll tell my old man then.

On his fifth week of training at Finchley United Football Club, Aron was professionally spotted. It is not just for theatre that people call that moment – the moment of being discovered – a footballer's dream.

For Aron certainly, it unfolded exactly like one.

One day, right after a game in which he coolly dribbled past four defenders to score his seventh goal, he saw the coach and the scout huddled together having a chat. They kept their voices low. A few words carried in the chilly North London breeze.

Athleticism. Coordination. Ball manipulation.

Aron grinned.

Incredible touch. Unbelievable balance. Proprioception.

Aron grinned wider. That will do, he thought. Thank the Lord, he thought.

The scout walked towards him. I look at him, the scout said, no longer whispering, and all I see is speed. How would you like, he said, clapping a hand on Aron's shoulder, to one day play in the Premiership?

Fact: Out of 1,500,000 youngsters that play football
      in the UK only 180 make it as a Premier League
      professional.

Fact: Aron was earmarked to be one of the 180.

Fact: Football became Aron's life. School, class, homework,
      books were relegated to the backburner, where
      slowly and silently, they burned. Nobody noticed.

Fact: Aron was a bird. He flew.

Fact: Aron was actually only a boy. He fell.

The injury announced its presence in the middle of a tackle by means of a loud 'pop' that Aron heard despite the noise of the cheering crowds and knew, instinctively and immediately, that it had come from inside his body. Within minutes, his knee swelled to the size of the football he had just kicked, and despite willing himself otherwise, his mind grew weak, and his body capitulated. In an act of almost unbearable humiliation, he found that it couldn't even support its own weight and he fell to the ground.

He was seventeen years old, playing for the Queen's Knights Academy. A wonderkid scoring wondergoals. A season away from signing with the first team. Provided of course, they all said smiling widely, that all goes well.

All goes well.

All goes well.

All goes well.

Three little words carrying so much weight.

Three little loaded words.

What next?

If circumstance is the confluence of chance and choice, it begs the question: how much chance, how much choice?

For it was not Aron's choice to meet Dr Rubenstein of 21 Harley Street. Ever, in his whole life. No offence to Dr Rubenstein of 21 Harley Street.

It's your ACL, Dr Rubenstein announced, pointing at the translucent blue film with his gloved index finger. Surgery plus complete rest. Nine months, maybe longer. Maybe shorter too, he added, looking at Aron's face. I'm sorry, he said gently, I know you're a footballer, but there's nothing we can do but wait it out, this is just bad luck.

That sound, did you hear it? That was the sound of a dream breaking.

All Aron really remembers of the hospital were two things: the anaesthetic smell that was present everywhere at every moment of every day, and Carol, about whom you could pretty much say the same thing, for it is a fact that Carol was there when they put him into the anaesthetic sleep, and Carol was there when he woke from it. And then Carol was there for the entire nine months he spent off the pitch in rehab, without whom, if he is to be honest, he wouldn't have made it, for the truth is that while his body was being forced to rest, his mind had never been more restless.

He followed the game religiously. He watched, with bad grace and burning impatience, his team play match after match after match. Without him. He noted, petulantly, many of the players who had started under him overtake him easily and effortlessly. Don't worry, Carol said, bringing him his lunch tray, your moment will come.

His first few times back on the pitch had felt great. It's like you never went anywhere, his teammates said admiringly, no one can get the ball off you. Great tekkers, mate! In thirty minutes of football, you haven't lost possession once! I'm back, Aron thought, as he danced around the last defender and curled the ball into top right hand corner of the net. And how!

A few weeks in, when he was playing a friendly against a rival North London club, is when he felt it, that now-familiar, dreaded pain, followed by a crippling fear that stopped him dead in his tracks. That was when he knew. He already knew. Before they called him into the meeting two weeks later, he knew. Before they uttered those words, he knew. It was a two-minute conversation. This time they were not smiling widely. That was a good clue. But jokes aside, he knew. One always knows.

And yet, hearing them say it… hearing those words spoken aloud, the starkness of those words, their matter-of-fact unambiguity… unchangeable, unalterable, unrepairable, unredeemable, reverberating around the room, ricocheting off walls, bouncing on the floor, hitting the ceiling – playing keepie uppies with his life – had come as a violent shock.

The heartbreak followed.

Slowly as the realisation sunk in, the conception of a future entirely different from the one dreamed of, a future without prospects or possibility – *without football* – his mind went listless, and a totalising pain set in. The business of internalising a truth-absolute that is so fundamental and so final was much, much harder than he had ever imagined.

What do I do now? he thought.

The answer – NOTHING – made him more terrified than he had ever been in his whole life.

This final phase or stage of the rejection process – like the final stages of a terminal illness – was when, as he put it to people later when he could get himself to talk about it, the mindfuck started.

The rest, as they say, is his-story.

> The next stop is…
> The next stop is…
> The next stop is…

Malfunction on the automated announcement system. Apparently, it too is stuck.

Sniggers from the passengers. Murmurs of discontent. Typical. They think. Nothing in this place works. They think. All that tax money. They think. And nothing works.

Baker Street station, the bus driver mumbles apathetically into the microphone. Sherlock Holmes Museum. Madame Tussauds. Harley Street.

Harley Street, Aron thinks to himself. Somewhere on that street was number 21. Lucky number 21.

Blackjack.

EIGHT

Four people, three conversations, between one stop and the next. The slipstream of rush-hour traffic.

It's like this. While he knows that many people riding a London bus would prefer no one and no conversation, being in close proximity with other humans has never bothered Aron. He would even go so far as to say that it is a kind of treat for someone of his inclinations, meaning that for as long as he can recall, he has always been interested in humans and more specifically in the observance of human behaviour. Joe will often paraphrase – and with undisguised disdain – the alleged Margaret Thatcher quote about how a man over the age of twenty-six riding on a public bus should consider himself a failure. Well, Aron thinks, all he has to say to the ghost of Maggie by way of a reply is that failure or not, at least he can claim he has lived in the world, because this… looking at people's faces, listening to them talk, hearing their stories, imagining their lives… is for him part and parcel of partaking in the human condition – this to him, is life. He once heard a famous novelist on the radio say that voyeurism was the single most important qualification needed to be a good writer. On that basis alone, Aron would be a good writer. But then, there was the problem of grammar, which understandably – given the profile of the novelist – perhaps did not occur to her to mention. No matter. We know what we know, and what we don't usually does not even enter our minds to consider.

And so.

Four people, three conversations...

The first of these conversations comes from a young girl in her late teens sitting on the seat next to Aron. She is wearing some sort of loose black garment that is draped around her body like a bedsheet, but with holes cut out on the sides from which two very skinny, very pale arms emerge. She has long straight hair that is streaked partially blonde and partially black, going all the way down to her waist. Aron personally thinks of the colour-combination as what he would call 'acquired taste'.

The girl is on her phone for the whole time, and even though Aron knows it is not polite to make other people's business his business, the thing with public transport is that it can't be helped. It's not like he's *trying* to listen...

I just told them, she is saying. Just like that. I mean I didn't plan it that way. Like I agonised over it for weeks, like how I should tell them and what I should say, and my reasons, and I rehearsed this whole big speech and everything, but then when it came down to it, I was like fuck it. So, I just said it. Like straight out.

She pauses to listen to the person on the other end, and then continues. Do you *think* they were cool about it? No, come on, obviously, they were shocked. Like I never expected them *not* to be shocked. I mean, I don't think they were expecting it *at all*. Like I never dropped any hints or anything along the way, so it's not like they were like even remotely prepared. She starts laughing. Yeah, I know right!

But you know what Em, it's not like it's some impulsive thing I just thought of like last night and I'm making this *huge* life decision based on some like stupid whim. I mean it's my *life*. I've been thinking about it for a super long time. Like I'm not an idiot. She rolls her eyes which Aron notices are a very unusual and beautiful shade of green. The colour of jade. Even though they *think* I am. What? No. The weird thing is they started screaming at each other and blaming each other and it's like I wasn't even in the room or this wasn't even about me. I mean, bloody hell, my parents can be so narcissistic, it's not even funny. Like, you think you've seen it all and heard it all, but nope – they keep surprising you like a gift that keeps on giving. Like seriously, I must have just stood there for like twenty minutes while they were just going at each other. Ridiculous, irrelevant stuff too, like she was yelling at him for mixing up the whites and the colours in the washing pile and leaving cups of half-drunk coffee all over the house that apparently *she* has to pick up every night and he was like you can't even take a shower without making the whole bathroom wet and totally random crap like that. I mean can you even believe that shit! Finally, I was like, guys, *seriously*, this isn't *about* you!

She nods vigorously into the phone. I *know* right! Amazing how married people can be so utterly beastly to each other. It's so boring. Anyway, the point is it's done. It's been the single most stressful part of this thing I swear. Just thinking of *how* to tell them. Like I don't need their permission, but it would be nice if I got their understanding. Shit. Hang on, I'm getting off the bus. Yeah, I'm on the top deck and I'll like totally fall down the stairs and kill myself if I'm doing two things at once, so hang on, okay. Two secs.

Of course, the other thing about public transport Aron concedes as he sees the girl walking down Baker Street still talking into her phone, is that sometimes you don't have the faintest idea what someone is talking about. And of course, the chances are that you will never find out.

The next person who sits next to Aron is a short, slight man wearing a Jewish skullcap on his completely bald head. Aron has never seen a skullcap worn from this close up and he is overcome with a sudden curiosity to know how it stays on, balanced on the crown so perfectly. He may not be highly educated in science and things, but he understands the general concept of gravity. Like the whole thing with apples falling off trees and all that. So, he's looking right now, and he can't see a single strand of hair, let alone any pins or clips or anything one would logically expect to hold the thing in place. And yet this apple ain't falling off the tree...

So... how?

But soon enough, Aron is distracted by something else, namely the man's posture which is so unusual, it is truly remarkable. His upper body is a perfectly perpendicular line, spine sitting flush against the back of the seat. The head is held erect, neck extended, chin up, eyes looking straight ahead. The lower body, similarly, is a straight line, parallel to the ground, buttocks tucked away, thighs touching, knees together, legs absolutely straight. Like a human replica of the number four.

Carol, Aron thinks, would be mightily impressed. His mother is always banging on to them about the importance of posture – sitting straight and standing tall, as she puts it. It's important, she says, especially for boys who look like J and you. You two ain't kids no more and things change for all of us when we stop being kids. But they change more for some folks than for others, she adds cryptically. Anyway, the point is: white people don't like to see boys that look like you slouching, it makes them nervous. Then she gives a great big sigh that comes deep from her belly and makes her shoulders heave. And Lord a Jesus, we all know it's best not to make white people nervous.

Maybe the Jewish guy was given the same advice by his mama, Aron thinks, 'cause he sure as hell following it. Aron watches carefully; nothing changes. From his statuesque position, the man doesn't budge for almost the entire duration of his journey, although it is also true that his journey is only one stop long. Still, even for this short amount of time, he manages to stay completely immobile. Even his heavily lidded eyes appear not to be blinking although Aron knows this is not humanly possible. Then, so suddenly it seems to surprise the man himself, he opens his mouth and yawns cavernously.

Excuse me, he says clapping a large and noticeably hirsute hand to his open mouth but looking straight ahead as if he is speaking to no one or nothing in particular, except maybe to the front window. Didn't sleep all night, he says. Neighbour's dog, he adds mysteriously, providing no further explanation.

A second later – still looking directly ahead – he asks if the bus will be stopping at Golders Green and Aron, knowing that the front windowpanes aren't exactly going to be replying anytime soon, says that it does. Then for no real reason except that he feels like being friendly, he decides to add how he'd been there once to attend a mate's uncle's nephew's bar mitzvah at the synagogue on Dunstan Road. The man half-smiles but says nothing, and then at the stop for London Business School, which is very far away indeed from Golders Green, he stands up as enigmatically as he sat down and just like that, he's gone. London *Business* School, hunh! Carol would have said if she was here, shrugging her broad shoulders and grinning her wide infectious grin, maybe he had some *business* to do!

The thought of his mother just then sends great beams of

warmth through Aron's heart. A wonderful woman, Carol – when he and Jordan and C'mon were kids, he had believed Joe when he told them their mother was Superwoman. Joe usually graced the claim with one of his trademark winks, but Aron chose not to pay attention to the nuances of that detail, for it is human nature to believe what we want to believe, and Aron truly believed he was the child of a superhuman. It was true, certainly, that all what Carol did on a daily basis seemed beyond the capability of an average human, for she left for work in the morning and returned home in the evening, yet their home was always spick and span, fresh meals on the table every night, not a speck of dust in sight. Yvonne needed false teeth, Carol was on it. C'mon needed a dress for the school gala, Carol was on it. Homework, football matches, prize day, you name it, there was Carol, true and trusty, permanently cheering her family on. Which is what makes that brief period of her disappearance even more baffling and impossible to understand, but Aron only knows what he's been told, which in truth is not very much. Still, that was all before his time, and for as long as he's been alive, Carol's never not been there.

Thinking of his mother in this way always makes Aron feel guilty about the bad stuff he had gotten himself mixed up in not that long ago. Not that she knows or is ever likely to find out. But *he* knows, is the point. He knows how it would make her feel if she did ever find out. Although he is a changed man now and his mother must surely believe in redemption, Aron thinks – after all, she married Joe, who at the time he met her, was, in his own words, a newly redeemed man. Bless her heart, it ain't just because it's his mum, but the woman was full of goodness. Even how she spends her days looking after old people at the care home on Garnet Road. It ain't all fun and games, Aron knows that; most of the residents in that place needed complete care, a lot of them couldn't eat or drink unassisted, some needed help bathing, a few had lost control over bladders and bowels... And minds. Oh yeah, some of them were totally crazy too; Carol had come home just the other week with a bruise on her forehead because this one man she had looked after from *time* got up that morning, picked up the flower vase on his bedside table and decided to throw it at her. So, he knows what his mother does for these people, and he knows too that she doesn't do it for the money. Even now she does it, even to this day, even though she herself ain't young no more, even when Joe is always telling her to stop and rest – no rest for the wicked she will smile and say, keeping busy keeps me young Joe, you don't want no old woman sleeping next to you, now, do you?

It's a fond reminiscence. Aron smiles fondly. She was a good woman, Carol, if there was ever such a thing. And so, if she ever discovered that he'd been involved with those brothers, acting like a big guy, thinking he's some kind of roadman, it would be certain to break her heart. Once again, he's glad he got out when he did. It's a feeling he's had recurrently for some time now, a great gladness that comes from inside him, a kind of gratitude that he was able to conquer the evils of greed, to dispel the illusion that so many young people like him are fed these days, this bullshit that a person can get rich quick without putting in the work, 'cause you only got to open your eyes and you realise it's fake, it's all fake, ain't nobody got rich by pimping, by dealing, by sitting on their arse, by offending and reoffending. Or even if they did, it came at a steep price, 'cause he knows those people and he knows that not a second goes by, they ain't thinking that one day they gonna be taken away from everyone they ever loved.

It is a grim thought and Aron is thankful, just for this moment, that the seat next to him has not been taken. He allows himself to spread out a bit though he's skinny enough not to need the extra space. But this, he thinks, is the very definition of luxury, innit, indulging in something that is not a need. Still, you can say he's doing it for mind-space, if not for body-space. For this precise reason – meaning because he is taking a moment to indulge himself on the top deck of a London bus – he happens to be turned sideways, his back against the window, body angled directly towards them, when the two women appear at the top of the stairs.

Now, it is an indisputable fact that certain reactions of the human body are not completely under our control. For example, in the instance when two or more people appear at the same time in our visual frame, our eyes tend to single out one person, who coincidentally also happens to be the most attractive of the group. Funny that. The mechanics of this are so instinctive and automatic, it doesn't even fully register in our consciousness.

Can't really explain it.

But.

No exception this time.

She could be anywhere between twenty-five and forty-five, stylishly dressed in a low-cut cream top and high-waisted cobalt-blue trousers that highlight her figure, which seems to be the intended purpose of the outfit. In the crook of her arm is a handbag that Aron notices matches her trousers in both colour and texture, as if they have both been cut out of the same material. A plenitude of glossy black hair is tied back in a low ponytail that falls loosely over her left shoulder. Her face is naturally tanned, the lips naturally puckered, the eyes, Aron notices, are very elaborately made up with a turquoise-blue outline on the top and bottom lids that lend her a kind of alert, animated look. All in all, it is a face that perhaps one would not call beautiful in the classical sense, but it seems to Aron that she is a woman who tries to make the most of what she's got. It is a quality Aron appreciates in people.

The woman she is with does not have this quality. That is as much as Aron's eyes will register before they move – involuntarily of course (of course, of course) – back to the first woman. She must have noticed Aron looking at her or maybe she is just used to people looking at her because she acknowledges him with a small, sweet smile as she takes the seat directly behind him. Her friend slides in next to her. Aron swivels his body back to normal position because it seems weird to be half-looking at them. One of them, it is impossible to tell which one, although it would not take a genius to guess, smells faintly of roses.

But you are from here, the pretty one says in distinctly accented English, it's different for you. Here, it is simply one of those things that happen. Sad but not some terrible tragedy. For me, in my culture, it is a totally different thing. Divorce is not that common still and there is a big social stigma associated with it. I can already imagine the horror of my parents if I even suggested it. My father will probably be shell-shocked and not know what to say at all. But my mother! God, my mother will more than make up for his speechlessness. My mother has always been obsessed with what other people think. For her, this will be like death. She sighs. And then of course, after the initial shock, she will find some way to blame me and use the children as pawns and try to talk me out of it. By the way, she's already said before that she thought I was way too independent and free-spirited and just because we live in England where women act that way and try to pretend they are superior to men, it doesn't mean we should forget who we are or where we come from and how we should behave as women. We are daughters, wives and mothers, she believes, before we are ourselves.

But surely, the Englishwoman says, you don't believe that sexist nonsense.

No, of course I don't *believe* it. I'm just telling you how she thinks, and that somehow or other, she will make it my fault; it's nothing new, she always has. Even with the most trivial things. Once she went into a mad rage because she heard me use a term of endearment towards my daughter. You need to stop Englishing yourself, she said to me. Calling your children sausages. It's unhealthy, it will damage them permanently. You should have seen my mother! Her face was red. She was really angry. It was incredible to me how angry she was, like she genuinely believed I was damaging my children. But, coming back to my present situation, the only place where I think she raises a valid point in all of this is regarding the children. We can't *not* consider the children. I mean, I know in such situations everyone always says it is better for children to have their parents in separate spaces rather than be in the same house with arguments and unpleasantness. But I don't believe that to be true. I think that is a fiction, a story we tell ourselves to make us feel better about the thing we have done, albeit unintentionally, to them. No, my mother is right about the children. It will dismantle their lives.

The woman next to her sighs. These things are always so much harder when children are involved, she says. Especially when they are little. I mean at that age they don't really understand anything. I don't know about yours, but ours cannot even entertain the thought that we might have a life of our own that does not involve them twenty-four-seven. It's like we have no other business on this earth except to play mummy and daddy to them for the rest of our existence.

The pretty woman gives a small, high laugh. Yes, she says. Ours are the same, but they use us for different purposes. They adore their father. They go to him when they want fun. They come to me when they are in distress. It's like asking someone to make a choice between fun and distress. Toy shop or the dentist's surgery. What do you think they will choose? Although I would never make them choose, obviously.

Obviously, her friend says. Nobody wants a *Kramer vs. Kramer* situation.

I love that movie, the foreign woman says ruefully. The kid was amazing in it. But it was so sad. I think I cried through the whole thing. And that was before any of this was personal. If I saw it now, I can't even imagine what it would do to me.

Wait, the other woman says suddenly, and Aron knows she's leaning forward because he can feel her breath, warm and unpleasant, on the corner of his neck. That funky glass building – isn't that where Nick works?

Aron looks out of the window. They are just crossing the Wellington Road roundabout, and there it is, a tall, uber-modern-looking building that looks like it is made entirely out of infinite facets of mirrored glass. The effect is both spectacular and surreal because everything of the world that is reflected in it is reflected right back at the world, like a kind of artificially forced self-awareness.

Yes, the woman says sighing, he's probably still in there. Probably be there till midnight. Sometimes I think he makes excuses to stay late just to avoid being with us. Or maybe it is to show us how important he is.

There is a rustling sound from behind, followed by the rich aroma of chocolate. It makes Aron realise he hasn't eaten since that chicken mayo sandwich at lunchtime, not counting the Coke and crisps he finished before boarding the bus. Sorry, the Englishwoman says, you don't mind do you, I just haven't eaten all day. Would you like some?

No, no, I'm fine, comes the reply, I'm good. I'm not hungry.

The woman sighs. No wonder you're so skinny. Anyway, I guess the good thing is that you guys are here and whatever happens and whatever you decide, hopefully your kids won't subscribe to those archaic ideas about women.

Yes, the pretty one says sadly. Yes, it's strange, I was thinking that exact thing earlier actually. I mean, it doesn't help matters that I happen to earn more than Nick.

Or that you're more beautiful, the other woman says with a tinge of awe in her voice.

This is met by a short silence in which Aron imagines the woman behind him is making some kind of gesture of modesty that effectively dismisses the idea.

You're sweet, she says after a pause, and maybe beauty is power too in a way, but I was thinking more of financial success, money as power, and in that regard, really, it is me against two people, Nick and his ego. With the children stuck in the middle. But as you say, the only saving grace is that we are here and not in my country. In my country, the choice would be obvious, and my husband wouldn't even have to do anything to make it go in his favour. I mean, honestly, he could lie on the bed like a corpse, and I could run around all day long like a crazy person organising their lives and still they would pick their father because in my country it is the default option. It's ingrained, branded into the brain from the minute you are born. My sister and I grew up that way too. That's why my mother has the ideas she has. It is totally normal for her. All the women there think that way because it is the only way they know. It's how their fathers acted, then their husbands and then their sons. The men dictate everything, they do not allow the women to make a single decision, it is not even a matter of considering who has more expertise in this or that, it is just the done thing that the men make all the decisions, personal and professional and financial, including what cut of chicken to buy from the supermarket to cook for dinner. But the cooking of the chicken, ah, but that is a different matter. In that they are helpless and totally dependent on the women. So needy! Just like their own children. That's why the children side with the men, you see. They are one and the same if you think about it.

The Englishwoman laughs. That's actually so on point. You know, the other day…

But Aron never learns what happens the other day. There is a vibration in his back pocket followed by the joyful notes of the ringtone which Aron had purposefully picked upon procuring the phone, going through the whole list of available options, shortlisting a few, selecting finally the one he considered the happiest. If he'd picked a she-phone, he remembered thinking at the time with a grin, the least he could do was make her happy. Yo! he says, trying his best to conceal the phone with the palm of his hand because in the newly switched-on fluorescent glow of the bus lights, it suddenly looks a whole lot pinker. Wha'g'wan bruv! Nah, nah man, just ridin' the bus home innit. Oh really, naes, naes. Yeah man, sure, for sure. When would dat be den? Tonight? He hesitates. If you could see him, you'd see him with his eyes closed, his face clenched as if he is fighting something, willing it to go away, to leave him. Monsters. An army. They are familiar to him. He recognises them all too well. With extraordinary effort, he replies, and he surprises himself how composed it comes out. Nah, he says, not tonight mate, nearly gone seven already, bare tings to do innit. Yeah, another time, definitely, gimme a bell bruv, anytime, anytime. Yeah, yeah. In da hours, blud, bae for now, peace out, yeah.

He puts his phone away pensively. Over the past few months, meaning since he got himself tangled and then thankfully untangled in the bad stuff, he has come to realise rather philosophically that while 'yes' may be thought of as the diametric opposite of 'no,'

God never intended for it to be so simple. Christ, no. Ain't so straightforward in real life 'cause of that complicating influence called temptation. Those were the monsters in his head – the collective forces of temptation. The sweet, irresistible promise of brotherhood. Bonding over a drink. Then two. A joint. Then two. Then more. Caned before you know it. Gets you every time. So easy to say yes, innit. So hard to say no.

Nyla said it to him once too. Not in any direct way, 'cause she's not spoken to him about all of that and what he was doing in any direct way. But she's hinted at it. The problem with getting *involved*, she said, is once you in, you in. And you in deep. And you listen to me now, A, when you in deep, you in deep, ain't no easy way out. She's right of course. Except the only problem is that when most people get involved, they are very far away in their own heads from realising concepts such as the immutable nature of mutual exclusivity.

Aron looks out of the window.

The streetlamps are on now, small clusters of brilliance along the road. A few shopfronts glow. More light shines from second and third-floor windows. People home for the night. But even as dusk deepens around the city, it will not shush. No, this is central London; always busy, always heaving. So many people, all going somewhere, all with a plan. And him, Aron Wilson? He also – finally, finally – has somewhere to go. He too has a plan. He's not going to let this one slip. We make our own luck, Carol always says.

Behind him, the two women are still engaged in their conversation. Yes, of course they know, the foreign woman is saying. It's been kind of hard to hide. You try to protect them, but we live in the same house, and they hear us arguing and well, they're not stupid. The other day he struck me across the face so hard, I thought I would lose my two front teeth.

Aron puts his ear buds back on out of some vague sense of respect he feels the situation is owed. Stormzy fills his ears. R&B, afrobeat, a real gospel choir, strings. Intimacy, regret, anger, resignation. Innovation. Emotion. Necessity is the mother of invention.

I mean he justifies it as jealousy...

Aron turns up the volume.

... I do it because I am jealous, he says, and I am jealous because I love you...

Aron drums his fingers on the window.

... but what will he say when he's killed me, how will he justify it then?...

But Aron's not listening no more.

... what will he tell the children? What will he do with the body?

Lay Me Bare.

(Says Stormzy)

NINE

They've erected an elaborate system of temp lights in the middle the street. The location of the lights is highly inconvenient, right at the mouth of the road, so when it is red, the turning traffic has nowhere to go. The whole problem is especially amplified at rush hour when the volume of traffic is so high, even a small back-up causes the whole system to collapse. This is the thing with big cities, everything is fine-tuned to work on such a tiny margin of error that it simply cannot accommodate anything outside of that. From the front window, Aron can see the impossibly long line of cars snaking its way around the orange and white cones that stretch endlessly ahead. London's a great city, the Professor man had declared. Aron slightly disagrees. It *will* be a great city, he thinks. When it is eventually done.

The number 13 groans to a halt behind a black cab. Someone somewhere blares their horn loudly and protractedly. A series of honks inevitably follow. Aggression needs but one leader to let rip.

Aron looks outside his window. They are stalled right by that posh soap shop. Lush, it's called, sells bath bombs and things. All kinds of different colours and shapes and textures and whatnot. Stuff don't even look like soap. Look like something you could eat.

Expensive as fuck. Always someone outside that store handing out free samples on a tray. Red-headed girl there now wearing a black apron, looking bored. People gathering around her in hordes. No one, Aron concludes, not even rich people, can resist a freebie. Nah. He edits the thought before it's even complete. No one, *especially* rich people, can resist a freebie. Is the whole reason they rich, innit.

The shop makes Aron think about his father.

Joe used to sell beauty products. Before he retired. Before he sold beauty products, he was an alcoholic. Before he was an alcoholic, he sold soap. When he was an alcoholic, he lost all the money he had made selling soap. Every last penny, all gone, dissolved, just exactly like the soap he sold. Aron's not a gambling man, but ten quid says the exact amount Joe lost could be matched, penny for penny, to the cost of the new upholstery at the local pub. 'Recently refurbished', the sign claimed. What do you know! 'Thanks to the unwavering patronage of one Mister Joseph Wilson', it should have said below that. Zero sum gain, as the wise men say. As for Joe, found himself on the street. Which happens occasionally when one has drunk away the rent money. Joe struggled. First a little, then a lot. Finally, even the pub refused to extend him credit. Sorry mate, the bartender said apologetically, I'd lose me job. That for Joe was it, the watershed event. Or, in other words, what some folks would call rock bottom. When The Lamb and Lions turns a man away, you know it's gone to pot. A choice then lay before him. Below was asphalt. Above was sky. Rise or fall, Joe's own father, the Antiguan preacher, used to say, rise or fall. Joe rose. Sought help. Received it. Rehoused by the council. Under strict conditional guidelines: quit the bottle. Get a job. Keep the flat. Or lose it. Easy as you make it, really. It wasn't, as a matter of fact, 'easy', no matter how many ways you stretched the imagination, but Joe had made his choice. A new wave of consciousness washed over him. A renewed awareness of this timeworn concept called life. The thing is, Joe liked life. Joe wondered at life. Joe wanted to live. That's the choice he made then – he chose life. Joined a local AA group, cleaned up, made a plan. Beauty products. Exactly like soap, only better. Same graft. More margin. Did that for exactly ten years and then retired. That had been nearly twenty years ago. He has always applauded himself for timing it all so perfectly because not long after he retired, the profession itself seemed to retire. The internet had just been born and as it turned out, that baby was so big, a whole heap of businesses had to die just to make space for it to exist. But it wasn't any particular gift of foresight that led to Joe's retirement. He'd just had enough. Experienced the struggle. Understood it. Overcome it. Now, he wanted to enjoy the other side. Slow down. Live. All the way until he died.

I milked it when it was good, mate, that's all I can say, he says sometimes to whoever will listen. When door-to-door was booming, Joe Wilson was at the door!

It doesn't take much to get Joe to talk. He loves an audience, his own father's habit. Gift of the gab. Imbibed from those early years of listening to his father deliver sermons. Or maybe these things are just in the blood. Genes, as they say. Aron smiles to himself. Yes, his father is naturally loquacious, loves to tell stories, loves to reminisce about the good old times: London ain't what it used to be innit. Different city. Different people. Nobody got no time for nothing no more. Back when I used to go round ringing people's doorbells, they'd offer me tea and biscuits, a slice of cake sometimes, if it were my lucky day. Now-a-days folks just go ignoring the doorbell, innit, pretending they ain't home. At this point in the story, Joe always shakes his corn-rowed head, which is still beautiful, and the beauty belies his age. Come to think of it, Aron concludes, when it comes to beauty, all that matters, Joe's still got. Good skin. Good bones.

Good teeth. Or one could summarise it simply by saying 'good genes'. On this one, there's no debate.

Joe moved to England with his mother – Aron's grandmother Yvonne – when he was eleven. On a boat. All the way from Antigua where his father, Noble, was a preacher in the parish of Saint Philip. Sad thing, Noble preached one thing, practised another. When Yvonne was convinced that no amount of prayer could save her husband's soul, she wrote to her brother in England and secretly arranged for safe passage for herself and the boy. Sometimes Aron will ask Joe about his grandfather, but what Joe remembers is patchy. At least of Noble the father. He remembers a bit more of Noble the preacher. Tall and handsome with a naturally charismatic personality, he was not easily forgettable when he stood on the pulpit and performed, for that's what it was for him, an elaborate performance where he was the star. And the congregation, his audience – adoring and mesmerised – sitting at the edge of their seats, hanging on to his every word, lips quivering, bodies shaking with passion. Outside of the pulpit, when he was not performing, he was a different man. Best for everyone not to open that box. But yes, Joe remembers his father's sermons, maybe not the words necessarily, but how he used to cast a spell upon the whole room, make them forget about the heat and the sweat and the stickiness and stand up from the edge of those seats in a frenzy, no persuasion necessary, and puff up their chests and stick out their rear ends and sing and sway. Praise the Lord! Oh, the atmosphere in that room, the ecstasy! When the kids ask about their grandfather, this is the part Joe tells them. He lost his way, this is the part Yvonne tells.

Yvonne is still alive. Ninety-two years young. Age has had a strange effect on Yvonne's body. Her breasts have grown longer and longer over the years and now relax at her waist, while the rest of her has shrunk, smaller and smaller. The result is a peculiar sight to behold. Best for everyone not to open that box either. Never mind. Her brain is in place, exactly where it needs to be. And so, she is thankful. When de brain stops tinking, dat is the day come to meet de Lord, she says sagely. Says other things too, she's got no problem speaking, the problem's with hearing, because it's pretty certain to everyone that Yvonne can't hear no more. She's got a hearing aid she keeps buried in her undergarments and false teeth she soaks in a glass of rum. She's got her reasons for both. Nobody asks. Yvonne lives with Joe and Carol in a little bedroom on the top floor that she's personally decorated. It looks like Christmas all year around in that little room, complete with tree and reindeer and snow. Arranged under the only window in the room is an elaborate nativity scene, shepherds, sheep and angels bought over the years from various North London thrift shops and added to the collection, but the baby Jesus is authentic, carried like Mary in Yvonne's own arms across the four-thousand-mile distance from Antigua. Me no trust dese English tings, Yvonne says, turning up her nose and making her nostrils flare, all made, as you will see, in China. Well, I tink de Chinese know 'bout as much of de baby Jesus as me know 'bout de Peking duckling...

Yvonne gets on with Carol like a house on fire, which everyone, especially Joe, considers mighty strange since mothers and wives aren't meant to get along at all, let alone like a house on fire, but being a wise man, he knows when he's got a good thing going and he's not in a hurry to extinguish those flames.

Aron doesn't know this of course, but Yvonne played a big role when it mattered.

Derefore, a man shall leave his farder and his mudder and hold fast to his wife, and dey shall become one flesh. You still a preacher's bwoy, Joseph, Yvonne told Joe all those years ago when Carol decided to come back home, and dat is Genesis 2:24. Forgiveness is forgiveness, matters nuttin' whose sin is more sinful, we all God's children. De devil come over us all sometime or udder, dat is de troot Joseph, and it is de job of love to drive it away.

And so, for all intents and purposes, Carol views her mother-in-law as a saviour; after all she saved her marriage, and for that very substantial past debt, she is willing to let a lot of stuff go. Plus, Yvonne is naturally fond of Carol. Never had any daughters, never had any children but Joe, and for her, acquiring the Jamaican Carol via Joe is as good as if she were her own daughter.

Your mudder, Yvonne often tells her grandchildren, was only a shy little ting when Joe bring her home dat first time. Looking down at her shoes de whole while, I could see only de top of her head. Pretty braids and schoolgirl shoes and shifting her weight in dat peculiar way from toe to toe. Me still remember de happy day, when I say to myself, me always wanted a darter, and Lord a Jesus – dis is she! Only good ting dat came out of dat whole beautification biznezz, if you ask me.

It was true. Joe met Carol selling beauty products. Post the struggle, when he was a reformed man. Sold the lady of the house two bottles of perfume, walked away with her money and her daughter. Good old Joe, years of graft finally paying off, for he couldn't possibly have gotten himself a better deal. Aron knows the story. They all do. Joe tells it often, when they are all together on a Saturday evening sitting drinking rum after dinner. Your mudder, she opened the door for me that day, Joe says. It was raining and wicked black, although it was only gone three in the afternoon and when she open the door, believe – her face was like the sun! When I looked at that face, I said to myself, now Joseph, ain't she just the prettiest thing you ever seen in your whole life! Carol will always blush at this point, no matter how many times the story is told. She was so young, your mudder, Joe says, but fine-looking even then, innocent-looking, yeah, big open eyes. Hair in neat little braids starting here, at the top of her head, skin so light like tea with too much milk. Hello, she says to me, leaning on the door in her red-and-white checked dress that hung so modest below her knees, hello how can I help you? Lord, I thought looking at her, if only you knew the ways! At this point in the narration comes the comedic bit where Joe throws back his perfectly shaped head and starts laughing and even though it's not that funny, he's laughing so hard, it's hard not to laugh with him. So, before you know it, Carol is laughing too and Jordan and Aron and even C'mon, which is saying something. Yvonne as well, chortling, succumbing to her son's infectious laughter, sometimes with her false teeth in and sometimes not. And then, Joe continues, your mudder's mudder Ernestine – bless her departed soul – come rushing out like a Montego Bay hurricane, ready to shoo me away but change her mind after taking one look at me 'cause – here Joe plumps out his chest – most folks wouldn't *conclude* it if they saw me now, but I weren't a bad-looking brother in my heyday. Nuttin' too shabby now either Joe, Carol will pipe in and C'mon's various kids will make faces like it's not cool, though inside they like it, they like that their grandma and grandad are still romantic with each other, despite things not always being easy for them. Listen: Joe continues, so you got the mudder making a big fuss over me, offering rom cake and spice tea. And me, I got eyes only for the daughter. And the daughter, more interested in her books, 'cause that's what she done the whole time after she open the door for me innit, sitting cross-legged on the carpet with a book in her hands and looking up at me every few minutes over the book with those big open eyes. Meanwhile, your grandma Ernestine, deciding between two different perfumes, spraying one on each thick wrist and holding it up for me to smell to tell which I like better, what goes best with the natural perfume of her own skin. But one is Bergamot and Sandalwood innit, and the other is Lavender and Sage and the two cannot be compared – ain't nothing similar about them. So, I tell her I cannot go choosing, it's like picking between apples and oranges, impossible to choose, and she sits down in her chair and shifts her backside this way and that and fans her face with last Sunday's sermon and makes like she dealing with some great difficulty and then buys them both. Lucky day! Luck makes a man bold innit. Shall I, I slip in slyly before I get up to go, take your telephone number so I can bell you next time, maybe when I got something special for a special lady like you? Oh yes, she says, oh yes, what a good idea! Carol peeks at me over the book and she rolling her eyes but she smiling too, I can't see it because the book's blocking my view, but I know, I know, and that knowing is the thing that makes me double-bold. So I ring the very next week and announce that I got some new hand cream that will make Grandma Ernestine's hands soft as a baby's bum. Yes, yes, she says, how about half past two? So, there I was again innit, at half past two on the dot, rubbing cream on your grandma's hands. Put some on Carol too didn't I, held her hand for the first time, never looked back.

Aron has not told Joe about the suit-shop job. Not told anyone in his family because in truth he never believed it until he was there – physically standing there this same morning in that posh air-conditioned room with the new clothes smell. It seemed too... improbable. That sort of thing didn't happen to people like him. Breaks, you could call it. Second chances. Nah, people like him didn't get no second chances usually. He was lucky. He knew it. Joe would be glad. Proud too. Joe understands the struggle. He's been through it, survived it and views it – meaning a brother's ability to survive the struggle – as a kind of honour that brings him one step closer to freedom, to the most authentic version of truth. Aron thinks of the look on Joe's face when he tells him and the thought of it makes him chuckle. He'll surprise him with the news tomorrow. Carol too. And Yvonne and Jordan and C'mon and all her kids whose names he sometimes finds impossible to remember, but to whom he is Uncle Aron. Unfair advantage they got, only one of him, innit, only one name to remember and so many of them. It's good timing, this day being Friday and all. He usually goes home on the weekend. His parents live not far from him, on Mountfield, down the road from the church, that location being of great and non-negotiable importance to Yvonne. He'll mention it casually over lunch or something. So, listen, he'll say, you'll never guess where I landed myself a job!

The bus is passing by the mosque. Behind it is one of the routes into and out of Regent's Park. Aron can see people exiting the park now that it is dusk, walkers and joggers and dogs and lovers, all returning to their respective homes. At the mosque they are doing their evening prayers; he can hear the call of the muezzin, rising above the noise of the traffic, penetrating and enigmatic. Aron considers himself a man of faith, although he is not a believer in the way that Yvonne is, or Carol or even Jordan. It is important, he thinks, to put one's faith in something, if only because the alternative – to put one's faith in nothing – seems too depressing to consider.

A faint breeze comes in from one of the open windows of the bus. It is still hot, even though it is approaching seven o'clock in the evening; he can feel the stickiness under his clothes. Must shower when he gets home, he thinks, he hopes the shower is working properly; it's been giving him trouble the last few days, starts off okay, then the pressure plummets leaving only an annoying trickle. The other day, took him twenty minutes just to get the soap off. So. Shower first. And then? Food. He needs food. There's leftover beef stew and noodles in the fridge that Carol gave him to bring back the last time he was there. She'd cooked way too much that night because Mohammed Ali had come round – he was the boy C'mon was currently sleeping with. That was his real name, really. He was a tall, heavyset boy from Hull who liked wearing tight T-shirts that showed off his incredible musculature. Aron wondered if at least some of C'mon's various children belonged to him. Difficult to tell, seemed equally indifferent to them all. Liked C'mon though. Liked his food too. So, Carol had cooked all that extra dinner on account of him. Packed the leftovers in a box, sent them back with Aron. Good for Aron, it had fed him three meals. He doesn't know how much there's left. Else, he can always whip himself up some eggs. He's good at eggs. Makes them just right. Even C'mon who fusses over everything admits he makes some banging eggs. And then? Sleep? Catch the game on telly? Or ring Nyla to come round maybe… maybe, yes. She's the only one he's told about the new job, she's been so excited about it, she's definitely gonna wanna know how it went. He grins at the thought of Nyla. She was one *fine* woman. Focussed too. Knows exactly where she wants to go.

He frowns absently at that thought. He feels like someone had just said that exact thing to him recently, only he can't now remember who. He's chatted to so many people already, he's not used to such long bus rides. Maybe he needs to sort himself out with a book or something from Monday. Borrow one from Jordan, Lord knows he got 'nuff to spare. Better than wasting time. Time is precious, he knows that now. Didn't before. But as they say, better late than never. Which as it turns out, is a saying about time. It comes to him suddenly, who said that thing to him. Was the pregnant lady, definitely. Said that thing about knowing where one comes from. It's true. He needs to know, he's put it off too long. Whatever it is, he can handle it, he's a grown man now with a proper job. But he knows it won't come from Joe or Carol. They're joined together at the hip, united in their silence, never is he going to get one of them to betray the other. Nope, if he's going to get anything at all, it'll have to be from Yvonne. A true believer, she's never lied in her life, and at ninety-two, Aron knows she's not about to start now. Too close to the end to start sinning. Too risky. Yup. He'll ask Yvonne tomorrow. She's the only one who'll tell it how it is.

TEN

Nyla! Nyla! Nyla!

Gold hoops on her ears. Tight curls closely cropped. Tortoiseshell glasses. Blue jeans and a long wool coat, all the way to her ankles in this pretty coral colour. She looked like the sunrise. At the tills of Leon's Food & Wine on a cold evening in November.

I know you, Aron said reverentially, for beauty like that must be revered.

She cocked her head slightly. Looked at him. Sighed. Turned back to Leon who was examining her eggs to make sure none were broken. Pursed her lips. Leon laughed, a wide-open gummy laugh.

No, really. I ain't just saying that 'cause you pretty. You *are* authentically pretty, but I ain't just saying that because of it I mean. I live round here, don't I? Ask Leon, he'll tell you, same as you, you Jamal's little sister, innit? See I *told* you I know you, he finished triumphantly when she turned around in surprise at the mention of her brother's name.

Yeah, so? she said, recovering with remarkable aplomb, you know my brother. That don't mean you know me.

Man, where you been though, Aron said, last time I saw you, you was this high. He raised his arm about three feet off the ground.

Inside her glasses, she rolled her eyes. I was that high when I was seven.

Aron grinned. But that's what I'm sayin' innit. Where you been since you was seven?

She ignored him. How much for them eggs, Leon? None broken, yeah?

Not a single one, princess. That'll be eighty-nine pence and I thrown in some Fruity Mentos for Clive, I know he got a strong weakness for them multi-coloured ones.

Aw, Leon, you're a sweetheart, she said, I'm sure my dad will appreciate them greatly. She smiled and Aron standing on the side noticed how everything just lit up electric when she smiled. He'd come into Leon's wanting smokes. Now looking at her, he's forgotten what he wanted.

I'm Aron, said Aron. What's your name? Can you believe I don't know your name even? And me and Jamal, man, we been mates since we was this high. The arm went back up. A little higher than the last time, an optimistic bid for a bit more credibility. Nothing ventured, Aron thought, nothing gained.

This time it was Leon who rolled his eyes, shook his wise old head. Kids these days, he thought in his mind, hopeless, ain't got no idea how to even begin to chirpse a girl.

But what's your name, Aron said. Can I ask you your name at least?

Uh uh, she said shaking her head, lips pursed.

Aw, now why you being all like that? I'm just chatting to you, just being friendly. Sister of my blud deserves some friendliness, innit? he grinned.

She set the eggs on the counter and put her hands on her hips.

Look here, man. You think just cause you some exotic brother, a girl's gonna give you her time? Well, think again, 'cause I ain't fooled so easy by those underwater eyes – they even real or you buy 'em at the opticians on the High Road?

For you? They real, he said, laughing. And they only for you – *I got eyes only for you*. He sang the last bit out in a nice-enough voice.

And then – finally – she laughed.

Her name was Nyla. They lived on the same estate, different blocks. He walked her home that evening. She let him carry her eggs. By the time they reached her door he had successfully convinced her to have a coffee with him. Only coffee. Only harmless. When's the last something bad happened over a cappuccino. Nah. He weren't like that. *That* type of brother. He was safe. He liked her that's all. She had nothing to worry about with him. Only a coffee. Very respectful. Very safe.

They stopped awkwardly outside her door, she with her back to the flat, him facing her, hands in his pockets. Aron noticed three doorbells. One was glowing, presumably the one that worked. The other two were crossed out in an X with a black marker. One had the words NOT WORKS in addition to the X in case of a total failure of imagination.

So… he said.

So… she said.

From the other side of the door, they heard sounds coming from a television that was clearly turned all the way up to peak volume. Lots of raised voices. Something about America's President gone building walls in Mexico.

Um, she said, I can take those now.

97

He handed her the packet of eggs with both hands like it was a ceremonial offering. He wished in that moment that he had something else, something better, to offer.

Thanks, she said, pursing her lips. Even in this short time, he had already learned it was something she did when she was trying not to laugh. In her, he found the trait adorable.

So… he said.

Inside her glasses, she widened her eyes. Amused. Knowing there was nothing forthcoming.

She decided to proffer a gift of her own. A gift of sorts. It was generous of her; the impact was instantaneous. You was a good player, she said. We all thought you was a great talent.

Wait, he said. You know me?

Of course. You was a good player. I just told you.

You know, Aron said, animated now, they wrote about me once. In the *Guardian* paper, no less. Never read the *Guardian* paper in all my life, 'cept that one time. Joe bought it, that's my old man innit, right here at Leon's shop, matter of fact. Read it out to everyone who would listen, yeah, and even to those who wouldn't. Man, he was so proud, Joe was. They called me a pacy, technically talented midfielder. All sorts of other stuff too. Gifted and shit.

I bet you was, she said kindly.

My knee innit? That was the problem. Every time I thought it was getting better, it started to hurt again. Dark times. Touched my head didn't it. I was proper depressed. I didn't wanna talk to no one. I just didn't even wanna play.

She said nothing. She knew her brother Jamal and this boy standing in front of her right now, trying so hard to be brave, had both started at the academy together. Later she heard he had been released. Jamal stayed on, played with the North London Legends then signed with Brentford. Done alright for himself. Every boy's dream. Not every boy gets to live the dream though; it ain't just about talent, she knows her brother's been lucky.

But I'm alright now, Aron said, I'm good. Great, actually. Moved on from there, got my body right, got my head right. That's the main thing, innit. Up here. He touched his fist to his temple, tapped it twice.

She nodded and he noticed a sudden softness come over her eyes. And maybe that was it, maybe that was what melted her finally, the heroic cheerfulness of that grand statement. So triumphant, so tragic.

I'll see you… he said after a minute, deciding right then that it was more than just her face that struck him or her sexiness even – 'cause *man*, she was sexy. Nah, it was something else he liked about her… her confidence, the way she held her head high and proud. Even just the way she lit up a room with her smile like that… Saturday, three o'clock, that good for you? I'll pick you up, yeah? Right here, at this very spot?

Yeah, she said, smiling as she left him that night. Sure. Right here is good.

And it was good. Everything was good. Everything was going smooth and friendly. They saw each other when they felt like it. No expectations. No disappointment. Nothing about got to spend Friday night with me. Or who were you with. Or where. Or why. Then, four months ago, ten-thirty on a Friday night, she phoned him, said she was on her way to his. He had been all excited, like a small child, but what he had in mind, clearly, she did *not* have in mind, 'cause she took off her coat, that's it, gone no further than that. Placed it carefully on the couch, the one part that wasn't soiled or damp from where the water was leaking from the upstairs people's bathroom. Then sat herself down next to it, legs together, hands on her knees. We need to talk, she said, looking all serious. They had talked. Or she had talked, more like. Something about steps. That they were on this step and she wanted to know did he ever want to take it to the next step. Did he even think about it? That's all, she said, that's all she wanted to know – did he even think about did he want to take it to the next step.

He didn't, was the truth, but somehow he knew instinctively that right then was probably not a good time to speak truth so he just sat there dumbly on the cardboard box with a cushion on top – clever improvisation for a second place to sit if one wanted to face the person sitting on the couch. Not that he had mates over for conversations of the sort that needed sitting across face-to-face. Or girls for that matter.

Anyway, so there they were, sitting face-to-face. And he understood that in asking if he wanted to take it to the next step, that *she* wanted to take it to the next step. 'Cause that's what girls do, is when they want something, they put it on you.

Aron Wilson, she was saying in a tone of exasperation. You even listenin'?

Uh oh. Calling him Aron Wilson like that only got one meaning. Means he was in trouble. Definitely, possibly in trouble.

An untimely drop of dark brown water missed her coat by an inch. Practically a sign. She flinched. Looked up at the ceiling. Pulled the coat closer towards her. Sighed. Opened her mouth.

Listen, A, she said. When I was younger, all I wanted was to have fun. We all did. Was the thing. And ain't nothing wrong with that. But I done all that. *Now* the thing I want is a steady life. And a steady guy. A good guy. Someone I can count on. Someone who'll stick around. Steady job. Steady head. I seen this shit with my own dad, man. You think this place is bad now? Aron watched attentively as she moved her hands to mean it weren't just the flat she was talking about, it was the whole thing – the block, the estate, the neighbourhood, this life, all of it. Speak to my dad and he says growing up in this place was like growing up in a war zone. Why'd you think Jamal started kicking before he even started speaking? Clive! Clive pushed him and pushed him and pushed him. This place was *grim*. Football was literally the only legal way out. Wanted something better for his son, 'cause he seen how his own life turned out. She shook her head. One job here, another job there. His whole damn life. Tell you something, A? If you everywhere, it means you nowhere. You gotta be somewhere. You gotta be someplace. *One* place. Then move up from there. You know. The shit my dad did, got him no respect, man. No respect. And this is the thing: if no one gonna be respecting you, you gonna stop respecting yourself. Works the other way too. If you ain't got no respect for yourself, ain't no one in the whole damn world gonna respect you. It's a circle. She traced a large imaginary circle in the air. Then she traced it the other way around. See, don't matter where you start, you gonna end up in the same place. You understand what I'm saying? she said.

Yes, he said, not understanding a thing.

She smiled that electric smile. That's great, baby. Is just that we been together six months now and all I need to know is: is you is, or is you ain't, up for doing this properly?

Aron stared at her. He knew he was meant to be thinking 'bout circles and steps. But right now, he was only thinking 'bout her curves. She had 'em in all the right places. Not skinny like some of the other girls he'd been with. Actually, like a lot of the girls he'd been with, 'cause seems the only thing most girls wanted these days was to be skinny. Not Nyla. Different that way too.

She was a big girl. Big, beautiful breasts he could bury his head in between and lose himself. Even her nipples didn't fit fully into his mouth, it drove him crazy. And other things about her drove him crazy too. Private places, so warm and inviting, like the Caribbean Sea. Jump right in baby, let me engulf you in my waves…

He liked big girls.

He liked her.

He *likes* her.

He likes that they have fun.

He likes that she laughs a lot and is funny and finds him funny.

He likes that the sex is so good.

He likes that they can talk about stuff after, her head on his chest, or his head face down between her breasts like it belongs there.

He frowns. He's not ready to go steady. But he doesn't want to lose her either. He knows such girls are hard to come by. Take his sister. Or her friends. All just the same. Wanting everything and doing nothing to earn it. This one's different. She cares about her own life. Works hard. Just the other day after he had reluctantly emerged from her Caribbean Sea, she started to tell him about how all these clients were always asking for her when they called in for appointments, her first, above everyone else. My slots are always full-up, she said. Every day, all day. And I know it ain't the same with the other girls. I know 'cause I see them, sitting idle, flipping through magazines or just on Facebook, wasting time. I ain't even got time for lunch most days, yeah, I'm so busy. Know what that means, she said, not waiting for Aron to answer, it means that one day, if I start my own place – and with that, her eyes gone all bright like two shining stars – maybe I could try takin' 'em with me, all them clients blatantly wanting only me to do their nails, waiting days for me even when the other girls got free slots. Think about that, A! My own place. Nyla's Nails. She rose from the bed, gracefully, like a lioness. Drew an imaginary banner. Nyla's Nails. In neon-pink letters. Just like a dream.

Had she inspired him?

Maybe that would be taking it too far.

But it had been a kind of awakening, a stirring up of his personhood. All this talk of plans and dreams, rather than being some illusory thing to be ridiculed, had done something quite different to his entire sensibility. It had made him realise, in an almost poetic way, that everyone – Nyla, him, *everyone* – needed a reason to exist in this world.

So, he'd quit the drug thing. That was true. And got the job at the suit place. That too was true. He doesn't want to think all that was on account of her 'cause that's admitting some shit about commitment he's not ready to do. But he knows she hated his getting involved. Hated when he said he needed to chip and she'd ask where and he'd lie and she knew it, and he knew, she knew. Hated even when he bought her stuff or took her out to the expensive restaurants where there's different people who seat you and different people who serve you and different people who pour you your wine. He took her once, didn't he, to the Italian place near Maida Vale station and ordered some fancy wine that came all the way from some place called Poo-Lia the waiter said, twenty quid for a bottle too, and she didn't say nothing, but raised her right eyebrow the way she did, all the way into her hair, like she working out in her head, how can he do that, where'd he get the money from. Not like other girls that way. Oh, he knows those girls, just take and take and take, don't care where or how, so long as they get shit. This one's... different. The other day he overheard her talking to her girlfriend on the phone. Made him fill up with warmth, just listening to the pride in her voice. Did I tell you, A's training to be Head Cutter, he heard her say. Deep, rumbling laugh involving every part of her body, from her toes to her eyes, made him wanna laugh just hearing it. Haha Tamy, that's a joke one, you givin' me giggles now. Head

Cutter as in the *tailoring* business, he ain't going around cutting people's heads off! Cutting *cloth*, at one of them snazzy men's places in the city. Yeah, 'zackly, tailoring for them city types. Suits and things. Bankers go there, innit. Lawyers. Professional people. Politicians. Boris Johnson. Prince William. James Bond. Whoever the current one is. That's who he'll be mixing with. That's who'll remember his name.

ELEVEN

So easy to get involved. So easy. You're over here. Over there is some shit. And then, fuck-knows-how, but you're over there. In the shit. Just like that.

Nine months ago, he done a favour for a brother. That's all he done. A favour. Package needed delivering. The brother in question, bloke by the name of Eldon Bailey, was stuck babysitting his kid sister 'cause their mum didn't show up after work like she said. Sitting in some dodgy bar by herself pissed off her head probably, he said to Aron on the phone. My sister's only two though, I got this job to do, but can't 'zackly leave her alone now can I. What if she burn down the flat with herself in it? Or throw her doll out the window and then jump out herself to get it? Okay, okay, Aron replied, I get the picture. He sighed. What 'zackly you need me to do? Easy, Eldon replied cheerfully, you won't *believe* how easy. All Aron had to do, he said, was show up. Show up, that's it. That is *literally* it! A simple exchange. You get yourself to my place. I give you a packet. You give it to the brother. That's it. Like that game we played when we was kids innit, pass the parcel. I pass to you, you pass to him. Easy peasy. You meet him inside the barber shop on the High Road. *Inside*, yeah. He'll recognise you, don't worry about that. I just gotta tell him look out for a brother with blue eyes. So, you give him the packet and he gives you cash. Count it though. Three hundred 'zackly. He hesitated. You get fifty. For your troubles. It's too much to be honest 'cause it ain't really *that* much trouble, but still. I'm fair like that. You help me out bruv, I help you, it's like that, innit. We take care of each other.

It had been the easiest fifty quid Aron had made in his life. Hard after that to stop. Told Eldon he wanted to help out some more, get involved. And then. Fifty here, eighty there, *two* hundred once, like winning the lottery. Just to hand over a brown paper bag to someone he didn't know and would never see again, didn't even know what was inside, didn't care. No small talk, no bullshit about the weather, nothing about what's your name and which ends you from and none of that unnecessary drivel. Just swap and chip.

All gone marvellously, innit. For the first time in his life, he had money in his pocket. Freedom to do whatever he wanted. Go to the cinema. Eat sushi. Buy a new pair of creps. Take a girl out someplace nice. Not confined to free shit. Or cheap shit. There was a brief period of total happiness Aron can remember when it had seemed impossible that anything could go wrong.

But then it did.

And now. He gets on the number 13 at Lord's. Eldon Bailey. The brother he done the favour for all those months ago. Aron doesn't notice him till he's on the bus, top of the stairs, turned around, looking the other way. At first, he finds it hard to believe that it's actually him. I mean, meeting like this! On the bus? He had thought he would never see him again, didn't think he would see none of them again, once he'd declared his intentions to the people who handled the money, procured the goods, made the decisions – the big men. That weren't easy either. Declaring his intentions just sudden like that. It took some serious bottle. But he done it, what counts. I can't carry on no more, he said. With all of this thing I mean. I gotta chip. Clean up. Get serious. I ain't no better than I am, I don't need nobody to tell me that, but... He put both his hands in his pockets and sighed deeply. This ain't what I had in mind for my life basically. It don't really matter on account of I ain't disrespecting nobody, but I done this for five months now and I feel like I got no sense of who I am no more. So. Basically, I'm out. I wanna be out.

They were cool about it. They gave him dap. They wished him luck. They didn't mention his one fuck-up. They didn't contact him again. That was two months ago. He's been clean ever since. No weed. No alcohol. Just a couple of fags here and there, not too many. When he told his siblings, they didn't seem to understand. To be fair, he veered skilfully away from revealing too many details, didn't let them in on the deep shit, just that he'd decided to sober up and settle down, get a real job. C'mon snickered over the phone and referred to him as Saint Aron and then promptly wanted to know if he had any 'left-overs' in the flat that she could 'borrow'. She'd be happy to come round and relieve him of the headache of disposing it. Alcohol or weed, don't matter which, anything will do, innit, I ain't picky like that, you know me, I ain't one to *discriminate*, she laughed. Jordan was his usual philosophical self, cautioned that it wasn't necessary to go to the other extreme, life was all about balance, finding the middle path. Nah, Aron replied. Lemme just do it this way bruv, see if I can. His brother laughed. Scene, he said.

And now he's here on the same bus, after all that. His former associate, Eldon Bailey. Baggy jeans. Two baseball caps. Ear buds. He's got his back to Aron, but he's gonna turn around now, any second. And he does. Their eyes meet. Recognition flickers, then deepens. Alright, blud! Aron says. Eldon grins. Takes off his ear buds, saunters up to the front, sits down on the empty seat next to

Aron. Long time, bruv, he replies. They clap hands. A complicated handshake follows. Aron heaves an internal sigh. That weren't too bad, he thinks with relief.

What you doing these ends? Aron asks.

The cricket, blud, Eldon says, adjusting his long legs in front of him. My man Jofra Archer's in there right now innit. What a man. GOAT, for real. Had myself some spare tickets. He shrugs. Went like gold dust.

Where'd you get 'em, Aron asks, exactly the question one mustn't ask a tout. Eldon loses his smile. He's got a great smile. Perfect teeth. Losing his smile is like when a cloud passes over the sun. Darkness everywhere.

Aron deflects. Onto himself. Don't really understand the game myself now, innit. Not like football. Football's easy. What it says on the can, innit. Midfielder, defender, attacker, goal. But cricket? Cricket's all 'bout some *complicated* shit, bruv. Third man. But where my first man and second man? Know what I'm saying? Technical and shit. Need all this gear too. This and that. With football, just need a ball, innit. And a foot. The deflection works. Eldon finds this funny. The smile comes back in exponents. He really does have a nice smile, Aron thinks. Teeth so perfectly aligned they could put a dentist out of work.

The tension eases. They move on from the cricket. Life. Music. Brothers they know. Speaking of, did you hear Curtis Ambrose blagged a job in music production, assistant to assistant studio manager at AudioHaus, Eldon says.

Is it? AudioHaus? Over in Wembley?

That's the one.

Woah, they big, man, real big. Good for him. That was his dream, innit. Aron shakes his head and laughs. Good for him, man, *good for him*. All that brother ever wanted to do was make music.

Yeah, that's it, that's it. Club-standard equipment and shit, state of the art, know what I mean. And your sister? Miss Seemone? How *she* doing? Eldon asks and the smile on his face tells Aron what he suspects but didn't ever wanna know and is now confirmed. He keeps his face inscrutable.

She good, man, she good. Same, you know?

Still with that white guy? Eldon wants to know.

Which white guy, Aron wonders, been so many, like counting blueberries in a Tesco's box.

He decides to take the path of least resistance. Nah, he says. That was over a while ago now, innit. Didn't work out for one reason or another.

Eldon peers into his eyes. She onto someone new or what, he says.

Dunno man, can't keep up with her love affairs, innit. Changes men like most girls change clothes. Makes me all muddled in the head, to be honest.

Well, you say hi to her from me now, Eldon says jovially. You tell her Eldon says come and give him a nice, friendly visit when she free sometime. We had a good time, you know. We had fun. Nice girl, your sister, peng too obviously, but real nice, that's the important thing. Sweet-hearted. Maybe confused sometimes, but – he shakes his head emphatically – ain't we all, man, ain't we all.

Once again, Aron finds himself in the position of having to change the subject 'cause what can he say about his sister? She's been in love her whole life, and yet somehow, when it matters, she's still ended up alone. Romantically, that is. Mathematically, she ain't alone, far from. She's got six kids with another on the way and sometimes even she can't keep track of whose father is who, it's so messed up. Just thinking about her makes him all flustered. He mops his forehead with the flat of his hand. It would be simpler if he didn't care. But he does care. That's the problem. He wants to care. He wants her to know he cares. She is his sister. But despite the noblest of intentions, what can you do with a girl who thinks the mere fact of her being born on this earth means she deserves the sun and the moon simultaneously and all together, packaged and delivered straight to her door? Always been like that, since she was little. When she was eight, she decided she wanted a horse. When she was twelve, she decided she wanted a prince. When she was nineteen, she decided she wanted to be a singer and move to New York. Deadly serious every time and when she got no horse and no prince and no New York, she moped around for weeks in a state of utter disbelief like why me, how could this *not* happen to me *again*? And still nothing changed. Even now, same story. Her needs grow costlier as she grows older but the gap between what she wants and what she can have stays constant – wide and unbridgeable and to Aron's comparatively simple mind, hopelessly incomprehensible. He looks out of the window thinking what can he talk about now.

The bus is still stuck near Lord's. Something up front is obstructing traffic, but whatever it is, it's too far forward to tell. Directly ahead, at the zebra, a group of school kids in uniform have just exited the stadium and are trying to cross the road. A harried-looking man with floppy hair and glasses holds up one hand to the oncoming traffic in a human stop sign. The other hand is making wide sweeping gestures from the pavement upwards, telling the kids to hurry up. The kids, in no obvious hurry, are clustered in little groups on the crossing, hollering and chatting and laughing, oblivious to the presence of the man, or the traffic, or, for that matter, of the world outside of their own heads.

Bare heads innit, Aron remarks.

Eldon rolls his eyes. England vee New Zealand, blud. Summer evening in August. Lord's. Home of Cricket. What'd you expect?

Now, speaking of expectations, Eldon's talking about did Aron know the extremely hilarious thing what happened to Marcus.

Marcus who, Aron says.

Footballer Marcus. Didn't you used to play with him way back when you was playing for the Legends?

Oh yeah, Aron says with a sudden, sharp pang of sadness for the dream which had so brutally slipped away, *that* Marcus.

Yeah, bruv, so *that* Marcus gone and become a priest.

He done what?

Become a priest bruv, Church of England vicar, believe! But get this. Poor kid. His own father went in. So, he become a Father. Father Marcus. Eldon starts to laugh. Peels of laughter, sudden and spontaneous. Exactly like a child. Someone somewhere in the bus shushes them. Eldon starts to laugh louder. Footballer Marcus to Father Marcus, ain't that just the funniest thing. For *real*, fam, I ain't joking you, honest to God. I was with him just this Friday night past. *Father* Marcus.

But wait, Aron says. His dad went in? I knew his dad, bruv. Rolled with him, didn't I? We did some shit together way back when I was cheffing at that Chinese place on the High Road. Ellis Sinclair. He's a good guy, I always liked him. When'd he go in? What for?

Eldon stops laughing. Baby face looks almost manly for a split second. Possession, he says in a hushed tone. Got careless. Fool. Five years. Mixed up with Fast Freddie and that lot. *You* know. Who you chipped from.

Aron's just about to ask more questions about Marcus, like where he is a priest, in which church and can Aron go see him 'cause he's been thinking lately about his own faith, but suddenly the white woman from two rows behind is saying, excuse me, excuse me, in her white-woman voice. Aron can't be sure who she talking to, Eldon or him, so they both turn around. Excuse me, she says, addressing Eldon for sure, 'cause she's staring at him in this immersified way with her small grey eyes.

Excuse me, she says. But by any chance, are you related to Nelson Mandela?

Am I what? Eldon says back.

Related to Nelson Mandela. I was wondering if by any chance you are related to Mister Nelson Mandela of South Africa. You look just like him, you see. Something about the nose, the way your mouth is structured, even your ears really, now that I look at you properly. You could be his grandson or something.

The way my mouth is *structured*?

Yes, dear, the placement and the shape. The texture too. Just like his.

Eldon laughs but Aron knows enough to know it is not a laugh of humour and should not be mistaken for one. If there is a comic side to this, there is none. Eldon don't see the joke even though he's laughing. Inside the laugh is a thinly concealed anger.

I ain't Nelson Mandela's grandson, he says.

Alright, dear. It's just the resemblance, you see… it is uncanny.

Is it? Well, sorry to disappoint you lady. Now if you'll excuse me, me and my mate here, we got some gangsta business to do.

The lady opens her mouth, but no sound comes out. The old man next to her has shut his eyes and is pretending to be asleep. Aron looks at him with interest, blud looks dressed like he's going out to fight a snowstorm or something. Just looking at him makes Aron feel hot.

Ain't this some bullshit, Eldon says to him, not bothering to keep his voice down. I mean you really gotta be white or something to think I look like Nelson Mandela. What she on about? Think she can make me the grandson of some saint-man and that make me all nice and noble so *she* feel safe on the bus? Like some kinda Zen-Buddha transference of good karma bullshit. Am I dreamin' or what? I'm sitting on the bus, minding my own business. Now, I'm part of some bollocks Japanese physics experiment. Now, Imma wear my shield. Now, Imma get ready to be transferred into. Now, I'm Nelson Mandela's grandson. Fam, that person is bare buki. I mean I ain't ejucated or nothing but even I got more sense than that, innit.

Aron grins and shrugs manfully cause there ain't much to say really in these kind of situations.

On a whim, he rotates his head and looks all the way back. The maid is still there, no one on the seat next to her.

Eldon's phone rings.

The bus stops at St John's Wood. People cross the street in hordes, office types, all of them typing into phones, oblivious to the world around them. Just like those kids he had seen earlier. But if that was innocence, then what was this? Ignorance?

He too had been like these people that one single time he fucked up, stuck inside his own head in exactly the same way. These people or those kids, whichever way you wanted to look at it, ignorance or innocence. Seeing no danger even while being smack in the middle of it. Except for one vital difference – he had no teacher holding up his hand stopping a bus from running him down. No protector.

It was wrong from the start; he sees it now, he didn't then. The venue agreed upon was a community hall at the back of a church. The timing was all wrong, a ballet class was about to begin. Little girls in tutus were streaming in holding their mothers' hands, the mothers, every last one, looking at him with that peculiar look like, *why you here*. Brother taking delivery of the package was already there waiting, standing at the back of the room by the piano with his hands in his pockets, looking bait.

You're late, he said pleasantly to Aron. He sounded French.

He was tall and very dark and had a kind of gentle, charming way of speaking so even when he was blatantly making an accusation it was like he was saying something endearing.

I ain't late, Aron said. I ain't never late, as a policy. Gives you grace the one time you need it.

The man shrugged. Okay, he said agreeably and took the package from Aron's hands so nimbly, it took a second for Aron to register it was gone. Well now we're attracting attention, he said, so let's finish this outside.

Just gimme the money man, it takes a second, Aron said, but not that forcefully.

The Frenchman smiled. Takes a bit more than a second, my brother. You're going to need to count it, aren't you. How do you plan to do that with fifteen pairs of maman-eyes on you.

He followed this with a little MJ moonwalk on the slick imitation wood floor. He was good, Aron had to confess. Later he would wonder why he hadn't made the simple connection. Enacted right there in front of his nose. The biggest hint of all. Smooth Criminal.

Aron shrugged. It was true. The room was full now, mothers and daughters. A slender swan-like white woman in a black ballet costume was in conversation with one of the mothers. Both women were looking at them. The white woman caught Aron's eye and began to walk towards them.

Uh oh, Aron said. Looks like she mean business.

See. That's what I'm saying my friend, the Frenchman said in an unruffled voice. Could have been avoided if you hadn't been late.

But I already told you, I ain't...

The man held up his hand gently, like he meant no malice.

Détends-toi, c'est cool! Chill, man. It's all good. Let's finish this outside like I said. It's quiet behind the church. I'm just going to stop by the men's room, been holding it in all the while you were late.

Aron shook his head. Why you keep saying that. I ain't late though.

But you were, the man insisted, but that's okay, we're all late sometimes. See you there. He cocked his head sideways.

I'll take that then, Aron said, reaching for the packet.

The man smiled and took a small step back, smooth, like a little slide, never taking his feet off that shiny wooden floor. I'm going to make a pee. I'm not swimming across the ocean to Algeria. We are in the house of God. Where's your faith?

Fool! He should have taken the hundred quid and chipped. Instead, Aron, moved by the talk of God and faith, sighed and shrugged and stepped out of the side door seconds before the ballet teacher arrived. She stared at him for a full minute through the glass panel, then turned gracefully on her heels and began conducting her class.

Aron waited in the churchyard, back by the smooth silent tombstones for nearly twenty minutes, empty hands in empty pockets, whistling a tune, while through the ancient, latticed windows of a crumbling medieval church, little black girls in bright pink tutus twirled round and round.

Aron slides his backside lower on the seat, puts his feet up next to where Eldon's are already tapping restlessly on the ledge. Tap tap tap. He's still on the phone. Aron sees a flash of some dark emotion pass over his baby face, but then he laughs boyishly into the phone, and there, it's gone, dissembled and diffused into the radio waves.

It's difficult therefore to know precisely what triggers the change in mood. Later, when he is running for his life, Aron will wonder if that's even important, this question of what triggered the change in mood. There was a change in mood, that's all, when something snapped, something popped, a breaking point reached, crossed, up and away over a threshold from which there was no turning back. That's all it takes sometimes, a second, a moment, the blink of an eye. For something to break. For the mood to change. In a bizarre moment, Aron wonders if it was the shoes. The fact of the shoes. His new ones, bright and showy like two orange suns, next to Eldon's own once-white ones, ripped at the toes, worn at the heels. Or maybe it was the phone call, whatever was said on that phone call. Or maybe it was the white lady calling him Mandela's grandson, blatantly pissing him off. He won't know is the thing. Not ever. Why did it happen, someone could ask him later and he would reply with the worst possible answer in the world – I don't know. 'Cause he doesn't and he never will. Why did it happen?

But it happens, is the thing. Eldon hangs up the call and says, where'd you get them creps, bruv, proper posh, innit.

Nowhere blud, just some guy flogging 'em.

Must have cost you bare.

Nah… not 'zackly real Nikes, to be honest.

Still, they wasn't free was they?

Nah… but they wasn't that much either bruv, look more expensive than they was, truly.

How much.

Dunno bruv. Can't even recall.

Thought you didn't have no bread and honey.

I didn't. I don't.

And the suit shop you working at? Just heard – Eldon points his chin to the phone in his hand – you get yourself a gig at some fancy-pants suit shop. You get it, fancy-pants – suits?

Oh that, yeah, haha, you give me the jokes bruv. Nah, not that fancy though. Basic gentlemen's store, is all. Just done my first day, innit.

Today was your first day?

Aron laughs. Yeah, that's it. *On the first day, God created light and called it day!*

The biblical humour, as intended, does not register on the other boy. His mind is on more practical matters. How much they paying you? he asks.

It is a direct question. Impossible to squirm out of. Aron realises this. He shrugs dismissively like it's no big deal. Like one-eighty a week, I guess, he says with deliberate nonchalance. Give or take. But I gotta pay out for tax and shit. So not sure honestly bruv, bit more than half that amount you can say, after the deductions and that. First day like I said, don't know nothing yet, not sure how I even blagged the job to be honest, mate.

So roughly a hundred then, Eldon says. Well, ain't that a coincidence. You know they took the hundred you owed them from me, yeah. Fast Freddie and those brothers I mean.

Aron baulks. He hadn't. They did? he says. Why'd they do that?

'Cause I made the introduction didn't I, blud. Recommended you to them in the first instance. So when you fucked up, I fucked up. Peak for you, peak for me.

I'm sorry bruv, Aron says and means it genuinely. That's a proper cock up, innit. I didn't know nothing 'bout that.

Well, now you do, so how'd you plan to fix it?

Aron looks distraught. Man, I got nothing.

Swear down now.

I'm proper skint, man, believe.

Eldon sighs and launches into a soliloquy. It's meant to be

instructive, but the bitterness within cannot be disguised. It cannot even be contained. It seeps out. Thickens and spreads. Aron presses his fingers to his forehead, like if he tries hard enough to will it away it will disappear, but Eldon's not ready to make anything disappear so easily.

You know something, he intones, Imma speak you a truth now. The route you taking ain't necessarily better than the one *we* taking. It don't make you superior to the rest of us, you know. Don't make you better than us. Soon 'nuff you'll be shut down by some white geezer for no reason. *Believe.* They ain't gonna *let* you get nowhere. And they ain't gonna tell you why. It's the struggle. Do you even understand the struggle? I understand the struggle. Four hundred years, bruv. You ain't gonna change four hundred years of history by working in some fancy-pants suit shop that give you the job cause you half-white. Half-white is no white, man, rules of slavery, one drop of black blood, make you *black*, bruv. As black as me. And me? I ain't gonna stand for no one disrespecting me. I ain't gonna be owned. I decided a long time ago, nobody steps to me. I take my own life in my own hands. Make what I need. Get outta here. Relocate to Spain. The Canary Islands. The Italian islands. The Greek islands. Any island but this island. Someplace basically where the weather ain't shite like *this*.

It's twenty-eight degrees out, Aron says quietly.

C'mon blud, you know what I mean, yo. Not today. Today's an exception innit. He smiles his disarming smile, but Aron knows it's not what it seems. Outside it might well be twenty-eight degrees. Right here, in this place between them, the climate is ice-cold.

Listen blud, Eldon says softly, so softly it's a whisper and isn't that way more terrifying than if it were a scream? It's gonna be like this. You gonna take me to a cash machine and you gonna give me what's mine.

Aron laughs, a funny, artificial laugh. Do I look like a brother with a hundred quid in the bank?

Eldon places a hand on Aron's knee. The gesture seems harmless enough, but the pressure is not gentle. No problem. You gonna take out whatever's there.

Blud...

Now.

Now?

Yeah, now. I see an ATM right there, across the street. C'mon.

Aw, man. You ain't serious!

Never been more. Yo, c'mon bruv. I wanna bun a zoot too.

Aron tries to stall. Driver ain't gonna let us off in the middle of nowhere bruv, he says weakly. Need to wait for the next bus stop innit?

But Eldon's up on his feet already.

They stop momentarily at the top of the stairs. Aron's mind is racing. Doing mental calculations. How much he's got in the bank. How can he get out of this situation. How can he make his friend change his mind. Try and be reasonable. Work it out... Or not? Find the opportunity and leg it. Lose the kid in the crowd. Jump into the Tube or something just as the doors close. Just buyin' time. Sort it later when the kid's cooled down. He's all crazy now. Don't know why. Trynna be the big man. He'll chill soon enough though. Can't reason with someone when they're unreasonable. He notices the maid distractedly from the corner of his eyes. She's talking to some Indian lady with nice hair.

Then they're running down the stairs, recklessly, two at a time, not holding the rails. Invincible and yet totally, completely, at the mercy of luck. Also, of the driver. One unexpected step on the brakes and they'd fly off, hit the ground straight on their faces, hard. Break a nose. Cut a lip. Or worse. Thankfully for them, the driver doesn't brake. The bus slows down and stops at a red light halfway between the St John's Wood and Queen's Grove bus stops. Eldon stands on his toes, springs upwards, so light on his feet, elongates his body, extends his arm all the way up to push the red emergency button above the rear doors. The doors swing open, the boys jump out, laughing – it is involuntary, they may be enemies to each other at this moment, but each knows who – what – the bigger enemy is. Behind them the system – ancient, impregnable, white – screams expletives into the microphone.

TWELVE

He sees the glint of metal in the suffused brilliance of the streetlight. Feels a searing pain in the taut muscles of his stomach. It penetrates his flesh, in and out, once, then twice. It is cold. The pain is deep.

And then, they vanish, both the metal and the pain. He feels something else, hot and sticky around the area of his belly button where twenty-three years ago the cord connected him to the womb that gave him life. Carol's or not, that question is still unresolved, suspended in time, in space, like all life's biggest mysteries.

He was never meant to know.

He falls to the pavement sideways, his head hitting the black tarmac, still warm from the day's sun. His ear pressed to the ground like that, he can hear the vibration of the footsteps running away from him, they are thunderous at first, then muffled, then they fade away, then nothing. He closes his eyes, then opens them again.

What had gone wrong?

An argument at the ATM machine concerning a missing wallet.

a

missing

wallet.

Merely an inconvenience when the world is not in crisis.

When is the world not in crisis?

A careless mistake misconstrued as a lie, a ruse, plain disrespect. Do you take me for a fool? I ain't gonna be owned so easy. Eyes flashing with anger. Stupidly, he had decided to run. But where to run? Where to hide? It only took a few minutes. One strong hand grabbing his shoulder. Turning him around roughly. The other hand reaching for something. Then the glint of metal.

And then, miraculously, he sees the maid. The maid! Yes, the maid crouching on top of him, she is on all fours like an animal, her hands grasping the top of his shoulders, her face directly above his, looking down at him. She is much prettier up close than she had looked from a distance, that first time he had spotted her down on the street from the top deck of the bus. For a second, he marvels at the dichotomy of this reality, the material reality of this girl, at how what had seemed aloof and slightly incongruous from a distance, seems pure, almost divine, from this angle, as though distance is not only a measure of the space between things, but also a measure of how easily perception is altered.

Yeah, Aron thinks approvingly, she's beautiful, the maid, even though her face is contorted right this minute in some kind of high emotion, mouth open, forehead creased, eyebrows all the way to her hairline in a look of – what is this look? He has never seen this look before, versions of it perhaps, but never like this, with this kind of intensity. She seems scared, swallowed up with fear.

But wait, what is this that just fell on his face?

Aww *man*, that look, it ain't just fear, it's some kind of sadness, she's crying! She's crying!

It was a tear he felt, and now he sees another one. Falling, falling, from her dark brown eye to his dark brown cheek, travelling that small distance between her face and his, starting as a tiny droplet in the corner of her eye, then gathering more tiny droplets along the way, like small tributaries that branch into a river before the whole thing empties into the sea. Her river of tears plops neatly onto his face in a miniscule splash, distorting its own perfect shape, breaking apart into the many tiny droplets that formed it in the first place.

He has never thought about crying before, not in this way, never stopped to consider the intricate detail of its mechanics. Now he sees it, unfolding cinematically, in slow motion, set to the tune of a song he can recognise but cannot at this moment name. It is a very dramatic song, the tune is haunting, cresting on sweet notes, then plunging downwards to explore the undertones of darkness, alternating between the two smoothly, with ease, fluid and free, boundless with possibility, like poetry, like love. Like love, like love, like life! He hears brass, he hears horns, he hears joy, he hears sorrow. The music is exalting, an interplay of rhythm and movement, shadow and light, cellos and trumpets, an aria, an epic, a fable. A fantasy.

A fantasy.

But *this*, this what's happening on the street, is not a fantasy.

She is shaking him now, her hands are on his shoulders, and she is shaking him violently, he is strong, he is sinewy, but she is shaking him effortlessly and he sees his own muscular body rattling like one of them baby toys, and it should hurt, logic tells him it should hurt, being shook up like that with such crazy passion, but it doesn't.

He feels no hurt, no pain. He feels nothing.

Her face, just inches above his own, is profoundly beautiful in an almost inexplicable way. He wants to tell her to stop crying. Stop that crying! he wants to say, what you crying for, look around you, look at this life, it is so beautiful, so perfect. He wants to say this and many other things, but when he opens his mouth, he finds that he can't. Inside his head, the melody is building in a slow, inexorable crescendo, shooting upward into the purple sky, and as the name of the song comes to him, so does the realisation that he knows exactly how it ends.

NORA

ONE

Nora stands at the bus stop, waiting for the number 13. Expectantly, she sticks her neck out. The vast expanse of Hyde Park lies directly behind her, a luxurious, bright green carpet. In front of her is Mayfair, home to some of the most expensive real estate in the world, landmarked by the arresting Art Deco façade of the Palace Hotel, from which Nora has only minutes ago emerged.

The bus is late. Of course it is late. It is never late when she is late, but today when she had feared being so late she's not even changed out of her uniform, it is late. As a rule, she always makes it a point to change back into her own clothes before exiting the hotel. She dislikes being out in public in her uniform, the prim black dress, the large white collar like a child's bib, her long, naturally wavy blonde hair pulled back from her face severely and coiled into a low, neat bun. This anxiety with the uniform, how she looks to the world when she is in it, is not just in her head, it's actually real; it's happened too many times now not to be real. The simple fact is that when she's in it, people stare, like she is anachronistic in some way, out of her era – a lady's maid in some 1930s movie. Well, she is a kind of maid, that part is true. The thing that strikes her most about these people is that they don't stop staring even when she directly meets their gaze, as if in their minds, she has dressed this way to *make* them stare, like a person in fancy dress out in the world wanting the attention, or they wouldn't be dressed in that way. For these people then, it causes no embarrassment to be seen openly gawking, why should it be, isn't that, they probably believe, the whole point?

She has pondered this before, this small example of collective group-think that makes some people no different from a flock of sheep and in a strange, empathetic sort of way, she cannot blame them for their lack of imagination, because it is true that being in her uniform out on the streets puts her out of context, and of course, out of context, almost nothing makes sense.

Nora has no particular grievance against the uniform per se. It is not oppressive or ill-fitting or hideously ugly or anything. She doesn't mind wearing it at work. That has never been a problem for her, mostly because everyone else wears it too. Also, she knows that it serves the important purpose of allowing staff members to identify other staff members, or to figure out why they might be in a certain place at a certain time. For example, if she, in her maid's uniform, was spotted in the cold storage scrutinising the various cuts of lamb, it would be as baffling as seeing someone in chef's whites folding towels in a guest's bathroom. So, in that sense, she actually appreciates the principle behind the uniform. It's perfectly functional and perfectly practical and in a way, perfectly symbolic. Also, on a personal note, it serves to keep hotel guests from unnecessarily fraternising with her, the ones who insist on staying in their rooms even while she is cleaning. Well, most of the time it does, anyway. Except of course that one time...

Anyway, she doesn't want to think about that one time. Just thinking about it makes her skin crawl. Best to train her mind not to go there. Though sometimes that is harder than one imagines.

The mind, as she has learnt, is a thing unto itself. She allows herself one terrifying moment of recall, then snaps herself back into the present.

It is a warm, windless evening, typical of London in August. Behind her, in the park, she can hear the hum of human sounds – children playing, shrieks of laughter, voices. There is something that happens to London in August, something magical in the air that draws people out in hordes – out of their homes and into public spaces, a kind of mass exodus. Yearly it happens, and yearly it comes as a kind of surprise. So many *people*, we remark unfailingly every summer, how are there so many *people*?

Nora cranes her neck again as if by repeating the action enough times, the bus will magically appear. Next to her is a Chinese lady wearing a cobalt-blue high-neck blouse over straight-cut trousers and pink trainers. Her hair is cut very short lending her a stern, almost austere look. She's holding a number of supermarket bags in both hands. Like Nora, she too is craning her neck forward. More accurately, she is craning her entire body forward, balancing on her toes, her tiny frame at a forty-five-degree slant, heels lifted clear off the ground. She has so many bags and is making herself lean so far forward that she looks on the verge of falling flat on her face at any moment. Nora doesn't know which bus the lady is waiting for, but whichever one it is, she is obviously irate at its lateness, because even in that impressive Michael Jackson pose, she is kissing her teeth, a displeased expression on her face. Tch tch tch she says now, her aggravation seeming only to intensify each time the wrong bus comes down the road and slows down in front of them. Unhappily for her, this happens all too often, for Park Lane is a busy road, and this bus stop in particular is a busy one, especially at this time of evening.

Outside of Nora and the Chinese lady, there are three other

people at the bus stop, including a harried-looking woman in a yellow summer dress carrying a pram designed for twins. The hood of the pram has been fully extended and there is no sound coming from under it, and so Nora suspects the babies inside – assuming there are babies inside, one can never be sure of these things – must be asleep. A couple of minutes later, the lady gets on the number 137, raising the enormous pram up the stairs and into the bus with the practised expertise of someone who has performed this action too many times to be daunted by it. Behind it, the number 74 draws up. The doors swing open, a few people get off and scatter rapidly in various directions. No one gets on. Both buses move onward. The remaining four people at the bus stop continue to wait. Nora shifts her weight from one foot to another. It has been a full eight minutes since she arrived; the bus is a full nine minutes late. The Chinese woman is still kissing her teeth, but by now she has set the orange plastic bags down on the ground next to her feet in a gesture of defeat. Behind them, a woman with big sunglasses and green hair sits on the bright red bench-seat and speaks rapidly into her phone in some Slavic language. Polish or Czech. This much Nora can tell. She has a good ear for accents and languages and things. When you are around people so much, so many of them foreign, you just pick these things up. Unlike the Chinese woman, this one seems unperturbed, happy to just talk on her phone and wait.

The last person making up the group is a man, tall and lean with small dark eyes and dressed in navy-blue overalls. He stands outside the bus shelter, to the far left of it, almost as if he is in two minds whether to bother with the bus at all. After a few minutes, when five different buses have come and gone, he makes a sudden decisive motion like a small stamp of his foot and walks off briskly in the direction of Marble Arch. Nora sighs and cranes her neck forward again. This time she is rewarded, for just there, turning the bend, is the number 13. She wonders for a split second if she should call out to the man, but then she has no idea if he had been waiting for the same bus. More importantly, it strikes her in the next moment that even if he was, it may not be an appropriate thing for her to do. What kindness had come instinctively to her as a child, she had realised later to temper, for she had learned, not without some slight cost to her innocence, that unexpected gestures of kindness, especially among strangers, were not always appropriate nor always appreciated.

The Chinese woman makes a noise that sounds like a grunt. The Eastern European woman finishes her call, slips her phone into her bag and rises languidly from the bench. In the early evening light her hair glows a bright, fluorescent green. The man in the overalls has disappeared among the throng of people emerging from a summer's day in the park. Nora steps forward onto the street and waits for the number 13 to stop.

TWO

At the top of the stairs, she scans the bus for seats. There is only one available space, just behind the staircase, by the aisle on the right-hand side. She is just about to make her way towards it when she feels eyes on her, the way one intuitively knows one is being looked at. She expected this of course, dressed the way she is, yet she cannot help but identify the culprit, and well, there he is, looking directly at her from the window seat on the front left side. The bus jerks forward in the instant she meets his eye, and she almost loses her footing and slips off the top step, not only because of the motion of the bus, but because he is the most unusual-looking person she has ever seen.

He looks young, her age, maybe younger, but he could have been older too, because of course he has the unfair advantage of genetics. The skin on his face is dark and supple, high forehead, prominent lips, a bone structure that alone makes his face beautiful. But the most astonishing thing about him are his eyes, which are a deep and penetrating shade of blue. Eyes like that would be remarkable even on a white man, but on a black man they look ethereal, like something out of someone's imagination or a piece of spiritual art hung in a sunlit corner of some Italian church. Painted by a celebrated master; subject unknown.

It crosses her mind that he might be wearing contact lenses, she knows you can buy those in a whole bunch of different colours at any high-street optician, but something instinctively tells her he's not. There is a casual confidence in his posture, the way in which his body is straight, but his head is turned, only to look at her. Even the look itself is distinctive – she cannot explain it, but it's not a look she associates with the way people normally gawk at her, this is a kind of open curiosity that one human shows in another, as a kind of reinforcement of the fact of being human. All that, and the beauty he wears so effortlessly on his face, seem to indicate to her that he doesn't need the aid of artificial enhancements; he already knows there is something different about him, unexpected and sublime, to be taken at face value. An act of faith.

She waits for the bus to stop at a red light, then makes her way to the empty seat. Beside her, on the window seat, is a middle-aged man with a heavily prominent nose and dark hair, receding at the top. Hello, he says when she sits down. Hello, she replies. Four rows in front, the blue-eyed black boy is deep in conversation with the large woman to his right.

THREE

My name, the man next to her says, is Filipe Silva. It's not, he explains, Phileepey, like they say in Spain. He is from Lisbon, he says, and his name is Filipe, pronounced Filipe, like the English Philip. He cannot bear it when people call him Phileepey, nor for that matter when they mistake anything Portuguese for being Spanish. We are two different countries, he says to Nora. Everything different. Different food, different language, different music. And most importantly, different people. Different governments, different histories, different leaders. They had Franco. We had Salazar. Different men. Can you believe, some people are so ignorant, they think the two are the same? It is true of course that they were both dictators, but that's where it ends. Franco was a counter-revolutionary; Salazar was a reactionary. Franco was loud and bombastic; Salazar was sober, a man of books, a scholar. Of course, the same distinction can be made between the Spaniards and the Portuguese of today, he says with a small smile. But the Spaniards might disagree with my assessment…

He shrugs lightly and looks out of the window. The substantial dimensions of his nose are even more pronounced in profile, dominating the landscape of his face so much so that the rest of it is indistinct, anticlimactic like one could imagine of a central mountain, tall and remarkable, throwing its surrounding valleys into the shadows.

... Or they may not, he continues. Sometimes people are proud of the way they are, even if that is perceived by other people as less than desirable. The thing is, he says, turning back to Nora and nodding his head thoughtfully, outsiders consider us to be 'enemy brothers', however I must tell you that is incorrect. In reality, Portugal and Spain are less brothers than enemies, and less enemies than neighbours. In any case – here he gives a long, exhausted sigh – I do not like it when people call me Phileepey, but the English, you tell them the same thing ten times and still they do not stop; it seems they have some trouble with their hearing. Or maybe it is trouble up here, in this department. He taps a finger to the side of his head. Sorry, you are English? he says looking at Nora apologetically, but whether the apology is offered because she might be English and he has insulted her, or simply because she might be English, is hard to tell.

Still, it is not meant to cause offence and Nora takes none. Well, she says, the answer to your question depends on what you think makes someone English or Spanish or Portuguese or from any one place. Is it where one is born, or where one chooses to live or what kind of passport one holds? Identity is a tricky thing, don't you think? I mean, I was born in England. I've lived my entire life in London. My mother was Irish. My father, I do not know. I don't own a passport. So, what am I? I suppose I do consider myself English. But it is less out of any great love or attachment for this country and more because this is really all I know.

I understand, the man says. We are only what we know, what we don't know doesn't exist for us. It is not relevant, let alone meaningful. But then, he continues, sometimes we come to know of certain things only later on in our lives, and then it can become confusing because now you may no longer be what you thought yourself to be when you only knew the thing you used to know. When that knowledge changes, you change too. Or at least some part of you changes. Take me for example. I consider myself Portuguese, but I have been in this country for twelve years. So, would you say I am now less Portuguese than I was? In my case, I think so, yes. My son, he is sixteen. He is totally English, even though his parents are Portuguese. But my wife? She speaks not a word of English. Not a word! She is more Portuguese here in England than she was Portuguese in Portugal. You see? All in the same family, and yet it has affected us so individually. Anyway, as I was saying, I came to this country twelve years ago. After the financial crisis you know. It hit our country very bad, the economic collapse. We are only a small country. Not big and powerful like Germany or like here. And for all the talk of the European Union, where was the union when we needed it? No union, only disunion! Each man for his own. How do you say it?

Every man for himself? Nora offers.

Yes, yes, exactly. Every man for himself. I always say, sometimes the real test of any relationship is when a crisis happens. Then you know exactly where you stand. In relation to the other party I mean, what they really think of you, how far they will go to save you. Also, you learn if it was the right relationship to get into to begin with. Straight away a crisis situation will tell you that, shine a light where it has been dark. You may be shocked to hear me say that in this current political crisis of yours – I mean Brexit of course – I do not blame the argument to leave, even though I am an immigrant myself. Yes, it's true. Of course, it has benefitted me for your country to be part of the EU, but it is not my vote that matters. Has it benefitted the British man, the common man on the street, that is the question. My opinion? No. The European Union was a bad idea to begin with, like a bad marriage, and like a bad marriage, at the first sign of crisis, it almost fell apart. The interesting thing is that most relationships do not get tested in their lifetime, not really, not in a drastic way. So, one just carries on. Are you in a relationship?

Me? Nora says with a bemused look. You mean, like romantically?

Yes. Sorry. Only if you don't mind my asking. It is a bit personal the question, I know, and of course we are only strangers.

No... no, I don't mind at all, Nora says pleasantly. But no, I'm not, not at the moment.

Well, the man says, when you meet someone, remember this. The way to decide if it is the right person is if, when you meet them, you are dying for them. You need to be dying for them. It might sound very dramatic, but believe me, that feeling just gets weaker and weaker with time so if you're not dying for them when you meet them, then... he holds his hands up on either side of his face, palms open... there's no chance. The different countries of Europe, they were not dying for each other. A German will always be a German first. A Frenchman will always be a Frenchman first. Anyway, as I was saying, the financial crisis destroyed my country, and particularly my line of work. I am in real estate. A contractor. In this country, they call it builder, but I prefer to say contractor. I am a trained professional you see. I have a degree in civil engineering. I was surprised when I came here, I realised you don't even need to go to school to become a builder. I don't like it. It is a craft, building homes, it takes learning, understanding, training. It's not something where you just wake up one morning and say, I am going to become a builder. In Portugal, you will not get a license without showing you have the right qualifications. Here, no.

So, the problem is I have to compete with such people here. It is very unfortunate because people choose builders mostly on price, whoever bids the lowest gets the job. Very few will take the time to understand what they are getting for the price. But, he sighs, there was no work at home. No jobs. It was a desperate situation. People were abandoning houses, half built, because there was no money. All over the place you saw abandoned houses, like ghost houses. He shudders at the memory. It was horrible. Here, sometimes I have to deal with people disrespecting my profession, but at least I have a job.

By the way, he continues, I only specialise in renovations. No new builds. No dealing with land and plots and permits and licenses. Too much headache and not enough margin. Renovations, for me, this is good. Good business. Only the minimum level of… how you call it in English… bureaucracy? Yes bureaucracy, maybe only some small permission needed from the council to cut a tree or make an extension or something like that. That is better for me. Also, there is something about renovations that is purifying, I find it like that you know – purifying. When you demolish an existing structure like a wall or a staircase, it is like you rid the place of its past. Past inhabitants, past stories, past ghosts. And then you rebuild. New people, new lives, new futures. Destruction of old, construction of new, destruction of past, construction of future. He nods his head a few times. Purifying, you see now why I use that word?

I like that, Nora says. I've never thought about it that way. It is quite beautiful.

Do you, he says suddenly, you wouldn't… you wouldn't have any need for renovations?

But before Nora can reply, he says, sorry, that was foolish of me. Of course, you are much too young right now. Most people,

138

they renovate in mid-life. All my clients are in mid-life. That is an interesting fact for you.

Nora laughs. I don't know when I'd ever have the money to buy my own place, she says, let alone renovate it. I live in a council flat with a flatmate right now, so sadly that puts me very far off from needing anything renovated.

Where do you live, can I ask? the man says, turning to her curiously. For the first time she notices his eyes. They are a very light brown, almost grey, and taken by themselves would be striking. It is a pity Nora thinks that his nose is so distinctive that one misses almost everything else completely.

I live, she replies, in North London. On the Elizabeth Road Estate. Do you know North London at all? It's on Boundary Road, kind of between West Hampstead and Kilburn. More Kilburn, frankly. We just say West Hampstead because it makes it sound posh. It's not posh, trust me. She rolls her eyes.

The contractor thumps his thighs. I know the place! he says, I know it well. It is very famous architecturally, did you know that? It is called Brutalism, the style of the construction, it became popular in the 1950s, which of course, he says with a small laugh, is much before you were born, but it was the kind of architectural design used for reconstruction projects after World War II. It is not just a style you know, it is also a philosophy. An attitude towards design. Simplicity, honesty, functionality over sentimentality and excess. Respect for the materials, the wood, the brick, the cement. Ethics over aesthetics, you understand? Coming off the war, you appreciate the context. For example, your building is made from raw, unfinished concrete. Minimalist. No unnecessary embellishments. Ugly to some, beautiful to others. But as they say, beauty is in the eye of the beholder.

That is really interesting, Nora says, turning towards him. That you should know all this, I mean. Like, it's a housing estate, not exactly a monument of historical or cultural significance.

The man smiles. But to me it is. It is my job, he says. My life.

Just then his phone begins to ring. Sorry he says to Nora. *Ola*, he says into the phone, *tudo bem*? and begins to speak in a stream of rapid Portuguese.

Nora looks out of her window. The bus is barely moving; outside, the streets are choked with the evening rush of people trying to get back home. She ponders what the man has just said. She has never even considered that the place she lives in could be, as he claimed, an architectural marvel. Or even remotely significant. In a strange way, it makes her feel proud, although it's not like she had much of a choice in picking it or anything, it was just what came up in the housing lottery. The same was probably true of most of the residents of the estate. Still, it is nice to hear someone say something positive about the place, usually all she hears about it is in relation to some violence or crime. Or else to homelessness and benefits. Easily stereotyped like these things are. Especially ironic when one considers that the Elizabeth Estate is comprised of over five hundred flats. But still, the stereotypes continue, to shape and to shorten, to confine and constrict.

She knows, first-hand, how multifaceted the estate is. Even just the matter of how differently different people lived. She sees it every day on the short walk back and forth from her flat to the street. There were the flats that boasted entire verdant gardens on their balconies – hanging baskets, glazed pots of different sizes and colours, pretty flowering vines draping down the stark concrete walls. Tidy entrances, bicycles on one side, boots on another, doormats that said WELCOME. Others... Nora sighs. Others were different... broken windows covered with layers of masking tape, sills thick with filth and grime, barren balconies, no plants, no

140

flowers, no sign of anything living. Not even, in some cases, of the inhabitants themselves, for often there'd be no curtains, no doorbell, no names. The people who live across from her, for example, have never had any curtains. Also, the strange habit of undressing in their living room. She doesn't know if one has anything to do with the other, but she's made it a habit to avert her eyes.

It's really a kind of miracle, she's often thought, this place which she calls home, being as large and diverse as it is. Her neighbours on one side are Saint Lucian, on the other side, Greek Cypriot, opposite her – Irish in flat A, Bangladeshi in B. Her own flatmate, Elena, is from Argentina. Everyone, different. Different habits, different customs, different tongues, different aromas of food wafting out onto the street, a real-life lesson in multiculturalism for curious visitors interested in a neighbourhood tour.

Sorry, the man says now, raising his body slightly to put his phone away in his pocket. That was my son. He's sixteen. I think I told you. The only thing he is interested in right now, is music. 'I Love Rock 'n' Roll'. He keeps screaming that song. 'I Love Rock 'n' Roll, I Love Rock 'n' Roll'. He sighs. I don't know what he's going to do with his life. His mother worries about him day and night. But that is a parent's right, no, to worry about their children? Doesn't matter if you are English or Portuguese or from Mars, if you are a parent, you worry about your kids. Perhaps in this way, we are less divided than we think.

He doesn't want to do what you do? Nora asks. I think it's fascinating, everything you've told me. She shrugs. I'm certainly going to go home tonight and look at the place in a new light because of it. I should be thanking you really. It's nice to meet someone who makes you look at something in a new light. It feels really nice.

The man laughs. Ah, no, no, thank you. That is nice of you to say.

My son, no he is not interested in construction. But it is not just in construction, you see, that one has to be interested. You also have to be interested in people. Yes, do not look so surprised, you look surprised. It is true. It is the part of the builder's job that nobody thinks about, but if you just stop for a second and imagine – I am creating the space in which people live. Where they breathe and sleep and eat and do the most intimate things in their lives, go to the toilet, get naked, make love. It is the foundation and the core of a person's existence – a home is everything! Without that physical structure, without a roof over one's head, one is just floating through the world, without direction, without, yes – structure. A home is where people put their roots down. It gives them permanence, a sense that they exist in the world, in a real space that is their own. Quite honestly, people don't think about a builder's job this way, but it takes a certain amount of empathy to do what I do. If I want to do it well, that is, if I have respect for the profession, which as I hope you now understand, I do. So, yes, I need to learn the psychology of my clients, their fears, their vulnerabilities, their hopes, their dreams. My son, maybe because he is an only child, I don't know, but he is not interested in people. I am interested in people. I see my clients not just as clients, but as *people*. When I am working, I get to see the internal workings of their lives. Their real lives, I mean, the part of themselves they do not show to the world. Sometimes I think it is because of the nature of my job, it is so troublesome and disruptive you see, that the person behind the job, becomes, in comparison, unobtrusive. Sometimes they forget you are there, they look at you as though you are part of the demolition, like a wall or a brick – something inanimate.

I know that feeling, Nora says with a small smile. I have experience with that too, strangely similar funnily enough, like when I am in a guest's room, cleaning it, to them, I become a part of the furniture or the bed linen, totally invisible like you said. But the strange thing is, that's how we are trained to be, unobtrusive – like to be no one is the ideal state. The guest's experience should be as if their rooms, their bathrooms, their considerable mess, has somehow just magically cleaned itself and the person doing the cleaning doesn't exist and the more you convince them of this, the better you do your job. Sometimes, these people – virtual strangers – share such intimate details about themselves, I don't understand how they can't see I'm there, and if I'm there, it follows that I can't help but hear them. But they don't care. And some of it is horrific, some of those things I wish I had never heard. Intimacies and family secrets and betrayals, you can't imagine some of those things they talk about even happen in real life. Terrible. My boss – she's Scottish – she has been doing this for fifteen years, and well, she says – eavesdroppers hear what they ask for. But in my case, it's not by choice, you see.

Yes! the man exclaims. Exactly! One time a couple had a big argument in the next room, and would you believe, the argument was about me! They forgot I had taken down the walls that very morning, so the room technically had no walls, meaning a few hours ago it would have been the next room, but at that time when they had the argument, it was the same room in which I was working, so of course I heard everything they said. It was regarding a painting they owned. A painting of an old man sitting on a chair by the fireplace. It is an incredible painting, I tell you. The old man, he is bent over with his elbows on his knees and his head in his hands, so you cannot see his face. The fists are clenched and that, just the clenched fists, the bent-over posture, that body language, it tells you everything. The man is tormented, grief stricken, engulfed in some terrible sorrow. He is dressed in a workman's clothes, all in blue. Blue bottoms, blue top. On his feet, he has on a workman's heavy boots, brown, laced up. Just like these, look.

The man lifts just his toes off the floor. There is something so childlike and innocent in the action that Nora feels a sudden burst of warmth towards him. Exactly like these shoes, the man says. And he is fully bald, he says, ruefully patting the top of his own head where his hairline has receded into a V shape. Like I am myself very soon going to be. I don't know much about art I have to confess, he continues, but this one, it hit me hard, it hit me here. He makes his hand into a fist and taps his chest with his knuckles. In *here*. How do you explain that? You cannot. You cannot explain why something suddenly hits you in here. He repeats the gesture and sighs deeply. It is just a picture, if you think about it, just something someone drew, a stranger. So, what is it about that image drawn by one stranger, depicting another stranger, that affects someone in that way? And you know, after I thought about it for a long time, I realised it was because it was not a stranger in that painting, but me. *I* was the subject of that painting. I mean, I know I was not the subject of that painting, of course, but I could have been, that is what I mean. It was like I was seeing a future version of my own self. And somehow the artist had seen that version of me already, like he was a kind of god who could see things before they happened, and then reproduce them with such unmistakeable clarity. I found it profoundly moving, unspeakably... yes, unspeakably moving. It made me want to weep, every time I looked at it.

Indeed, it so happened that once, when they were both there, the man and the woman, the owners of the house that I was refurbishing, that I looked at the painting and I was overcome by a moment of emotion I could not control and I sat down amidst the rubble that I myself had created that morning when I had taken out the old tiles, and I began to cry. It was like a melancholy

144

had gripped me, but the extraordinary thing was that inside the melancholy was a happiness, and so intense was my happiness that it was causing me pain. I do not know how to explain it to you, but I knew immediately what it was. In Portuguese, we have a word, it has no direct translation into English, but it is something like a deep longing, a nostalgia for something that is lost, or perhaps it was never there. It is that unexplainable emotion that I was feeling.

Anyway, that's what they were having the argument about, the couple whose painting it was and whose house I was renovating. It was not, as you might have expected, about money or how I was robbing them. Which is the most common complaint people have of their builders. No, it was this painting. The man thought my behaviour was unacceptable. I had been hired, he said, to perform a service, and for me to do such a thing as to be crying openly on the job showed a lack of professionalism and perhaps even an unsound mind, and could someone with an unsound mind be trusted to do such important work, intricate structural work that involved creating a safe space in which they were soon going to have a baby?

The woman argued that that was the purpose and point of art, to move someone suddenly and when they least expected. That's what made art beautiful. That it touched each person in a different way and who could say who it would touch and in what way. And so what if I was a contractor, I was still a man, a human being, with a beating heart. It is what, she said, made Van Gogh the genius that he was. They had this entire conversation not even realising I was there, although I was there the whole time.

The painting, the man clarifies now to Nora, was not the original of course, but a replica that you could buy off the internet quite easily. He had since bought one for himself that he had put up on the walls of his own house and that his wife hated because she said she had not seen anything more depressing in her whole life. Why, she pleaded with him, would you put up a painting of an old man crying?

Then she threatened to leave me if I didn't take it down, he says.

Your wife threatened to leave you because of a painting?

No, the man concedes after a short pause. That was just an excuse.

And did you?

Did I what?

Take it down.

No.

And did she leave?

No.

Nora smiles.

But now, dear English girl, *I* must leave *you* and get off at the next stop, the man says, bringing his knees together. I have a meeting with a client whose house I am currently renovating. He is a busy man. Very busy and very fussy. He needs to be updated two times a week, wants to know point-by-point, what has been done, are we on schedule, how much money has been spent, how much is left. Every last detail. But he never has time during the day. So we always need to meet late in the evenings after he finishes work. He told me that during the workday, he doesn't get up from his desk, not even to go to the bathroom. Someone has to bring him food and if they don't, he won't eat all day long.

Gosh, Nora remarks. That's crazy. Is he the Prime Minister?

At this the Portuguese man laughs heartily. No, no, not the Prime Minister. This man, my client, he works in the city. At a Hedging Fund. You know, trading. Hedging the markets. Makes millions, he tells you straight to your face that he makes millions – but still he wants to save pennies. He tells you that too. I want to save pennies, he says, every single one. Every corner you can cut

146

without compromising quality, do it. That was his instruction to me when I started. He said it's the same strategy he approaches with his work. Exploit every opportunity without compromising the law. Of course, the consequences for bad judgement are huge, both in his case and in mine. He breaks the law, he goes to jail. In my case? A wrongly installed skylight, bad plumbing, faulty electricals. He shudders. You can – how do you say in English – draw the conclusions.

He shrugs and then his lips curve into a small, private smile.

You know, he has a very beautiful wife, this client of mine. I agree to these late meetings even though it is a great inconvenience to me, only to look at her. She never says anything, just sits there and listens while the man talks, but it doesn't really matter to me. That is between them, who talks, who listens, who makes the rules, who breaks them. It is not my concern. As long as she sits there on the sofa in front of me and I can look at her, I am satisfied.

He stands up and hands Nora a business card.

If you ever decide to renovate your home, give me a call. I will remember you. You have a very nice face. A kind face. If I had a daughter, I would wish for her, a face like yours.

FOUR

At Marble Arch, a woman gets on the bus, dragging the hand of a reluctant child.

The woman is short and plump, very young, with an eager round face and frizzy, blonde hair. The hair frames her face from below her ears, all the way around, so in a way she looks like a child's drawing of the sun, a halo of yellow waves converging on a circular orb. The girl accompanying her, who looks to be about nine or ten, is dressed in a pretty navy frock with lots of elaborate frills at the hem. Her fine brown hair is tied up in a high ponytail and decorated at the very top with an enormous navy-blue bow in some kind of silky, shimmery material.

They stop momentarily at the top of the stairs. The woman has the expectant expression of someone who is deciding where to sit. Even as Nora watches, the look changes almost instantly to one of determination. Holding the little girl's hand, she marches steadfastly down the aisle. The little girl follows. When they pass Nora, the child looks at her pointedly and scowls.

Come along now please Anastasia, the care worker says in a high, bird-like voice, must I pull you along like a tow-truck all the time? Are your feet stuck to the ground?

148

Anastasia says nothing but apparently allows herself to be towed to wherever they are going. Do you want the window seat, Nora hears the care worker say from somewhere behind her. Well, if you aren't going to say anything, then I'm just going to have to decide for you now, aren't I?

Nora knows a care worker when she sees one. They all look exactly the same. Not in the superficial sense, that is. But in a deeper, interior way that Nora recognises instantly. Tall or short, thin or fat, young or old, they all carry that same eager look on their faces, the same indefatigable aspect in their demeanour. Especially when a case number is with them. This one is being taken to a prospective home. Nora knows that too. Taken to a prospective home she does not want to go to. In clothes she does not want to wear. Anastasia is probably not her name.

Nora had grown up in care. Four different homes from the age of six until seventeen. Her own home, meaning the place she had been born, Flat 22, Clive Court, Willesden Lane, NW6, she has almost no memory of at all. Neither of her father. If you can even call him that. The man who had biologically birthed her would be a more appropriate title, since even the use of the term 'father' presupposes a certain minimum relationship with someone, whereas of this man, she knew nothing – no name, no description, no photograph, no story, nothing. A ghost.

Of her mother, where once she remembered everything, even little things like how her gums showed when she smiled or the way her hair smelled after she had just showered, she now has only a faint recollection of a small wiry woman with straggly blonde hair and large brown eyes, open wide as if in a state of constant panic. That's all. That and a few memories of the little time they shared together. Most everything else is gone, almost like along with the person, the memory of them too has been taken from her. Rather than viewing this as an injustice however, Nora views it as a kind of blessing. It is more destructive, she believes, than constructive, to be haunted by the minute details of someone who was once so vital to her and now exists only in some sort of unreachable parallel reality.

She was called Claudia. Claudia was bipolar. Nora did not know Claudia was bipolar, she was too young back then to know anything of the labels ascribed to people who are different from other people, but she knew her mother was not like other mothers. Mainly because unlike other mothers, Claudia was actually comprised of two separate people: Happy Claudia and Sad Claudia. Happy Claudia was wonderful. She took Nora to school every morning, picked her up every afternoon, standing at the school gates, crouching on her knees with wide open arms. In the evenings, they read together or sang songs or played games. Happy Claudia cooked fresh meals every night, spaghetti and meatballs or haddock and chips, the delicious frying smell filling the little space, making Nora's mouth water. They ate together on the small kitchen table and talked about things and then Nora helped her wash up. On these days, Claudia smiled a lot and laughed a lot and hugged Nora all the time and told her how she was the most precious thing in the world.

Then suddenly, when Nora was at her happiest and the days seemed warm and sensationally bright, an enchanted time of sunshine and light that couldn't possibly end; without warning, Sad Claudia would arrive, and nobody knew if Happy Claudia would ever come back. Sad Claudia was a different Claudia. Where Happy Claudia was attentive and loving and caring and kind, Sad Claudia disappeared into her bedroom and never came out, sometimes for weeks at a time. Various neighbours from various flats in Clive Court, wiser to Claudia's condition than her own daughter was, brought Nora food. Sometimes. Other times, she made do with beans on toast or bread and butter. Sometimes these same neighbours who sometimes brought food, took Nora to school. Other times, when no one came, she stayed at home and played all day long with Gabriella and Faye, her two beloved dolls, smooth and wooden, faces painted in carefully by Claudia when she was Happy Claudia – round blue eyes, thick black lashes, rosebud lips – while the artist herself, like a less fashionable Banksy, was nowhere to be found.

Years passed. Happy slipping undistinguished into Sad and Sad into Happy. Nora got used to never knowing what to expect from one day to the next, Happy Claudia full of sweetness and love, or Sad Claudia, full of darkness and dread. Then came 'the day'. Nora remembers 'the day' because it was so dramatic, perhaps the most dramatic day she had experienced so far in her short life. On 'the day', a strange woman with a sweet face rang the doorbell, asked Nora when she'd last been fed a proper meal, and upon hearing the answer, burst spontaneously into tears. Then she took Nora to her own flat two floors up. This upstairs neighbour, who introduced herself as Germelle, was only a young thing herself, not even eighteen, moved just a few months ago with her large family from Jamaica. When Nora entered number 23, it was like she had entered a different world. Reggae music blared from somewhere. The smell of something rich and spicy wafted in from somewhere else. The small space was crammed full of Jamaicans ranging in age from two to ninety, and to Nora's amazement, they were all laughing, singing, cooking, eating all at the same time. And dancing… dancing, dancing, everyone dancing. Dancing while laughing. Dancing while cooking. Dancing while eating. Nora had never seen anything like it in her whole life. Germelle gave Nora a hot bath, scrubbed the dirt off her body with a loofah that turned from white to brown to white again and served her a meal of something salty and fishy, muttering to herself the whole time, while Nora said nothing; never said anything at all. The next morning, a care worker turned up to Nora's home and took her away, and Nora never saw Claudia again.

If stepping into a small flat filled with dancing Jamaicans had been dramatic, then Nora's actual going away had been the most undramatic thing in the world. Shouldn't there have been, Nora wondered for a long time after that, something ceremonial to mark the occasion of bidding a final adieu to her mother? Lights flashing, trumpets blowing, a hundred saluting guards? But Claudia did not even get out of bed. Later, when they were on the bus and Nora was pretending to be asleep, she overheard the care worker talking on the phone. Poor child. Couldn't get the woman to open her eyes. Cold as a dead fish. It would be many years gone when Nora would realise – in a totally different context – that sometimes the power of one's private fantasies can be so overwhelming that one forgets that life is often smaller, sadder and less thrilling than it is cut out to be.

So, Anastasia, the frizzy-haired care worker is saying in her high-pitched voice, if they ask you what you like doing, what are you going to say again?

The reply, if there is one, is not loud enough for Nora to hear.

Anas-*TA*-sia-I-didn't-*HEAR*-you, the care worker repeats a minute later, in a sing-song voice that to an untrained ear cleverly conceals the note of warning inside it.

Reading, the girl with her well-trained ear replies gruffly.

Good girl. Reading, drawing pictures and playing educational games. We went through this, remember?

Remember. Remember. How can anyone forget…

152

Nora's first family was a Norwegian couple who looked more like brother and sister than husband and wife. Both were big and tall like giants, with cropped golden hair, so pale it was almost white, and blue eyes so clear they might have been made of glass, or air; they looked not real, an illusion, like you could poke a finger through the eye and bring it out cleanly on the other side.

There was something about them that terrified Nora, although she could never – still can't – put a finger on exactly what. Unsurprising then, her inability to provide a suitable explanation to her own care worker, a kindly middle-aged woman with an efficient, brisk manner and a face afflicted with rosacea, as to why she had run away from the split-level terraced Victorian on Compayne Gardens, NW6, in the middle of the night and would rather be dead than be sent back to them. It was not as though they had been unkind to her in any way, she admitted. The house was clean, she had her own room, her own bed, they fed her on time, sent her to the local school, even helped her with her homework. They never raised a finger on her, no, not so much as raised their voice, which was always very soft, and you had to strain to hear the whispers of their slow, deliberate English. No, it wasn't any of those tangible things that one could point to and say 'that's it, that's what it was.' This was... different, hard to isolate, harder to vocalise, impossible to justify – a kind of chill that started in her spine and travelled all the way down, branching into her legs until it reached the very tip of her toes, an unspoken fear of the fact that although they were *always* there – one or the other or both – no matter which way she looked or where she went, staring down at her with their blue-blue eyes, asking her if she was okay in their soft-soft voices – she felt they were not there at all, that they were a magician's trick, a delusion, a madness.

The second 'family' Nora stayed with was a lady called Miss Mandy Jones. Miss Mandy Jones was petite and pretty, as proper as they came and as posh as the Queen. Also, obsessive-compulsive, uptight and more than a little neurotic.

Literally everything that Nora learned of life and how to go about the business of life, she learned from Miss Mandy Jones. Over the course of five years, Nora received a rigorous education in many essential aspects of personal and professional development, such as good behaviour, manners, personal hygiene, tastes, hobbies and interests – all things that Miss Mandy Jones believed developed a disposition for reasoning, forming ethical character, and providing a base for skill and knowledge. In other words, as she explained to Nora, it was her wish to inculcate in the young girl the Aristotelian idea of the 'education of the senses'.

The singular thing that Nora did not manage to obtain in her five years with Miss Mandy Jones, was love.

Perhaps this small detail must not diminish the worthiness of Miss Mandy Jones in anyone's eyes, for she was an excellent teacher and everything that could be taught, she taught. But love. How to teach love?

Never mind.

The first thing Miss Mandy Jones did was to re-christen Nora, Nora.

Gertrude? Is that what the nice pink lady from Social Services said your name was? Well then. Let's call you Nora, shall we? Because now that I look at you more carefully, we can't possibly call you Gertrude anymore. Mostly because you're rather pretty and well, as names go – it's not.

That done, she began Nora's education. She taught her to talk properly and to walk properly and to sit with her legs together like a lady, and not apart 'like a vagabond displaying one's panties to the whole blessed world'. She taught her to fold a napkin on her lap and to eat with a knife and fork and to keep her elbows off the table. She taught Nora how to pucker her lips and say please and thank you instead of making a grimace and saying yeah and neh. She taught her to brush her teeth for two minutes twice a day, and wash her face for one minute thrice a day, and put on a pair of the finest silk stockings without making them rip. She taught Nora how to make a bed perfectly and wash the dishes perfectly and make a perfect apple pie that was perfectly soft in the middle and perfectly crisp on the edges. Every night, she brushed Nora's hair one hundred times exactly to make it shine.

And then one day, when Nora's hair was shining so bright it could well have been made of gold, everything changed. The very thing that made Miss Mandy Jones, Miss Mandy Jones, disappeared for good. She met a man.

Nora was twelve. The man, Tony Aggett, was tall and skinny with a long, fleshy nose and thin lips. On his first visit to the house, he looked at Nora in an expression of what could have been either extreme distaste or extreme desire, it was hard to tell. Before his fifth visit, he had issued an ultimatum to Miss Mandy Jones:

Miss Mandy Jones and Nora

Or

Mrs Mandy Aggett and no Nora.

The day the care worker came to take Nora away, Miss Mandy Jones, soon to be Mrs Mandy Aggett, stood outside the blue door of her small, neat, perfectly kept house on Frognal Lane, NW3, legs together, feet together, toes pointed ever-so-slightly in, and waved goodbye to Nora without shedding a single tear.

The third family who agreed to take Nora into their home consisted of four people: a man, his wife and their five-year-old twins, one boy, one girl. Together, they constituted the Smiths of Flat 18, Daisy Court, St Leonard's Road, Cricklewood, NW2.

The only peculiar thing about their otherwise totally domesticated lives was that late at night after the twins were put to bed, the man liked to dress in the woman's clothes and the woman liked to dress in the man's clothes. It was impossible to tell if they cared if Nora saw them or didn't, because the first time she did, they ignored her completely and simply carried on as if she wasn't even there, until eventually, she went back to bed. In the morning, there was no mention of anything at all, and Nora wondered if she had dreamed the whole thing up. Until, that is, it happened the next time, and the time after that and the time after that. As far as Nora was concerned, these peculiar goings-on had terrified her at first, then shocked her, then amused her, and then, nothing. Eventually she came to think of it simply as a thing people did to entertain themselves. Some people watched movies on Netflix; others cross-dressed at night and went back to making tea and toast in the morning.

Still, as it turned out, what she did or didn't make of it didn't exactly matter. She was but a grain of sand on an overcrowded, public beach, insignificant, worn down by time and tide. No, Nora did not matter; the system was what mattered. The system had standards, values and beliefs, a code of conduct, answerable in full, at all times and in all situations. The system had a reputation to protect. And the system was not impressed.

One night, the care worker dropped in unannounced, 9pm on the dot. Right in the middle of the act. Her pink face turned beetroot red. She let out a little muffled gasp, marched up the stairs to where Nora slept, pulled her covers off the bed, packed the belongings that were in plain sight, to hell with the rest and took the girl back with her that very night. Hail Mary, Holy Mother of God, pray for us sinners now, she intoned, dragging Nora forcefully by the wrist.

Jane, dressed like John, and John, dressed like Jane, stared at her sadly with their elaborately made-up eyes from where they lay on the blue-tiled kitchen floor. Upstairs, one twin slept, and the other twin cried. But which was the boy, and which the girl? Your guess is as good as mine.

The last home Nora stayed at was on Hornby Close in NW3 and belonged to Theodora Wilson, a thirty-five-year-old schoolteacher at the local Swiss Cottage primary. Theodora was young and full of life. And then, one day, very suddenly, she was still young but no longer full of life. Back then, it had seemed to have come out of nowhere, no warning bells, no nothing, but when Nora thinks about it in hindsight, she knows the signs were always there if you looked carefully enough, peeking out through the gap, under a crack. The tiny trip on the way to the kitchen causing the lunch tray to wobble and fall, the inability to screw shut the lid of the jam jar, slipping in the shower before she had even turned the water on, the strange twitch that developed in one of her eyes and around the mouth. But the problem with being as full of life as Theodora Wilson was known to be, is that the benediction becomes its own curse – it fools a person into believing that their way of being is their inviolable natural state, the state that they were born in, and the state in which they will continue to exist.

No one noticed anything was amiss. Not Nora, not the schoolchildren, not the schoolteachers, not even Theodora Wilson herself.

Until that is, she did.

One morning, without saying a word to Nora, Theodora telephoned the care worker and asked for the girl to be taken away. My mother died of Motor Neurone Disease, she explained to the care worker when she arrived. I know exactly what's going to happen to me.

She was laughing hysterically when she said this.

Frightened by the unnatural display of behaviour, Nora let out a loud, involuntary scream. Shh, shh, the care worker said. The poor thing cannot control this emotional expression, she whispered to Nora, patting her arm. It is a symptom of the disease.

I don't want you to have to care for me, dear. The idea was for me to care for you, Theodora said to Nora as she hugged her goodbye, laughing the whole time, while Nora cried and cried. It was the closest she had ever come, in her whole life, to attachment. She was seventeen years old.

The following week, the care worker in consultation with her co-care workers decided that Nora, only months away from being legally an adult, was now old enough to live on her own, provided she got herself a job. This last part they did not think would pose for the girl any insurmountable challenges. She was presentable enough to look at. Blonde, that was always a plus. Slim, that too. Spoke very little and only when spoken to, a great plus. And of course, the biggest plus of them all, the blatant act of genetic defiance – no trace in the child of the madness of the mother.

She was put on the housing waitlist for Camden Council and made to register her name on several job sites advertising vacancies for candidates that matched her specific skillset. Less than two months later, Nora applied, interviewed and procured a job in the housekeeping department of the Palace Hotel on Park Lane, W1. Exactly three days after she received her job offer, she was informed by the council that her bid had been accepted for shared tenancy in a flat on the Elizabeth and Bevin Estates on Boundary Road, NW8.

You lucky, lucky thing, the care worker said, scratching her acne-afflicted cheeks.

'You have one week to accept the offer,' the letter stated. 'If you do not accept it, you can stay on the waiting list (or bid for other properties), but you may be put lower down the list. You may be taken off the list temporarily if you keep rejecting offers.'

Nora accepted both offers on the same day. That evening, the care worker bought Nora her first ever glass of wine. I closed your file today love, she said, clinking her glass with Nora's, let's drink to closing your file.

Well, this is us, isn't it? the frizzy-haired care worker announces at Portman Square. Chop-chop, time to get off. Best behaviour now, Anastasia. Everyone loves a good girl. You know that now, don't you? Yeah? Don't you? Can you at least pretend to be listening to what I'm saying? Everyone loves a *good girl*. We know that, DON'T WE? Yes. There we go, that's better, there's a good girl.

FIVE

Good girl. Good girl.

There is something about those two words that make Nora's blood run cold. That's what *he* had called her. Good girl, he had said, good girl.

Looking down on her. While she was kneeling on the floor. While he was making her do all those horrific things…

Good girl.

His name was Bahram, but he went by Barry. He was from Iran. He told her how he'd escaped the regime in 1978 – before you were born, he added softly – with friends, some of whom were close confidants of the Shah; it wouldn't have been possible otherwise. It was the Shah himself who had aided their escape, he explained, before Khomeini took over and Iran went to hell. Barry now lived exiled in Qatar and worked in oil. He'd been very successful – he used the word fortunate – and over the years, had amassed great wealth.

He had checked into the hotel for just under two weeks. Specifically requested the Eisenhower Suite. Upon check-in, he had been offered a complimentary upgrade to the Terrace Penthouse, owing to the length of his stay and because he was a repeat guest, both of which metrics the Palace valued greatly in terms of measuring client profitability, but he had refused it. The Eisenhower Suite is where he wanted to stay, he insisted, it was in the specific history of that space that he was interested. I wanted to see what it felt like to sleep on a bed in the room where Dwight Eisenhower planned the Normandy Invasion, he told Nora later. I mean, imagine, the largest seaborne invasion in history and all masterminded right *here*! I have stayed at the Palace before, he continued, several times in fact, but I preferred to be frugal then, choosing the more basic double rooms over the suites, I didn't want to spend the difference, although I had it. But now, as I am fast approaching my last act on this stage of life, I would like to indulge myself a little.

That took Nora by surprise, the thing he said about this being his last act. He didn't seem that old certainly – he couldn't have been more than fifty, just from the way he looked, which, Nora had to concede, was not the way anyone looked if they were old or infirm. He was of medium height and lean, with a V-shaped body that seemed to have been achieved not without some effort. His face was long and narrow with a well-defined jaw, a sharp, straight nose, and full lips. His hair was black and glossy with just the odd silver strand here and there, but his beard was completely black and very neatly trimmed – like his body, it seemed something that he took great care to maintain. But it was the eyes Nora noticed first. His eyes were dark and deep-set with a certain intensity about them, the whole aspect only amplified by a pair of thick, bushy eyebrows that sprouted untamed in all directions, a fact that struck Nora as an odd contrast to the neatness of his beard. Yet, despite these features, which individually were rather striking – one could even call some of them beautiful, the depth of the eyes for instance, or the straightness of the nose – put together, they seemed not quite to work, and in the end, the man's face could not objectively be called handsome. He did however look young. And that is what surprised Nora about his paraphrasing of that famous Shakespeare line. His youthful looks must belie his real age, Nora concluded, for those words he had uttered so calmly had seemed to her to be so final, and even a little bit sinister.

The first time Nora cleaned his room, she hadn't expected him to be in. The 'Please Clean Room' sign had been placed outside the door and in her almost-seven years of doing this job, Nora had learned that most guests preferred to have their rooms cleaned when they were out. There were always certain exceptions of course. Sometimes, guests stayed in because they were tired or unwell. Other times, she'd see them sitting at the beautiful antique writing desks, multiple laptops open, simultaneously typing while speaking into their phones, happy to bear any disruption her presence might cause, because the alternative, she was told in very serious tones by the Head of Housekeeping, could cause markets to crash and entire governments to collapse. What Nora found funny was that even though some of these guests were clearly very important people, they all acted, when confronted by her presence, as though *they* were inconveniencing *her*. It was true, they would nearly always give her that same apologetic look and say something along the lines of how she should pretend they were not there and carry on as normal or how they promised not to get in her way or be too much of a bother. Nora didn't really mind either way. It was always easier to clean an empty room, that part was true, but even when it wasn't, she found mostly that the guests kept their promise of staying out of her way, reading or working or carrying on with whatever they were doing, barely registering her presence, not making any attempt to make conversation, most of them not even making eye contact, just looking up vaguely in her general direction to thank her when she announced she was done.

And so, when she entered the Eisenhower Suite and saw him there, sitting on the sofa in his powder-blue open-necked shirt, just sitting there doing nothing, not reading, not talking on the phone or watching TV or doing anything, she was only very slightly surprised.

Oh good morning, Mr Heydari, Nora said. Shall I come back when it's more convenient? Oh no, that will not be necessary, he replied. Please carry on, don't let me bother you.

Inside her head, Nora smiled. She could have guessed that line, word for word. He seemed soft-spoken, she thought, almost verging on shy, and had a very formal and refined manner of speaking, like you would expect of theatre actors who had been specially trained to speak English in a certain way. Nora noted just the tiniest trace of an accent.

No bother at all, Nora replied politely and started to change the linen.

After a few minutes, she heard him say: Excuse me, but would you care for one? When she looked up, she saw him gesture at the basket of pastries on the table in front of him, half-covered by a linen cloth. The blinds were fully open, and the morning sunshine bathed the room in streaks of golden light. He was sitting on one end of the sofa, by the armrest, legs neatly crossed, his whole frame captured in a slanting sunbeam.

I'm alright, thank you sir, she heard herself say.

He rubbed his chest with his index and middle fingers, the part just below the collar bone, and Nora noticed the thick tufts of dark chest hair that stuck out from where his shirt was unbuttoned. Ah, that's okay then, he said, I just thought… rather than all of this going to waste…

It's very kind of you to think of me, sir, Nora said and continued working.

Not at all, he replied, if you change your mind, feel free to help yourself. It's very bright today, he added after a few seconds, unusual for London.

Yes sir, Nora said.

He turned his body very slightly towards the window. Nice day to go wandering about town, he said, if one is so inclined, that is. I remember my first time here as a child, being dragged up and down Knightsbridge by my mother in the pouring rain. And then, when it got too much, even for her, she'd take me to Harrods, and we'd eat oysters at the Oyster Bar and wait for the rain to end. He laughed softly. Which it never did. By closing time, we'd eaten so many oysters and my mother had drunk so much champagne that we could just barely get ourselves into a black cab and return to the hotel. And then we'd do the exact same thing the next day. And the next, and the next.

His parents were both Iranian, he continued, but had British citizenship as they believed it offered certain geographic and strategic advantages. They had got one made for him too, right at birth. He had started travelling when he was only months old, and it had infected him, the travel bug. He had been to more than sixty different countries before he was fourteen, but he always travelled only with his mother, his father usually being too occupied with his work to join them. His father, he said, had been a businessman, a person of some repute in Tehran, and seemed to spend most of his time entertaining prominent people at their home on Fereshteh Street. There was constantly someone coming in as someone else was going out, he said, all sorts of important people of great wealth and power, business tycoons, foreign diplomats, politicians. Trays of drinks and snacks went all day long from the kitchen to my father's study. I remember helping myself to them as they were being carried across the house, some dates or a handful of olives. Always the freshest and of the highest quality of course – in these matters, money was no object. My father wanted nothing but the best, whether from food or from life. My mother came from a very illustrious family herself, he said, which explains my father's decision to marry her; it was in a way a union of empires as much as a union of hearts. He smiled. One agonises over certain decisions, he said, when this – he tapped the side of his head with his index finger – is in conflict with this – he tapped his chest. I suppose my father underwent no such agony. The two organs most responsible for the decisions we make, he said, were for him in perfect harmony. But, as I was saying, every July, my mother and I came here, first to London and then we would carry on to the continent, to Paris or Rome or another European city. But she would always say that of all the cities in the world, she loved London most. My poor mother, he finished wryly, she came like a pilgrim, every single summer for years, and I don't think she experienced London on a day like this more than a handful of times. Sunny weather always remained elusive to her. He sighed. I speak metaphorically, of course.

This type of weather is indeed rare, sir, Nora replied politely, for although she knew his expectation of someone in her role was to listen, rather than to speak, she believed after such a long speech that it would be impolite not to say anything at all. Then she added, you didn't want to go out, sir, to the park or to see the sights?

He smiled. Ah, but I am not here to sightsee, he said. It was business that beckoned. But my business matters take place mostly at night, at the restaurant or at the bar, so it leaves me during the day in the unfortunate position of having nothing to do. He sighed. I have been so many times to London, there is nothing left of it for me to see. I have no desire to go and admire the same sights over and over again. I have done all that: appreciated the scale of your Buckingham Palace, looked up wondrously at your Big Ben, marvelled at the crown jewels at your Tower of London, fed the pigeons at your Trafalgar Square, even got pickpocketed at your Leicester Square...

Nora noticed how, albeit in a manner of speaking, he had made all of these places 'hers', when the truth was that she had not physically been to a single one of them, with the possible exception of a drunken excursion out to Leicester Square with a group of friends on a Saturday night, which didn't, anyway, count.

... I do not consider myself a tourist here anymore, he continued. The charm of London remains of course, but the prospect of admiring its multitudinous marvels is no longer charming to me.

I understand, sir, Nora said with a brisk nod as she arranged the pillows with perfect symmetry.

He leaned his body forward, a curious look on his face. *Do* you? he said very softly, almost like he was speaking to himself. *Do* you understand? You see I have met so many people over the course of my travels and so few who really understand. You don't have to answer that, he said to Nora's relief, with a little smile on his face.

By then, Nora had finished cleaning the main room, with the exception of the floors, which were always to be left for the very end. She made her way in the direction of the bathroom. May I clean your bathroom now sir? she asked. He replied immediately, yes of course, of course, he said. Twenty minutes later, when she emerged, he was still sitting there in the same position, still doing nothing. I'll do your floors now sir, she said brightly, and then I'll be out of your way. This time he said nothing, and she wondered for a moment if perhaps he might have fallen asleep. When she was finished a few minutes later, she said without

166

expecting a reply, that's your room all done now sir, I wish you a pleasant day.

But then he said, will you be here tomorrow?

Yes sir, Nora nodded.

Good, good, the man said, I look forward to that. Would you like some of this before you leave? It would give me great pleasure. A croissant maybe, or a pain au chocolat. He pronounced pain au chocolat, pan oh sho-coh-la, exactly like the French would.

Nora hesitated but the gesture seemed so guileless and childlike, so unmeditated, that she stepped forward ignoring the voice in her head – never, never walk on the bedroom floor after it's been mopped – and tentatively reached for the smallest piece of pastry she could find. Later she would look upon this moment as the one that, had she chosen to act differently, may have changed everything. The road not taken, a nod to Frost.

Wonderful, the man said, making a face of delight like a small child, this is simply wonderful.

Thank you sir, Nora said, stepping out of the room backwards, holding the forbidden Danish in one hand, pulling her housekeeping trolley with the other. She paused after she shut the door and stuffed the whole thing into her mouth before she turned around in case someone was there in the corridor waiting to catch her in the act.

The weather was glorious for the next several weeks. Even the papers were full of it, an Indian Summer, they called it, and except for two days when it had threatened to rain (but not, in fact, rained), the Eisenhower Suite had no need for artificial light during the daytime hours.

Whenever Nora went to clean the suite during the period of the man's stay, she always found him sitting in the way she had seen him on that first day, in the corner of the sofa closest to the window, captured wholly in that precious English sunbeam. Other things appeared not to change either, or to change very little, trapping her, she realised later, in the illusion of stopped time. For instance, he was always dressed in a similar style – open-neck shirt, linen trousers – though never in the same clothes. It seemed he had a preference for light colours, the trousers ranged from various shades of beige to light grey; the shirts were pale yellow, or pale blue or pale green or pale pink, but pale always. He wore his shirts with the sleeves rolled up, exposing the hair on his forearms, which, like the chest hair that revealed itself from the open neck of the shirt, was dense and dark and curly. He always had the basket of pastries in front of him, from which on occasion she would see him eating something neatly on a plate, bringing the plate right up to his mouth so no stray crumbs fell anywhere. He never offered her any again, which she was grateful for, largely because the stress of thinking about how and where she should eat the thing outweighed any pleasure she might get from the thing itself. Another curious fact about him that Nora observed every time she came to clean his room, was that outside of eating the occasional croissant, he never seemed to be *doing* anything, not reading a book or flipping through a magazine or watching TV – nothing. And so, when she appeared for that one hour a day every day at eleven, it was almost as though her presence was a cue, transforming him from something else to the status of a sentient being.

He told her many things about himself. He spoke mostly about his childhood which, while seeming idyllic from the outside, he said, had been far from perfect on the inside. Mainly, he said, he was referring to his father's many affairs, his mother's silent acceptance of this fact, his own growing resentment of his mother's acceptance of his father's affairs – a train made up of three compartments, each carrying leftover baggage from the one preceding it. He had never

168

come to terms with it, he said, having neither confronted his father nor accepted it with the reticence of his mother. It remains, he said to Nora, even after all these years, still unresolved in my head. He was not really an only child as he had previously led her to believe, he confessed. He had once had an older sister who died five years before he was born. The poor thing, he said, her fate was sealed before she even had a chance to fight for it – she had been born with a single kidney and the other had failed right before her second birthday. They had tried everything to save her, the best doctors, the best hospitals – my parents were rich people, remember, he told Nora, both rich and influential, their network was vast and powerful – but the transplant had not worked, she had been too little and too weak, her body not yet developed to fully grasp the working of its own organs, how could it be expected to accept borrowed ones? It was a lesson, he said, eyes half-shut in contemplation, that the thing they say about money not buying happiness is not simply a dull truism. When it happens to you, and so harshly, you realise its profound significance. I mean, he said, another way of putting it is that money speaks its own language. But one forgets that one also needs to find someone who can understand it.

His parents had waited five years to have him. Five years was what they had considered appropriate; apparently there were certain rules relating to the amount of time considered appropriate for mourning, different depending on who had died – meaning, he said, the time period of grieving is different for a dead cat, versus for a dead dog, versus for a dead parent, dead child etcetera, you get the idea. Nora replied that surely there couldn't be a time limit on mourning; some people mourned the loss of a loved one for their whole life. True, he said, but you can't take it in such a rigid way, it's not meant to be a hard-and-fast rule as such, just a guideline, approximations based on studies of behaviourism; very smart people, Nobel prize-winning scientists, have dedicated their lives to these kinds of studies, you know, he said in what she thought was a slightly condescending tone.

Anyway, he continued, the point was that his parents, adhering to the guidelines as they understood them, had waited five years. Still, he had been born under a pall, his mother so fixated on what had happened to his sister that she ascribed the same fate to him. In practical terms, he said, this became a sort of living nightmare, as in her mind, she believed everything that existed around him might one day kill him, the swimming pool for example, or a pair of scissors or even the sun. As soon as I was old enough to walk, he said, she got rid of the dogs in the house in case they inadvertently bit me and brought on rabies. He was not, he continued, allowed to play any outdoor sport that involved even the smallest risk of injury, and since essentially all sport carried some inherent risk of injury, this meant that he was not allowed to play any sport at all. He didn't know how to ride a cycle, he confessed, for he had never learned, so terrified was his mother of him falling off it and injuring himself fatally. In other words, he said, my mother viewed my life as a game where large invisible balls were constantly being thrown in my direction with the ultimate aim of killing me, and to win the game was to avoid being hit by one of these balls. Her role in this game was to aid me in mastering this skill. The only activity, he said, if you can call it an activity, that she didn't consider too dangerous to kill me was flying. As in, not piloting a plane, by flying he merely meant sitting in one. He could not, he mused, explain this strange inconsistency; after all, he noted, planes do crash, but it was why he had started travelling at such an early age and therefore was, so early on in his life, so well-travelled. But almost everything else that a child would do in the normal course of childhood, was for me, forbidden because of my mother's certainty in her imagined fears.

Finally, he said, because of this strange dynamic, his relationship with his mother had come under unendurable strain, causing, in turn, a strain in the relationship between his parents, although, he said, theirs had been an unhappy marriage long before he had come into the picture at all. In any case, his mother's seemingly ceaseless paranoia with regards to him had been the last straw in the marriage and as a way to save it, they had imported an au pair from Switzerland to take over the job. The accent you might have detected in my speech, he said with the hint of a smile, is Swiss. She had died only recently, he said – her name was Bertha – in a small cottage in the Alps, died quietly in her sleep at the age of ninety-four. He sighed. It's difficult to explain, he said, how hard he had taken her death, for it was her that had taken the fear of death out of him. You have to understand, he explained, that my early preparation in life had convinced me that I was destined for death, not in the way we all are – he made a sweeping gesture with his arm – but in a singular way, as if I moved through life with an invitation card on my forehead asking death to drop in for drinks and dinner.

And so you see, he concluded, from my mother's example, that love is a tricky matter, it blinds you to certain things and sometimes you end up not realising that these things you've convinced yourself you are doing for someone out of great love are actually causing them great harm.

He had taken this lesson, he said, in letter and in spirit, when it came to raising his own family.

At this point, he stopped to fish out a beautiful tan-coloured leather wallet from his back trouser pocket. Look, he said, holding the wallet in one hand and beckoning Nora with the other: my wife. Would you like to see?

He showed her a passport-sized picture of a woman who was so exquisitely beautiful, Nora found it hard to imagine such beauty could even exist. Her dark hair fell in waves over her shoulders, her eyes were enormous and dark, like her hair. The angles of her face were so impressively structured, they made her look regal, like some kind of exotic queen.

She's so beautiful, Nora marvelled.

Yes, and look, my children.

He pulled out another picture from his wallet. This one, very slightly dog-eared, was a photograph of his wife, flanked on either side by a young woman and a teenage boy. The girl, who Nora took to be the man's daughter, was also strikingly beautiful and exactly, Nora noted, in the image of her mother. The boy also was good looking, tall and broad shouldered, already at that young age. Both women, Nora observed, were looking directly at the camera with the poised self-possession of those who have faith in the ability of a photograph to render – precisely – its reality. The boy, however, seemed to be looking at something behind the camera; his dark eyes looked empty, almost sad.

You have a very handsome family, Nora remarked.

This is from a few years ago, the man explained. They've grown up a bit now. Nazneen, that's my daughter, has a daughter of her own and she tells me, only last month, that she is expecting again. In fact, the news came only a day after my beloved Bertha died and did a fair bit to cheer me up. My daughter, he continued, married an American man called Richard, a professor of microbiology at Stanford. Sweet man. Slightly scatter brained like the proverbial mad professor, but infinitely patient. My daughter you see, he said somewhat sheepishly, is tremendously strong willed. But in her defence, he continued, she is of course extremely beautiful and it is clear that is why my beloved son-in-law married her, and well, if her beauty is the valued commodity, then accommodating her strong will is the price he has to pay to possess it. Like a very beautiful flower with a fragrance that attracts wasps. It follows that if you want the flower, you must learn to put up with the wasps. Apparently, my own dear mother used to be like that before all that tragedy involving my sister, which from what I hear, not only diminished the strength of her will but caused her to lose it altogether.

They all live in California he said, looking at the photograph, my wife and my kids and my granddaughter. This confused Nora slightly because he had previously mentioned that he lived in Qatar, but she chose not to seek any further clarification, nor did he choose to provide it. Instead, he moved on to the subject of his son. My son, he said, is a bit of a dreamer. He wants to be a poet. He read English here at Cambridge and is currently in the process of writing his first book of poetry. It's brutal I hear, he continued, the publishing world – my son tells me the chances of getting published are only between one and two percent. Can you believe that? When he told me this and I verified that it was indeed the truth, I felt I had never heard of more depressing odds in my life. Anyway, it's his passion, so he's not going to be dissuaded by mathematics. Much less by me. But as I was saying, based on my own experience with my mother, being so overprotective of one's children so as to dictate their every move, is debilitating to them; you may as well clip off their wings at birth so to speak. One must let children make their own mistakes and learn from them. Not mistakes that could lead to death of course, he added hastily.

Of course, Nora agreed, looking up for a moment from dusting the lampshade. There is a big difference between giving children the freedom to jump off the last step versus off the first-floor balcony.

He clapped his hands. What a delightful analogy, he said. You're a smart girl, aren't you?

He chuckled then as Nora began mopping the floor from the far side of the room backwards towards the door.

He's not married, my son. Lots of girlfriends though. Every time I Skype with him, there's a different girl in the background. Perhaps it is the only piece of advice I have given him that he has faithfully followed. Take your time to settle down, I told him, because marriage is such a delicate thing and takes so much imagination in some sense. What I mean, he said, is that you have to tell a story about your marriage, keeping on telling it, keep on enlivening it, reinventing it all the time. He sighed. There are so many different ways of looking at it. I mean, you can say that marriage is the beginning of something, but that means by definition that it is the end of something else. Of course, it depends on one's priorities, which one of the two happens to be more important, the beginning or the end. And one's personality, might I add. Some people are just more suited to a married life. I never found myself to be one of them. I mean, don't get me wrong. My wife and I, we enjoy a very harmonious relationship. We understand one another, and I would even go so far as to say, we help one another make sense of our own existence. It's just that I had no idea how much I would be giving up of what was meaningful to me, or of my conception of what a life should be. If I'd known, I'd have waited a little longer. But… He sighed then and opened up his hands in a gesture that indicated, 'it is how it is'.

What day is it today? he asked her suddenly.

I believe it's Wednesday sir, Nora replied.

Please don't call me sir, he said waving his hand brusquely as if swatting away the very idea. It's so maddeningly British. Such a bland and characterless word. Call me Barry. Or Bahram if you wish, but Barry will do. By the way, I leave on Saturday, he volunteered.

My flight out of Heathrow is at noon, so I will leave straight after breakfast. I guess when you come to clean on Saturday, I'll be gone.

The following day – a Thursday – when she entered his room to clean, she found it as immaculate as always, his striped blue-and-white pyjamas folded neatly on the foot of his bed, his silk slippers hidden away in a corner, his towels lying folded on the floor of the bathroom to be replaced. The sun streamed in through the large windows facing Hyde Park, casting its light in the usual corner of the sofa. But the sofa was empty, and Barry was out.

SIX

At Dorset Street, a woman gets in with a dog in her arms. Another woman, heavily pregnant, squeezes past her on her way down. It is difficult for the two women to fit side-by-side on the narrow staircase; the dog is enormous, like an adult sheep. Nora wonders how the owner has managed to climb those steep steps holding the dog like that, but there she is, on the top of the stairs, looking expectantly for an empty seat. It's hard to focus on the woman: the dog is so beautiful, it draws you to itself straight away – long delicate face, large liquid eyes, coat glossy and thick, and as white as snow. It seems to know it is beautiful in the way that sometimes beautiful people know this about themselves – it looks around the bus with the particular air of confidence that comes from being the cynosure of all eyes, more beautiful than everybody else.

Nora makes the mistake of making eye contact with the lady – she cannot resist, the dog is too beautiful not to elicit a certain curiosity; the owner seems the obvious starting point. It is only momentary, this eye contact between the two women, but that's all it takes. The lady makes her way purposefully towards the empty seat next to Nora. No form of acknowledgement is made either on the approach or on arrival. Staring straight ahead, the lady sits down, knees slightly apart, dog on her lap. Her body, while seated, is at a slight angle, turned towards the aisle. Nora appreciates the gesture – in non-verbal commuter-speak, it translates to what one would call 'respecting personal space'.

Now that she is right next to her, Nora appraises the woman more carefully. Disappointingly, she finds that she is disappointed. There's not much to look at, really. Fifty-something, dressed badly. Some sort of long, shapeless maxi dress that looks more like a nightgown. Red with small white flowers, puffy sleeves that make her shoulders look enormous. Large, oval face, oily skin. Straggly shoulder-length hair. The roots need doing. The rest is a shade of burgundy that is not even trying to be natural. The eyes are small and brown and deeply sunken in. Nose, long and narrow. Lips, thin and scabby at the edges. In short, the face of the woman is unremarkable. In striking contrast to the face of the dog on her lap, which is very remarkable. There is something incongruous about the pair. It reminds Nora of certain couples she has seen at the hotel where one of the two (usually the woman) is very, very beautiful and the other (usually the man) is very, very ugly. But then the one that is very, very ugly, is usually also very, very rich. So that explains that. What explains this?

The dog is licking itself all over. Self-love, Nora thinks, so important. She'd read in a magazine in one of the guest rooms once, that if one doesn't love oneself, one cannot love anyone else. Obviously, the dog couldn't have read that, it must just know. Extraordinary, Nora thinks, how much animals just intuitively *know* without psychologists having to tell them things. And yet, humans are considered the more intelligent species. A conclusion, made naturally, by humans. The dog yawns. A long, lazy yawn, as if it is bored by everything. Like can be said sometimes of extremely intelligent people. What a creature! Nora thinks admiringly, beauty *and* brains! She looks at it, almost respectfully this time, but the dog pays her no attention, it's back to licking itself. Now focussed intently on its front right paw, having just finished with its front left paw. So meticulous, Nora thinks, not a single unlicked patch.

The bus makes its slow, halting progress towards Baker Street station.

On the sidewalk below, she sees a couple walking, holding hands. They walk briskly, moving together, completely in sync. Nora's mind wanders back to her previous thought of mismatched couples – she's only just had one of those experiences a few days ago in fact, it's fresh in her mind. She had been cleaning one of the suites, one of the fancier ones on the top floors that went for a couple of grand a night. She had nearly completed the work, just finishing off mopping the floors, doing them as she had been trained to do, starting from the windows, working backwards until she reached the door to exit. She'd had her back to the door when the woman burst in, laughing. It had made Nora turn around with a little start, and then she'd seen her, the woman, tall and shapely like a catwalk model, blonde waves cascading down her shoulders all the way to her hips, face glowing, striking in her radiance. The man followed right behind her, carrying a whole lot of shopping bags with designer names inscribed on them, a fat, bald man, at least four inches shorter than the woman. Sorry, thank you, he said, noticing Nora. We leave bags and go.

Good morning Mr Alexeyev, Mrs Alexeyev, Nora said brightly, standing up straight, placing her mop behind her back so it was obscured, another thing she had been taught – mops were unsightly objects and so, as far as possible, hotel guests must be protected from the sight of them. I'm nearly done, she said.

Is okay, the striking woman replied, we are not in rush, we go get vodka. *Lyubeemiy?*

Da, da, lapooshychka, the man crooned, we go get vodka, sure. He looked at Nora. More simple like this, he said, you clean floor, we drink vodka. He nodded at her primly. I leave shopping here, he said, placing the bags down by the side of the door, then offering the woman his arm. The woman blew a kiss at Nora. Then linked arms with the man. And off they went. Wherever one goes to get vodka at 10am.

That's a very beautiful dog, Nora says now.

Bites, the woman says. Bites anything and everything. Bite your fingers off if you're not careful. One by one.

Oh, Nora says and shuffles in a bit, towards the window.

The dog stops licking itself abruptly almost as if it knows it is being spoken about. Shifts its weight, stares directly at Nora, still as a statue.

The bus is crossing York Street, inching its way towards Baker Street Tube station. Everything around here is Sherlock Holmes. Sherlock Holmes Museum, Sherlock Holmes Café, Sherlock Holmes Pub, Sherlock Holmes Pharmacy. Everything one needs to live happily, all on that small stretch of road. Knowledge, food, beer, drugs. Elementary, my dear Watson, elementary.

She's my ex-husband, the woman says.

Sorry, what? Nora says.

Mischa, the woman says, patting the dog's head. Mischa is my dead ex-husband.

Oh, Nora says, Oh.

Bit me.

The dog?

My ex-husband.

Your ex-husband used to beat you?

Biiiite. She turns to Nora suddenly and bares her teeth. No *beat*. *Bite*. Chomp chomp.

179

Nora's hand flies to her mouth to stop the gasp. She nods her head. Up and down, several times to denote understanding. She wonders momentarily what she should do. The woman is clearly mad, she thinks. Completely and irrefutably mad. Dangerous too, or just mad? Should I change seats? Nora ponders. Get off altogether and wait for the next bus? It shouldn't be too long, she thinks, at this time of evening, one of those singular rush-hour benefits. She adjusts her bag on her lap, unsure of her own mind on this imminent matter of fight or flight. The dog turns its beautiful face upwards and makes a whining noise.

Dead. My ex-husband. Died in Armenia. I am Armenian. Died of typhus.

Sorry, Nora manages to say but her voice when it comes out sounds choked, I'm sorry to hear that.

Don't be. He was an animal. Died seven years ago. Forty-nine years old when he died. Do you know, she says, animated suddenly, Mischa is a Samoyed. Samoyeds are supposed to be friendly, known for their good nature. Do you know what a Samoyed's nickname is?

Nora shakes her head.

Sammie Smile. That is the nickname given to Samoyeds. Because they are so smiley.

That's nice, Nora says.

An aggressive Samoyed is almost never to be found, the woman says. Well, what do you know, I found one. Never a more ill-tempered brute in the whole dog kingdom and she has to be the one I picked. She has destroyed my house. Bit the furniture. Bit the walls. Bit the carpets. Bit the curtains. Bit the plants. Flowers. Fence. Gate. Not only things. People. Bites people. Animals. Neighbours. Friends. Rubbish collectors. Bites the milkman. Bites the postman. Bites the cats. Bites other dogs. Bites *children*.

She stares at Nora with her small, dark eyes, scrutinises her, as if she is looking at her for the first time.

You are a nun? Are you a nun?

It's not a habit actually, Nora says. Just my uniform. For my work.

Strange costume.

Not a costume.

Strange work.

Nora manages a small smile. Touché she thinks.

I'm amazed she has not bitten you yet. You must be a very special girl. Are you a very special girl?

Without waiting for Nora to reply, she continues. Mischa is seven years old. In human years that is forty-nine. It's him of course.

The blue-eyed black boy from the front of the bus is on his phone and just then he laughs loudly, a big, happy chortle that makes Nora want to smile. Involuntarily, of course. His phone, she notices, is bright pink. Strange choice, she thinks.

We have to go, the woman sighs, gathering up the dog in her arms. Beauty, it comes at a steep price. Twice a day we have to take this bus. Mischa has to walk in Regent's Park. She will not make the poo anywhere else.

SEVEN

The entrance to Baker Street Tube station is obstructed by a group of teenagers. Two of them seem to be in a fight. One punches the other in the stomach. The other shoves him back. Someone else is trying to break them up. A girl pulls one of the boys back, looks at him entreatingly. He shrugs her off. An old story that never gets old. The incoming text makes Nora's entire handbag vibrate.

Gawd, she thinks, now she's going to need to find her phone. No easy task. Her bag's a mess. She left in a rush. For a bus that was late. Nothing new there either.

She reaches into her bag, her fingers recognising the familiar shape of things, keys, water bottle, lipstick, box of Smints, loose change, ah, there it is, that distinctive smooth, cool touch of glass – beautiful, fragile, like life itself – there we go.

She stares at it. It unlocks. Facial recognition. How far we've come. Whatever will come next.

One new text.

Nora already knows who it is from – her flatmate Elena, the last remaining person on earth to use text messaging instead of the several other, more popular communication tools on offer these days. The truth of the matter is that Elena barely uses her phone as a phone, meaning to make calls, because she works in a commercial kitchen where it is usually too loud to have any kind of comprehensible conversation. And she refuses even to install, let alone use, any social media, which she views as a corrupting influence invented by the American capitalist mafia for the explicit purpose of wasting people's time and taking people's money. It would be right to conclude that she has very strong feelings about certain things.

Eggs, grapes, what else? Quick. Am at Tesco's, the text asks.

Nora texts back her reply. Oooh oranges? Pls. Craving oranges. So hot. I'm dying.

Dios mio! It's 25 degrees on the rainy island! 25! Just imagine! So hot! I'm dying! Jesus. So English.

Fuck off.

Happily. Where?

Another text a second later. A picture of a bag of oranges.

Nora smiles.

Elena is from Buenos Aires. Specifically, from La Boca – which, as Elena explained when the two girls first met – deserves precise and particular mention because of its precise and particular character. It is a neighbourhood, as Elena pointed out, that some call home, others deride, and still others live in fear of, for La Boca is notorious for its ghosts that emerge after the sun goes down, from their graves of poverty, to rob and to kill. Not just legend that, *es verdad*, Elena confirms, with the confidence of someone who belongs comfortably in the first group.

Nora has seen hundreds of photographs of La Boca on Elena's phone, the cobblestoned streets, the colourful houses, the life-sized papier-mâché statues of Eva Peron and Diego Maradona. This is El Caminito, Elena said, pointing to a photograph of a small street bordered on both sides by spectacular rainbow-coloured buildings – probably the most famous image of Buenos Aires. In every guidebook in the world, guaranteed. She sighed. Makes everything look very cheerful. But nobody looks closely enough to see the condition of the buildings. You only see the colours. Trick of the mind.

But why are they multicoloured like that? Nora wanted to know that first time she saw the photograph.

Elena laughed then – a sharp, ironic laugh. That, *amiga*, is the whole comedy of the story, she said. You see the colours and it makes you believe that it is a happy street with happy people, because only happy people would paint their houses in all these colours, and it makes you want to go there too, because you too want to be happy, like the people living in those houses.

She wagged her index finger like a schoolteacher imparting words of wisdom to a benighted child.

I'm telling you, my friend, the creators of social media stole the whole idea from my city. The very concept of it, the psychology it sits on top of and relies upon! Think about it: you see photos of people on social media and they look so happy and you think their lives are a certain way. And you believe it, you believe what you see. And you too want for your life to be like that. You don't think to look inside. It's a trap. That's why I won't waste my time on it. I've already *been* inside, I spent my whole life inside and the difference between the inside reality and the outside illusion… she shook her head… I can't even begin to tell you. The history of these houses, there is nothing particularly cheerful about it. La Boca, you see, used to be a shipyard. Mostly everyone who lived there, all the men in my family for generations, were dockworkers. So, the houses were built from scrap material left over from ship building, corrugated sheet metal, planks, whatever they could find. Then they painted them. But there wasn't enough paint of the same colour to cover a whole house and they were too poor to buy more, so they mixed and matched whatever was available. That's why the houses look like that, different-coloured walls, doors, windows – like patchwork quilts. In English you have the saying, necessity is the mother of invention, and well, in this case, the whole story started from necessity, from poverty. Then the artists came into the neighbourhood and found inspiration and started painting all the houses on all the streets and then like so many poor places all over the world, it had a revival – she used her fingers to make exaggerated scare quotes around the word – and now, surprise, surprise, it is a tourist attraction. She sighed. Morning to night, she said, the tourists come and buy cheap rubbish from the streets and pay money to see people dancing the tango – not even real dancers, scam artists, all of them – then they go home and tell people how they risked their lives to go to La Boca, it's crazy how stupid some people are. At this point, Elena usually raised her index finger to the side of her head and repeated 'loco' a few times with an expression of undisguised disdain on her face.

Just thinking of Elena's face displaying that very Elena-esque expression makes Nora smile. She has a very expressive, soulful face, Elena, largely on account of her eyes, which are bright green and heavily lashed. In many ways her face is a sort of mirror for her consciousness, it refuses to hide what she feels, which can be equally joyful as it can be distressing to behold. But what you see is what you get, which to Nora is a blessing, for living with someone where the opposite is true, seems to her in theory to be an endlessly exhausting proposition.

From somewhere behind them, Nora can hear the persistent siren of police cars. She wonders if it's got anything to do with those boys fighting. It must be, she thinks; blocking the entrance to a major Tube station at peak going-home time was bound to invite the attention of the authorities. The police don't even come to La Boca anymore, Elena told her once, can't be bothered. Sometimes, crime is so far gone, it becomes beyond bother. Nora scoots over to the window seat and looks out, turning her head all the way around to see if she can tell what's going on, but a line of buses obstructs her view.

She goes back to thinking about her flatmate.

Face aside, the most striking thing about Elena is her terrific figure, which is ironic to Nora because Elena is a chef and loves everything to do with food, especially the consumption of it. She has a particular fondness for the kind of things most people would classify as high calorie but – rather unfairly Nora thinks – she is one of those lucky people who don't need to watch what they eat. The other matter of irony is that Elena came all the way to England to become a chef when British food, in the opposite manner of French or Italian cuisine, has largely been put in the limelight by those who lament its poor taste and supposed lack of imagination. But that is the point, Elena says earnestly when asked, if the status quo is *bad* food, it means there is opportunity for *good* food. Like a void, you can say, for me to fill. Why should I go to a place where everything is already amazing? What do I have to bring to the table? No. For me, I want my asado and chimichurri to compete with your roast beef and Yorkshire pudding, which by the way – a roll of the eyes here, a scrunch of the nose – is not even a pudding.

She works as a trainee commis chef at a renowned steak restaurant in the city, prepping vegetables for bankers whose wrist watches cost most than her yearly wages. It is currently her third year in the job, and although in the normal course of events she would need to stay in the role for another year or two, she is hopeful she can speed things up because she is considered something of a prodigy among her colleagues. Except that is by her immediate supervisor, the Chef de Partie, a tall, totally bald, allegedly misogynistic man called Rick, whom she refers to as Rickets.

She doesn't like him, clearly.

It's not just the choice selection of nickname that gives that fact away. You just need to look at her face.

Just the other day over dinner, Elena recounted an incident at work, that demonstrated, she said, without a shadow of a doubt, that Rickets was, as men go, the most detestable kind.

I accepted a delivery, she said, and later we discovered that almost half the stuff we had ordered was missing. So clearly, they left some of the boxes in the van or delivered it somewhere else, who knows. But I signed off on it, so it was my responsibility. I don't know what I was thinking. Obviously, I was not thinking. I was doing prep at the same time for the sauces, and sauces, she explained, shaking her head, are a nightmare, one small error and the whole thing is ruined. It takes complete concentration to achieve the kind of precision that is needed with sauces. At least, she confessed, at my level. But it's not an excuse. Multitasking is part of the job; if you can't multitask, you can't be a chef, simple. I messed up.

When she realised what had happened, she said, she admitted her mistake to Rickets immediately. I was so apologetic, she added, I was nearly in tears, that's how bad I felt about the whole thing. Amazingly, she reported to Nora, he said nothing at all by way of a response; he was totally silent, his face was impassive. But then three hours later, she heard him speaking to the sous chef. It's my fault, he said. I should have been there. No one was there to check. Only Elena. Can you imagine! she exclaimed to Nora over the dining table. Can you imagine what he said, knowing full well that I was right there in the kitchen, within hearing distance. *Sin vergüenza de mierda!* Now then, she continued, her dark eyes glinting, if *that* was not irrefutable evidence of female invisibility, then she didn't know what was.

Maybe, Nora suggested, he was just trying not to get you into trouble. Be the fall guy, you know?

Oh please, Elena countered. He's really not the self-sacrificial kind. Look, I know it was my fault. I work fifty hours a week. I am on my feet the whole time, surrounded by heat and stress, too much stress frankly, especially at service times, when everyone is screaming at everyone else. The pressure, while not necessarily a bad thing, can lead you to make mistakes. I made a mistake. So, tell me off. Rebuke me. I deserve it. But what he did, I find so disrespectful.

Maybe he is threatened by you, Nora said. You're young and you're talented and well, you're a woman.

Why would *he* be threatened by *me*! He already knows he's well on his way to being promoted to sous chef. A whole year earlier than expected. I mean, I hate him, but he's the finest saucier I've seen. But the things he says! The other day he was like why do you even need to work, you're pretty enough. Can you believe it! I mean the sexism embedded in that statement, as if, for a woman, beauty and absolutely every other capability must be considered in opposition. Many days I feel he is pushing me to quit, but I'm not going to let him have that satisfaction. The thing with this job, it's not just about talent, it's about – how to say in English – steeliness. Determination. You have to have a fight in you. It's good in a way I have Rickets: the more he insults me, the more the fight in me is sparked.

Have you considered, Nora said shrewdly, that the hate is actually love in disguise? You spend, as you said, fifty hours a week together in the same small space. Maybe he's scared of acknowledging his feelings, even to himself, so he manifests the opposite behaviour. It's common, especially among men, a form of self-preservation.

Elena rolled her pretty eyes. No. He actually does hate me. And since when, she added, narrowing those same eyes, did you become such an expert on men, Ms Freud?

At that, Nora chuckled. You forget, she said, how much I see in my own job, which although you may not think it, reveals so much of human behaviour. What people actually feel, and what they choose to show and the chasm between the two – she shook her head – unbridgeable sometimes. Anyway, the point is, hopefully, you get an early promotion and at least you won't have to report to Rickets anymore. Then you'll make tons of money, and you'll leave here and find a nice flat in in the nice part of NW8 and there won't be anyone to cook me dinner anymore. Nora made a face.

Ha! Elena said. No worries about that, *amiga*. Not moving out of public housing anytime soon. Honestly, I know I won't see a pay rise until I make sous chef at least. So, I'm stuck right here in this part of NW8 for now. And you're stuck with me. Feel free to take advantage of the cooking. It's literally the only thing I know how to do.

Which, Nora thinks now, makes Elena one of the fortunate ones – how many of us are lucky enough to be doing the one thing we know how to do?

The number 13 brakes suddenly and Nora is thrown forward in her seat. Twat! someone yells angrily from the back, when will they hire drivers who know how to bloody drive? She's tempted to turn around just out of curiosity, but she's distracted by the black boy with the blue eyes, who *has* turned around out of curiosity. Once again, she admires the unusual, startling beauty of his face. Now he's turned himself sideways with his legs stretched out, occupying two seats. He catches her looking at him. Their eyes meet for one ephemeral second, then he looks away. She frowns. He spreads out even more even as she watches, like he doesn't care, like it's his private living room or something. She hates when people do that in shared spaces. So entitled. She wonders if he's a footballer. Footballers are like that, the whole lot of them, think they own the world.

She's discussed this with Elena more than once, for Elena's one indulgence is football. It's true, Elena nods. They can be showy sometimes. And always surrounded by women. Wives *and* consorts.

Don't you mean escorts, Nora asks.

Si, si, Elena replies impatiently. Escorts, yes. This is what I mean. She rolls her eyes. Although I don't know why they need them at all, their wives are all so hot, do you know a single footballer who doesn't have a hot wife? But on a serious note, she argues, it's not entirely their fault. The whole arena of professional sports is structured in that way – it is a business, plain and simple, operating for profit, and the sportsperson themselves are a thing that can be bought and sold, no different than the cards with their names on it that small children trade. As always it all comes down to money. I mean if you think about it that way, football literally embraces the worst excesses of capitalist culture. Pay a person that kind of crazy money and what do you expect it will do to your head? Zero to hundred in a day. Like waking up in the morning and finding yourself at the summit of a mountain. Bound to make anyone dizzy. And it's not just the money either. It's all of it. The lifestyle. The women. The cars. The houses. Whatever money can buy. Which is everything these days. Education. Health. Clean air. Sex. Even love.

But you know what, she says, everyone talks about the ones who make it, I am more interested in the ones that don't. Mark, she says, referencing an ex-boyfriend who worked as a probation officer in Willesden, told me how there are gangs just waiting for these boys to be released from teams. They know they will be vulnerable, disillusioned. Easy pickings. An expression of pure disgust clouds her face. Preying on the weak. Like vultures. So *si*, it's entertaining to talk about mistresses and yachts, but what about the other side? She emits a low whistle. Those are the stories that are not talked about and should be. Let the footballers drive their fast cars and sleep with a million women. Maybe you think it's distasteful, but at least it's not harmful.

Still. Any small contempt she may feel for its ambassadors refuses to dampen her spirit for the sport itself. When the *fútbol* is on, Nora prefers to be out rather than watch her flatmate sitting in her undergarments in front of the telly eating junk and whooping and cheering in the most unfeminine way possible.

I *love* it, Elena says in her own defence.

But do you have to behave in that uncivilised way. Look at you! You're eating Doritos in your panties. Crazy!

I can't help it, Elena laments. It's *fútbol*! I am an Argentinian woman! My country is football crazy. Of course, if we are playing against Brazil, we are a completely different level of crazy. You don't even want to go near that level of crazy, you English people won't be able to handle it. By the way, the British brought football to Argentina, did you know that?

That then leads to a whole different discussion about what the British brought to various places and what they took in return. No matter how many times this is discussed, or with what level of critical objectivity, the two sides never quite seem to equalise. Power, Elena declares, is always unequal. If it was equal, you wouldn't call it power.

The lights have come on now, both inside the number 13 and outside, on the street. It strikes Nora newly how extraordinarily beautiful London is on summer evenings. Lush-leaved trees overhanging dark pavements. The still air shimmering in the glare of the car lights. The way the sun colours the sky pink and then moves behind the ancient buildings, backlighting them in its deepening glow. All this she notices, from her particular vantage point, as if she is a kind of god looking down upon the created world.

And then, at eye-level, a couple appear at the top of the stairs. They are holding hands. The woman is large-boned and ebony-skinned and more beautiful than the man who would be considered white under normal conditions but is presently alarmingly red presumably due to the unseasonably hot temperature, like a lobster when it is plunged into boiling water.

It is a particular affliction, Nora has to admit, confined to her people. She is equally susceptible to heat, burning easily in the absence of sun cream, her skin blistering, turning an unsightly pink. Not nearly as bad as this man, but not that far off either. After all, they share the same skin. And yet, it carries so much power, that fragile, delicate skin, so much invisible privilege.

The couple kiss on the lips, intimately like lovers, then, bizarrely, as the bus surges forward, they part ways. The man takes a seat two rows behind the black boy, on his own. The woman walks past Nora to a different seat and sits on her own. The seats next to both are empty.

Human behaviour, Nora thinks, is like trying to solve a Rubik's Cube. You get all the blues lined up, only to see that the yellows are no longer in place.

EIGHT

Nora has a problem. Or maybe she has a secret. Or it could be that she has a secret problem. Which is that Nora has lost all interest in sex. But even that is not accurate, not exactly, because to have lost something implies that you had it once, before you lost it. Well, Nora believes she never had it to begin with – her breasts grew, and her hips widened, and she began to menstruate, but the desire for boys never came. In a sexual sense, that is. For a while when she was in her late teens, she pondered whether her lack of desire for boys was because she desired girls instead, and she made herself look at girls, really look at them in a way she'd never thought of doing before. She started to force herself to look at women in a physical way, at the shape of their bodies, the curve of their breasts, and imagine how all that would look under their clothes, also the space between their legs, soft and wet, like hers, she made herself think about that. But there too – nothing. Which is when she first began to view it as a problem. It was a problem, that as the years passed and nothing changed, made Nora fearful, for if sex was a biological need, like eating and drinking and breathing, and she had no interest in sex, then what did that mean? Did it still make her a woman? Did it still make her human?

It was not something she could talk about, not to anyone, not even Elena, who she would probably call her only real friend. She can already see the look on Elena's face if she ever told her – disbelief at first, she'd probably ask Nora if she was joking, just pulling her leg to get a reaction, and then, when she realised Nora was serious, she'd probably feel pity. And there was nothing worse – Nora knew this all too well – than to be the recipient of someone's pity.

Sometimes, she wondered if her own childhood, roving and rootless, was responsible for any of this, because it was true that she'd never experienced intimacy at all, not between her parents or really anyone else in her life. She herself had gone years without being touched, even the odd hug or an arm around her shoulders came infrequently, unexpectedly, leaving her speechless against the rush of emotions brought on by something anyone else would consider so normal. With the two boyfriends she'd had, she'd enjoyed the companionship, but when it came to sex, she'd gone through the motions reluctantly, painfully even, pretending outwardly that she enjoyed it, praying inwardly that it would be over soon, that they would announce they were going to come, and then just come. In any case, she never understood why people did this – announce they were going to come. Nor why they needed to make all sorts of animal noises while in the process of coming. But the point was that even before all that started, she prayed for the moment when it would be over and done with and then, thankfully, they would pull out of her, and it would finally be finished.

Until of course the next time. Which always inevitably arrived, way too soon and way too often. And which she never refused for fear of offending the other person. And also, of course, for fear of being judged, of being considered uninterested. Or abnormal. Although it was abnormal, she knew that; no matter how much she pretended to be normal, she knew this was not normal. She had never had an orgasm from sex with another person. No, not even once. No matter how much she tried to manipulate her body in various positions to make it happen, it never did. For this purpose, then, she used a rabbit that she had acquired from the Ann Summers store on Wardour Street on her fifth visit to the shop, because it had taken her five visits to decide what she wanted, and if she even wanted it. The first time had been purely by chance, it had been her day off, she'd met a friend for a dim sum lunch in Chinatown, spotted the store on her walk to the bus stop and stepped in out of curiosity. She'd never realised until she stepped into the store that first time, just how many options there were for the explicit purpose of receiving pleasure, like two whole walls full of possibility! Different sizes and colours and speeds and whatnot. How did one decide which one to buy? How *does* one shop for a dildo? She was not the sort of person to ask for help with this sort of thing, even though the sales lady had approached her nicely and discreetly and asked if she'd like any. But all that had done was to make her terribly self-conscious and she had simply turned on her heels and walked out. A similar kind of thing had happened the next four times. She'd walked in, surveyed the dizzying number of options, picked up a few of the boxes, read the print description on them, felt completely confused and walked out. The fifth time, she just reached for the first thing that caught her eye. The print on the box read: 'Our Classic Rabbit. Back by popular demand'. The thing inside, partially visible through the see-through film, was bright pink and enormous and claimed to provide some 'fantastic internal excitement'. It's a gift, she said at the checkout, and then immediately regretted it before the words were out of her mouth as she realised this might be the one item in the whole world where it was stranger to buy it for someone else than for oneself. On realising her mistake, she turned bright red, and stared at the display of the cash register as it brought up the price – £30 – refusing to meet the salesperson's eye even for a single second. She paid for it with cash and walked out with the plastic packet concealed in the deepest recesses of her handbag. When she got home, she hid it in her underwear drawer and didn't look at it for a week.

When she used it, later that following week in the privacy of the shower cubicle, she was pleasantly surprised at the sensation it created in her body. Dopamine, she would read later, the "feel-good" hormone. Oxytocin, the "love" hormone. Whatever it was, this feeling, whatever was responsible for it, it was something she had never previously experienced and she saw the appeal, saw how they could get addictive, these substances, these chemicals, promising happiness, promising love. Like drugs, only produced by one's own body. Legal! Free! It made her understand for the first time why people did all kinds of frankly ridiculous things just to feel it. Love in return for sex, marriage in return for sex; job, promotions, careers, in return for sex. Money. Money in return for feeling this feeling. But still, *still*, having now experienced it, and, for that matter, enjoyed it, she did not understand the fuss. It was to her, as pleasurable – but no more – than having a freshly baked croissant still warm from the oven or a cup of hot chocolate on a rainy evening. But just like she could go days without needing a croissant or a cup of hot chocolate, she felt she could go days – even perhaps forever – without needing to orgasm again. She did, to be truthful, use the rabbit a fair bit, especially on the evenings when Elena was out, and she had nothing else to do. At times, she genuinely enjoyed it, that feeling of total-body participation in what was, in its best version, a pleasure so intense it almost switched her brain off for the duration of the thing. At other times, she found it tedious, the bright pink rubbery thing whirring inside her, unnecessarily loud, with its row of silver beads and creepy rabbit ears. And then when

196

the pleasure did come, she concluded that nice as it was, it was still somewhat of an anti-climax, just barely worth the tedium or the time. In short, if she were to summarise how she felt about the pink penis, her honest feelings would be nothing more dramatic than ambivalence.

The important thing as far as Nora was concerned wasn't that she had no interest in men. She simply had no interest in sex. She had plenty of interest in men. She had plenty of interest in love. She still wanted to be loved by a man – having eliminated women after careful consideration – but in a romantic, fun way that involved long walks and holding hands and talking and cuddling together on the sofa under a tartan blanket while watching a movie. Taking her clothes off and having a man put his thing into her private parts while he groaned and grunted and gyrated on top of her, she considered neither romantic, nor fun. She realised a long time ago that this made her abnormal. An oddity. She had even googled it. In turn Google, the definitive expert of all existing things, wanted to know if she classified herself as:

(Use "✓" to indicate your answer)
- *Having no interest in any type of sexual activity, including masturbation*
- *Never or only seldom having sexual fantasies or thoughts*
- *Being concerned by your lack of sexual activity or fantasies*

Nora considered the options, decided she met all three criteria – check, check, check – and carried on reading.

Dr Google then proceeded to diagnose her condition as asexuality, which it defined as 'a sexual orientation characterised by a persistent lack of sexual attraction toward any gender'. It informed her that at least one percent of people were believed to be asexual, which, she calculated, would make her one of around 78 million humans – a statistic that gave her an odd sort of comfort. She kept reading. The website went on to explain that the condition could be caused by several factors, physiological or psychological, meaning nature or nurture, which it conceded was an age-old debate that no one, not even experts whose job it was to figure out these things, had quite figured out.

So: then, what? Or what, then?

No matter which way one put it, the truth was that she, Nora, had no idea how to proceed.

She thinks about this now, sitting on the number 13, secretly watching a gay couple who cannot keep their hands off each other on the other side of the aisle. She should get it looked at, she knows that, by some kind of expert who could at least explain to her what options were available to someone like her. Was this a disease with a cure? Could it change if she met 'the one'? Or was she stuck with this, with the rest of the sorry one percent, for the rest of her life? Did this mean she wouldn't be able to marry? Have children? Would she have to keep lying to men about sex, keep pretending how she enjoyed it when it actually repulsed her? She'd heard people could be hypnotised out of these things. She'd once read about a woman with an irrational fear of spiders. It was a physiological fear, not just a mental one; the sight of a spider made the woman physically sick. And then she'd undergone hypnotherapy and she was no longer affected by spiders – to prove it, they'd showed a picture of the now-cured woman with a spider perched upon her forehead, grinning widely for the camera! If it worked for the woman, Nora thought, perhaps it might also work for her; who knows, maybe this was it, the great panacea, the cure for all phobias. After all, a phobia was a phobia, whether of spiders or of sex. The same, only different. We are all, she thinks philosophically, the same, only different. She frowns. Aren't we?

In front, on the seat directly behind where the blue-eyed boy is sitting alone, listening to his music, bobbing his head to the beat while he drums his long, dark fingers on the windowpane, is a man wearing a maroon baseball cap. She notices that it doesn't sit flush in the centre of his head, it is skewed very slightly to the left. He's got his arm around a woman sitting next to him and he's stroking the back of her T-shirt with the flat of his hand. Something about this bothers Nora, not that he's touching the woman but the fact of the cap being crooked bothers her, just even looking at it. She wants to walk up to him and straighten it, but of course she can't do that. Elena says she has OCD, but she says it like it's a joke. It's true that their flat is spotless, every dish in its place, every piece of furniture angled exactly so. Her own side of the tiny closet she shares with her flatmate is arranged perfectly, dresses and skirts in one pile, tops in another, dark colours at the bottom, light colours on top. Elena's section, she can't bear to look at and will physically turn the other way if it is opened in her presence. But whatever it is, whether it is as Elena says, a disorder, or simply a way of being, it suits Nora perfectly with respect to her job. She is great at it, plain and simple. No one can fault the way a room looks once she is done with it. Since the year she started, she has more or less consistently won the 'Housekeeper of the Month' prize (a free lunch at the fine-dining restaurant after closing time). New hires and trainees are instructed to learn from her; she's been promised a promotion is in the offing.

Of course, everything she has learnt, she has learnt from Miss Mandy Jones. She has no problem admitting this to anyone who asks her where she learnt to clean so well. No, she says openly, I didn't go to vocational school, I didn't even attend classes, I learnt by doing, at the home of a lady who taught me everything I know. Sometimes she feels bad that she didn't get the opportunity to thank Miss Mandy Jones properly. She has even thought of contacting her, surely it wouldn't be that hard to find her, after all, anyone can find anyone these days, the people at Facebook have made privacy obsolete. But she's held back because she doesn't know what to say exactly.

Dear Miss Mandy Jones,

Hello! This is Nora. You once took me into your home and looked after me after my mother was sectioned, and now I am the best maid at the Palace Hotel on Park Lane, and I wanted to thank you because you taught me how to: (pick one)

- *make a bed*
- *fold towels*
- *take smudges off glass*
- *clean the toilet*
- *arrange the toilet paper*
- *mop the floor*
- *all of the above*

It sounded ridiculous.

So, she dispensed with the notion. Funnily, Nora thought she saw her – Miss Mandy Jones – once, in the homewares section of the big Marks and Spencer's on Oxford Street. Nora was looking for a new kettle – earlier that week with no prior indication of anything being wrong, theirs had begun to sputter and spit and had finally died in such a dramatic way that Elena seriously suggested they bury it in a corner of the shared garden. So, there she was, in the Marks and Spencer's shopping for a new kettle. The lady she thought she recognised as Miss Mandy Jones was on the other side of the shop floor in the cutlery section, pulling out spoons and knives, examining them one at a time in meticulous detail before deciding whether to place them in her shopping basket or put them back in their place. Nora was quite sure that the lady was Miss Mandy Jones, it had to be Miss Mandy Jones dressed in that perfectly tailored pale-peach skirt suit, who else examines the prongs on a fork for a whole minute at a time? Delighted at the possibility of such a serendipitous reunion with her former mentor/carer and that too in the homewares department – which had to be a sign, surely – she was about to walk up to her, but then the lady raised her head, looked directly at Nora, and then looked away. After that Nora was not quite so sure anymore that she was the person she thought she was. She was, Nora had to concede, thinner and older and greyer than Nora remembered, so perhaps she had mistaken someone else for her after all. But then, a few minutes later, she was joined by a man who was unmistakably Tony Agget – the same beady eyes, the same fleshy nose, and it dawned on Nora like a kind of biblical revelation that sometimes it is true that you can be, even to people so vital to you, so totally and utterly forgettable to them.

The number 13 creaks to a stop on a red light. They have just crossed the flower shop on Park Road. When you walk by it on a sunny day, the air becomes perfumed with the smell of flowers.

NINE

Looking out of her window at the next red light, Nora witnesses a puzzling sight. A motley crew has gathered outside one of the large mansion blocks. There are so many people that even the spacious semi-circular drive cannot accommodate them all and a large number have spilled out onto the street. They stand awkwardly, some unsupported, some leaning against the gate posts. The gate posts themselves are wide and imposing and topped with gold lion's heads that seem both befitting and anachronistic at the same time.

It is the idiosyncrasy of the group that strikes Nora, for some of the people are dressed in pyjamas and slippers, others in gym clothes and trainers, still others have no shoes on at all. An elderly woman in a pink bathrobe has curlers in her hair. She is making elaborate hand gestures in a corner all by herself. Nobody is really talking to anyone else. Fire alarm! Nora thinks instantly as the traffic light turns green and the bus lurches forward; it has to be a fire alarm, for this scene unfolding in front of her – unlike many of life's unfolding scenes – has only one possible explanation.

All this then naturally makes her think of Yasmin, a colleague in housekeeping. Yasmin is Ethiopian with a small, doll-like face and huge almond-shaped eyes. She's tiny, barely five feet tall with a waist so small Nora could wrap her arms around three of her at the same time. She has long black hair that falls to the small of her back in hundreds of tightly curled ringlets. Nora has seen it in private, because in public, Yasmin wears the hijab.

Yasmin is only twenty-two, but she has three children already – three-and-a half, two-and-a half, and six months – who live with her mother and mother-in-law in Ethiopia. Her husband, Asif, who is also Ethiopian, works as a waiter at a restaurant in Paris, because he was denied entry into the UK, but not into France, while Yasmin was denied entry into France, but not into the UK.

Who knows why? she says shrugging her tiny shoulders when Nora asks her. Maybe English officer liked my face, didn't like Asif's. And French officer liked Asif's face, didn't like mine. Isn't it that French people and English people disagree about everything? So, with us too.

They made the decision collectively to live separately, despite the obvious drawbacks of the situation, because the money was too good to pass up. Of *course* they miss each other, she says emphatically in response to Nora's enquiry. They speak to each other twice a day on Facetime, once in the morning with their children and both grandmothers and various other uncles and aunts who live in the same house, and once at night, just the two of them. One day, they hope to be reunited back in Addis Ababa.

The reason the scene outside the apartment building makes Nora think of Yasmin is because Yasmin had once lived in the high-rise towers of the now infamous Norfolk House. Before, that is, it was burnt to a crisp. Of course, Nora knows – as do most of the people gathered outside this building in their dressing gowns – that even if, in the worst-case scenario, there was an actual fire in *this* block, it would most probably be contained. Not knowledge so comfortably contained by the residents of Norfolk House, no. For there is little similarity between this prestigious 1930s mansion block in a prominent neighbourhood in NW and the twenty-four-storey block of council flats in the dodgy part of W11, any Londoner knows that. Not in its architecture, nor its post code, nor in its residents, nor, as it turned out, in the molecular make-up of the materials used in its construction, which no normal person would think of investigating when moving their beds and sofas into a new home. No, London woke to the life-or-death-level significance of this only on the morning after the fire. In three days, the city was an expert on cladding materials. People became wiser. Smarter. Better-informed. They wanted to know what they couldn't see.

The narrative changed forever.

Now, even rich people viewing flats with savvy estate agents will say: we simply *love* the view (of the river, of the park, of the skyline) but tell me darling, does this building have any ACM in it? And they will look down nervously at their Jimmy Choos waiting for the estate agent to reply, but he is already gesticulating wildly with his arms and assuring them not to worry themselves even *thinking* about *that*, because *that* was horrible, *that* was gross neglect of duty, *that* would never happen *here*.

Immediately after the fire, Yasmin had slept on Nora and Elena's couch for eleven nights until the hotel offered for her to stay in one of their guest rooms until further arrangements were made. Damn right they should, Elena said strongly, when Yasmin told them about it. You are an employee and God knows they have enough guests staying there with enough money to save the NHS *and* the London Underground.

Why does the Tube need saving? Yasmin asked.

I don't know, Elena said. I just felt like saying it.

Elena liked Yasmin. It showed on her face.

Then again, Yasmin is easy to like.

Nora and Yasmin first became friends at work on account of what Yasmin refers to as 'the hijab incident'. Nora says that calling it that makes it sound more dramatic than it was. Yasmin says only people who have not experienced dramatic incidents would think like that. Nora replies that she has experienced sufficient drama to last many lifetimes but chooses not to elaborate further. Yasmin doesn't make the mistake of asking. High EQ and respecting boundaries are some of the many things about Yasmin that makes her likeable.

At any rate, 'the hijab incident' refers to the time – a week after Yasmin had been hired – when Nora interceded on her behalf upon finding out that the poor girl was up against Jane Macdonald, a well-proportioned, truly formidable-looking woman from a seaside town on the East Lothian coast called Drem. Jane Macdonald also happened to be the woman who had run housekeeping at the Palace Hotel, firmly and with an iron fist, for the past fifteen years. This, in Nora's opinion made the playing field uneven from the start, both from a power/position/rank perspective as well as based on pure physicality – Jane Macdonald could probably hide Yasmin in the front pocket of her blouse without anyone noticing! Hence, the compulsion – for fairness, for justice, for equal rights – for Nora to step in.

The bone of contention was, as one may have already guessed, Yasmin's hijab, although it was not the wearing of it that was the issue – that would be so 1990s-passé. Rather, it was the colour of it that became the sticking point. The hotel, as it was understood and communicated onwards by Jane Macdonald, wanted her to wear black hijabs exclusively, because black hijabs:

1. matched the colour scheme of the uniform
2. blended in with her hair
3. did not attract unnecessary attention

Yasmin, however, wanted to wear whatever colour she wanted to wear, because this was a freedom she had always enjoyed since she adopted the hijab at the age of five and was loath to be dispossessed of it now, at the age of twenty-two, by foreigners in a foreign country that clearly did not understand her culture.

But she was too scared to vocalise all this.

Nora found her crying in the staff ladies' room. A shoulder was lent. It was gratefully cried upon. The story was narrated. Half an hour later, Nora donned armour (straightened her dress, adjusted her cap, tidied her hair) and marched into the battlefield (Jane Macdonald's tiny office on the first floor just by the staff entrance). The duel began.

She has to view it as part of the uniform, Jane Macdonald said calmly.

Head coverings are not included in the specifications for our uniforms, Nora countered, armed with a sheet of paper outlining the specifications for their uniforms. Which means it's her choice.

Well, not exactly, Jane Macdonald said, only slightly ruffled by the thoroughness of the enemy attack. She is an employee of the hotel. She sniffed imperiously. And thereby, of me.

What are you, our own version of Supreme Leader Ayatollah Ruhollah Khomeini? Shall we now call you Supreme Leader Jane Elspeth Macdonald?

How do you know my middle name? the Scotswoman said suspiciously.

I know things, Nora said, which she hoped was a very cryptic and clever thing to say.

A look of concern passed momentarily over the Head of Housekeeping's blue eyes. Nora did not wait for her to compose herself.

As a woman, she said, playing her trump card, it's her choice to wear it. She sets the terms of her hijab, whether it is black and austere or colourful and ornate. She has agency. Take away that choice and you replace a symbol of power with a symbol of tyranny.

Jane Macdonald opened her mouth. She tried to speak but no sound was forthcoming. She closed it again.

And with that, the battle was won.

What you did there was a very courageous thing, Yasmin said later.

Not really, Nora said modestly. What was she going to do? Punish me with 148 lashes?

Yasmin smiled.

Well, she could have… you know…

Let me go? No chance. I'm the best they have. Even if I say so myself.

Well, *I* thought you were very brave, Yasmin said.

Nora shook her head. You don't know me. I'm not brave.

Well, I know you now, Yasmin replied, extending her hand shyly, I'm Yasmin.

In her free time, Yasmin makes handmade coasters from cords of cotton twine. Her speciality is macramé which is a technique using knotting rather than weaving or knitting. She learned the intricacies of the craft from her grandmother who learned it from her own grandmother, who was apparently descended from Babylonian slaves. The word macramé, Yasmin says, is derived from the Arabic *macramia* which means 'ornamental fringe'. Ancient Arab weavers, she explains, knotted excess thread along the edges of hand-loomed fabrics like towels and shawls into decorative fringes.

She's tried to teach Nora how to do it, shown her how to make the various types of knots – lark's head, square, alternating square, button, picot, spiral, and all the various combinations of half hitches – but somehow Nora's never seem to end up looking like Yasmin's. Your fingers are slender and agile; mine are just clumsy, Nora laments, looking hopelessly at a failed coaster whose centre has fallen through like a collapsed soufflé.

Meanwhile, Yasmin makes her final knot on a beautiful double-coloured pastel pink and green one. Here, she says, placing it in Nora's hand, take this. My gift to you.

I couldn't, Nora says, it's perfect.

But then all of Yasmin's coasters are perfect. Nora has been persuading her to try and sell them online – Boho is so *in*! And these are so gorgeous. They look like flowers! Just do it already, they will fly! You'll have a line of customers all the way to Japan.

But Yasmin claims she is afraid of HMRC and doesn't want to get mixed up in tax issues in a country that is not hers, which could create problems that could even remotely impact her job. I can't afford to risk this job, seriously. I'm black and female and Muslim – who will give me another job? Before 9/11, she says, it was different. Then I was just black and female. The problem with islamophobia is that it gave intersectionality a third dimension, like watching a car crash with 3D glasses. So, I have to be smart, and I can't afford to let my guard drop and do anything stupid. Anyway, I don't do this for profit. I do it for me. To make an example of human capacity. All I need is cord and scissors. No office, no fancy equipment, no machine, no licence, or degree or passing this certification and that test and this interview. Just my fingers and my eyes and the little tricks my *Ayate* taught me. That's enough for me. I stay fulfilled and I don't risk anything. Because, she says emphatically, making big eyes with her big eyes, if I lose this job, I'll be nothing and nowhere.

She obtained the housekeeping job (plus work visa and all relevant paperwork) in the first place because she had an aunt by some unknown degree of separation who worked as a housekeeper at the Ethiopian Embassy in South Kensington. The aunt, born and bred in West London, had never met Yasmin in her life, but still, was able to obtain for her a letter of support from the Ambassador's wife, which seemed to have done the trick.

When Nora asked why if she had friends in such high places, they couldn't just bring her husband in, Yasmin smiled.

You forget, she said, that even power is relative. My aunt is only a maid and it's still only the Ethiopian Embassy. They too cannot afford to use all their bullets recklessly. Plus, there is a difference. I am just a poor oppressed woman with a headscarf and possible, debatable, female genital mutilation. My husband is an angry man with jihadist tendencies who might be plotting to blow up the London Underground system. She shrugs. You see how it works? She adds with a laugh: maybe in France it is the women who make trouble. They have it written in their history, after all, starting all the way from Joan of Arc.

After the fire, when she stayed with Nora and Elena for those eleven days, they made her teach them how to do the Ethiopian dance, not because they were particularly keen to learn it, but because they wanted to get her mind off the death and the destruction she had just witnessed.

For the first four nights, Yasmin got up multiple times during the night, drenched in sweat and screaming with all her might.

Elena shook her head. How can such a little person make such a big noise, she remarked. Poor thing. It must be devastating for her. Maybe let's take her some water, she said to Nora.

I feel unmoored, Yasmin cried when Nora brought her the glass of water, like a boat drifting in these huge waves, carrying me I know not where. For the second time in my life, everything that was familiar to me has been lost. But, she said, at least I am glad to be alive. Seventy-two people died, she said. Seventy-two. It could easily have been me.

Yasmin said she considered it the will of Allah that she had been saved. He saved me by making sure I was not in the building that night. It was the first time since she moved to England that she had ever spent the night away from home. It hadn't been planned. Yasmin had gone to a friend's place for dinner – another Ethiopian girl who worked in the shoes department at Debenhams – they had stayed up late, eating and talking, and then watching a movie, in the middle of which they had both fallen asleep. When the movie finished, it was already past midnight and Aisha, her friend, thought it would be simplest and safest for Yasmin to stay the night there and go directly to work the next morning. I have spare things for you to use, she said, a toothbrush and pyjamas. Honestly, I don't like you going home by yourself so late, a single woman in a hijab, it's not safe. I have heard of people hiding in Little Wormwood Scrubs and jumping out and mugging people, especially after dark. Yasmin, too sleepy to argue, had agreed.

She first learned of the fire at 9am the following morning when she showed up to work and everyone was talking about it. She was shocked. She *lived* there and did not have a clue. Aisha called her seconds later crying hysterically. The fire had already been burning for eight hours. It was the most horrific tragedy London had seen for a while. He saved me, she repeated to Nora and Elena, eyes turned upwards to the sky, I don't know why He saved me. I don't know why He saved me and took those people. I don't know what makes my life worth saving over their lives. I will never understand. And then she began to uncontrollably sob.

It was Elena's idea that on the fifth night, they ask her to teach them how to dance.

I simply love to dance, Elena said quickly when she sensed Yasmin's hesitation. All Latin people do. I would love to learn a new dance. And Nora here, like all English girls, would love to learn any kind of dance.

Oh, shut up, Nora said.

Come on, Elena said, we are all here today, in this place, together. Who knows if it will ever happen again! Teach us a bit about your culture.

Okay… Yasmin said, still hesitant, but noticeably swayed by that piece of existential philosophy. Okay… if you really want to learn, I can teach you. So… the name of the dance is Eskista, and it means 'dancing shoulders', so you have to do it like this, look.

She made some incredible movements with her body that involved rolling the shoulder blades, bouncing the shoulders and tilting the chest.

Nora and Elena stared.

Don't just stand there with your mouths open, Yasmin said. In my village they say, if you open your mouth, the mosquitoes will go in. She laughed. Come on, copy me!

No, no, no, she said after a while. Nora, if you don't even try, I don't know how to help you. Elena, at least you are trying, but please. This is not the salsa. Stop shaking the bum. You need to shake the shoulders. I told you, the name of the dance is dancing shoulders, so you need to make the shoulders dance. Look, like this…

Later, all three collapsed on the couch exhausted and laughing, and Yasmin seemed, for the first time since the incident, less distressed.

My husband met me while dancing the Eskista, she told them shyly. There was a wedding once and the whole village was dancing, all the men on one side, all the women on the other side and he saw me, and he said after that he could not stop looking at me.

Speaking of her husband she says she hopes that he has not been unfaithful to her like she has not been unfaithful to him. But she confesses it is a hard thing to expect from a man.

When Nora looks shocked, she says: What? What is that face? What did I say that is so shocking? You think it too. Only you don't say it because English people don't say these things even if they are true.

Elena nods. It's true, she says. She's right. You think it but you won't say it. Always afraid of offending people.

Yasmin confesses to them that she is on the pill, because when she does meet her husband again, she does not want to have any more children. She also confesses that he doesn't know this about her, and if he knew he would be very angry.

Why? Does *he* want more children? Nora asks.

Of course. The men in my country always want more children, Yasmin replies. Because they don't have to look after them. Same for Asif. And, she adds after a moment's reflection, fathering children is a matter of pride. It makes him feel like a man.

Why, Nora wonders in her head, does it involve so much drama to make a man feel like a man?

Why, Elena says aloud, does it involve so much drama to make a man feel like a man?

Elena cannot imagine what actual horror Yasmin has gone through. I cannot imagine what actual horror you've gone through, she said recently on an evening when Yasmin was over.

Nearly four years have passed, and Yasmin still finds it difficult to talk about the incident.

No, Yasmin replied shaking her head, the people who were there that night went through the horror. The people who died, the people who ran out of a burning building. Them. Those people. My neighbour from Sudan, she was like a sister to me, the girl four floors down from Eritrea who was always smiling though her life was not easy, that old widower on the 21st floor, whose name I didn't know until I saw the obituary in the newspaper, but every day he used to tilt his hat and wish me good morning. *Those* are the people who suffered. Them and those they left behind. Me? I was one of the lucky ones. I escaped.

Como? Elena demanded through clenched teeth, *how* do you not feel anger?

I do, Yasmin admitted. At the beginning I only felt pain. I could not even think about that night. I could not speak of it for months, for nearly a year. Nora has noticed that even now, she will not talk about the specifics. She will not discuss the details of the people, she will not name them. Maybe, Yasmin said, that makes me a coward, but once the pain starts, I cannot make it stop. So, it is better for me not to let it start. But the sadness? That will never leave me, not for as long as I live.

Yes, but anger, Elena insisted, how do you not feel anger?

It is there, Yasmin said, in the middle of the pain and the sadness. Between those two emotions are so many others that come and go... anger, resentment, outrage, resignation. But who to direct the anger to? she asks. Who to blame? For weeks and months, she said, all of London was gathered outside the building. All these people, nowhere to be seen before, seemed to emerge out of the woodwork. Reporters, politicians, lawyers, human rights advocates, jumping up and down and behaving like zoo animals. Suddenly everybody was an expert on building materials and social housing and human rights. I don't know she said, what was more depressing, the incident or the response to it.

Sometimes something terrible happens and all people, everywhere, feel like they need to respond. Doesn't matter if they are connected or not connected, everyone, everywhere has to express some kind of opinion because they have to show they care. So all these people screaming and shouting, about how can this happen and something must be done right now. But then, something else happens, some other disaster in some other form in some other place, and this one gets forgotten. The real issues, the deeper issues, are just lost, buried under all the shouting, and in the end, I wonder what is really done that could make a difference.

The whole thing, just even the fact that something like that could happen in a country like this, seemed incredible to someone coming from a country like hers. People at home, she said, could hardly believe her when she told them about it. After the incident, her husband, along with the rest of the family in Ethiopia, was insistent that she go back home. At least at home, her husband said, we do not live in combustible tower blocks. Yes, she told him, but the fact that it has happened to me once means, statistically speaking, that it will never happen to me again. Plus, she said, the money from the housekeeping job was good. It would easily pay for two children's school while her husband's earnings would pay for the third child, plus all the other expenses of food and supplies and running the house. So really, combustible house or not, they couldn't afford for her to go back.

Anyway, she said, when it is our time, it is our time. At least, that is what I believe. Death is a part of life, she concluded, looking at the girls pointedly, and Nora noticed how her dark eyes shone with a liquid fire, one day or another, it comes to all of us.

It is funny that all these abstract thoughts come flooding into Nora's head from just a fleeting glimpse of a sight seen through the window of a moving bus. But sometimes that's all it takes, a flash, a whisper, a shadow, a whiff. At the heart of all of this is the inscrutable fact that there's something unnerving about the idea of people gathered outside their homes against their will. Something profound. Something philosophical.

TEN

She doesn't notice him straight away. She's replying to Elena who's texted asking what she fancies for dinner because she, Elena, fancies cooking that night.

Anything you like, she types, I am easy.

The reply from her Argentine flatmate comes before she's even finished typing: I know you're going to say something lame like WHATEVER YOU LIKE.

Her own message goes through immediately after and she smiles as she reads the response it's received: HA! I knew it. So English.

She's still smiling when she looks up from her phone.

And then the smile freezes on her face.

How quick the reaction is, as if a poisoned arrow has just penetrated her skin. The colour drains from her cheeks and she feels sick like she has been hurled forward and turned upside down, her stomach's been squashed and now she needs to throw up. She looks down at her hands and finds that she has balled up her fists so hard, her knuckles are white. She takes a deep breath, holds it in, intertwines her toes inside her shoes and forces herself to look the other way, out of the window.

CALM. FOCUS. DISTRACT. BREATHE.

But she finds she cannot breathe. She shuts her eyes. Opens them again. Her heart may have stopped. The city is still moving. Out on the street: a bald man in pink spandex running alongside the bus. A cluster of teenage girls in school uniform. An older couple holding hands. A woman pushing a pram. Another woman pushing a wheelchair. Boy with his leg in a cast. Dogwalker with 1-2-3-4-5-6-7-8… eight dogs, father and son cycling side by side, dressed in matching gear, dark-haired man hunched over a mop, cleaning the pavement in front of a café… like a story, Nora thinks, the chapters unfolding in front of her, snapshots of friendship and love, determination, dedication, acceptance, family, toil… disconnected and yet connected, distinct and yet of a piece, occupying in her head a single frame, like a photograph taken in panoramic mode. Blurred. Insignificant. Irrelevant in her present reality. Reality… Catastrophe. Other people's lives… so secondary in relation to one's own.

A few seconds later, once she determines that she has composed herself enough to face it, she sneaks a rapid sideways glance at her neighbour. The breath finally comes out, ragged, bursting with relief. It's not him. Of course it's not him, every logical bone in her body had already told her that. She knows he has probably never stepped foot inside a public bus in his whole life, she knows that, rationally she knows it is impossible that it could have been him, but it's crazy, the resemblance, it's uncanny. Instinctively, she shifts her body away from him, crossing her legs and squeezing herself as close to the side of the bus as possible. But even as she's doing this, she wonders if her body language could be perceived as blatantly offensive because the man next to her is wearing a skullcap and the long flowing garments that announce his religion plainly. She thinks of Yasmin. What would Yasmin think of her! Instinctively, she reverses the action and now, she wonders if she's overdone it. But if she's moved too close to him, he isn't aware of it, because he's already dropped his chin to his neck and shut his eyes.

The fact that his eyes are closed gives her the opportunity to look at him. She scrutinises his face. No, she thinks, she's not losing her mind. Same narrow face, same sharp nose, same pointy chin with its neatly trimmed beard. Only the eyebrows are different. These ones are neat, two arched black lines. But the rest! What's that word people used? Doppelgänger? Sitting beside her is not him, it's his doppelgänger. This gives her a vague sort of consolation. But now of course, she cannot separate the two. Looking at him, this perfect replica, makes her think of him. The imperfect original.

And everything he had made her do.

It had happened on a Friday, the day before he was due to leave.

She was in the bathroom, cleaning the bath. The Palace Hotel advertised itself as having the deepest bathtubs in London. It wasn't a false claim. She had to physically get into the tub to clean it, there was no way a normal-sized human could reach the bottom of the thing from outside it. That's where she had been, standing inside the tub, bending over absurdly from the waist, when he came up behind her and put his arms around her chest.

She didn't know – doesn't know still – why she hadn't straightened up immediately and screamed or done something, anything. But she did nothing, just stood there, bent over, frozen like a statue while he squeezed her nipples with his fingers and something firm and hard pushed against the inside of her thigh. Writhing like it was a thing alive. Well, of course it was alive, she would think later, it was part of his body, and *he* was alive, but it felt to her in that terrifying moment as if it was a separate thing altogether with a mind of its own, some kind of wild and wilful creature. It sounded completely crazy in hindsight, ridiculous, but that's how she felt then, like even he who owned it could not in that instant completely control it.

Then he was leaning forward, his body pressing down directly over hers, weighing her down so forcefully she had to clutch the edges of the tub to keep from falling. In that position, he began to kiss her neck, the back of it, and then the sides, first one side, then the other. This beauty spot, he said, his tongue licking the side of her neck, below her right ear, I have been waiting to claim this beauty spot for weeks. Did you know you had it, this beautiful brown spot, just here? He flicked his tongue, warm and wet, over her skin. Did you know, hmmm, did you know you had it, sitting there against your pale skin, just waiting to be loved?

Sir... Barry... please, she heard herself say but her voice was strangled, the words amorphous.

Please, what? A plea of some kind. Unconvincing, even to her own ears. So, of course, he hadn't stopped. How long is time when one finds oneself ensnared? A mouse in a mousetrap. Unsuspecting. Stupid. Who knows? Not the mouse. She does not know how long he carried on while she stood there, silent and still, and let him. Let him carry on, although she felt sick, *demented*, with fear, at the thought of what he was going to do to her. And then from somewhere deep inside her, some little courage emerged, and she whipped around, startling him. He drew back defensively, but only for a second. For that second then, that one precious second, she entertained the idea of kicking him in the nuts or biting his arm or doing something damaging and deranged like that.

But what then?

Even if she overpowered him (unlikely) and managed to get out, what then? She knew at the back of her mind that at the end of the day, her word wouldn't hold, that she'd be told she had misunderstood his intentions, surely (she would be told) he was just being friendly, he wouldn't have meant anything *bad*, then she would be made to sign something that guaranteed her silence, and then after a month or two, when it had all died down, she would probably be fired for something totally unrelated and wholly insignificant.

He was too important; she was too unimportant. He was too rich, and she was way, way too poor.

To fight this fight.

Her body must have slackened in some kind of subliminal internal resignation, because after that she heard him say: You really don't want to? She looked at him then, astounded by the extraordinary nature of the question and shook her head. No, she said, finally finding her voice, although when it came out, it sounded eerily without distress, please no. Okay, he said in a hoarse whisper. Okay, if that's how you feel, I won't force you. I won't make you do what you don't want to. Okay? Gratefully, she nodded. Thank God, she thought. Thank God. She had pleaded. It had worked. It must have been some kind of misunderstanding. Maybe she'd given the wrong impression. Maybe it was her fault.

Right, he said then, straightening his body, relieving hers of its oppressive weight. Come on out of that bath then. You look ridiculous standing inside an empty tub like a lost child. Here, let me help you. He held out his hand. Stupidly, she took it.

Tell me honestly, he said when she was out, placing his index finger under her chin and staring intently into her eyes. Is this how you really feel? You're not just saying this because you're being coy? Or because you are embarrassed about what you are? Ashamed of the differences between us? Because if that is the case, then I would ask you to not let that be the cause of any constriction. Put all that aside and answer me this, you really don't want me to fuck you?

No, she said, still so measured, still so calm. But who was this person speaking on her behalf? It wasn't her – she wasn't measured, she wasn't calm, she was terrified. No, she repeated slowly, I don't. He sighed and said, in that case, just blow me.

Her eyes grew wide with alarm.

I'm respecting your wishes, he said, in the manner of a man who has been expertly coached on the art of compromise, I won't fuck you from behind like I wanted to.

He moved closer to her then, standing with his legs slightly apart. Still looking directly at her, he unzipped his trousers. She watched aghast as he reached into his underwear and guided his cock out. It was small and smooth and dark, much darker than the colour of his skin, and it was fully erect, perpendicular to his body, defying gravity. He adjusted its position in his hand. She noticed how it was surrounded by a tangled, unruly bush of dark pubic hair.

Stop staring please. Have you never seen a penis before?

Nora looked away. She'd only ever been with two partners. She said nothing.

Or perhaps you've never seen a circumcised penis before. Well, now you have. Kneel please. Kneel down on the floor in front of me.

He put his hands on either side of her head and thrust his crotch towards her face. It smelled of sweat and faintly of urine. She resisted the urge to gag, instinctively placing the tip of her tongue on the roof of her mouth to block her throat.

Come on, he said with the slightest note of irritation, come on please, I can't stay hard forever...

The London sky is blushing.

Daylight has faded, nightfall is yet to come. It is that in-between time of silhouettes and shadows, when people return home and lights come on and music begins to play on old-fashioned stereos.

The number 13 is approaching the end of Park Road. The broad façade of the mosque looms on the right. Behind it lies Regent's Park. Directly opposite it, across the road, is the new wing of the Wellington Hospital – The Platinum Centre – where people come from all over the world to be treated, the equipment is so state of the art. Faith on the one side, Nora considers, science on the other. Both, she thinks in answer to the question that inevitably pops into her mind, human existence: it needs both. When they stop at the red light, Nora can hear the deep voice of the azan floating down from the roof of the mosque. It is enigmatic and soulful and totalisingly beautiful. This is the call to Isha, the final prayer of the day. Nora wonders briefly who the people inside are praying to. What god is this that heeds their prayers?

That day in the bathroom, she too had prayed. Prayed it would never happen. Prayed that even if it did, it would be over quickly.

It had happened. It had not been over quickly.

London Central Mosque, the automated bus-voice announces. The bearded man next to her opens his eyes, slides off his seat and makes his way to the stairs, alternating his grip on the rails from one hand to the other, so his gait is unsteady, a kind of lumbering forward. A large white woman takes his place. A large white boy, with a nervous look on his face, trails immediately behind her. He's got her face, exactly. He stops when she sits down and stands in the aisleway next to her, clutching the railing with both hands, and looking hesitantly down at the floor. There are seats at the back, the woman announces imperiously, looking up at him. The boy mutters something under his breath but doesn't move. Stand if you like, the woman says, can't say it won't do you a bit of good. The boy flinches but remains in the same position, clutching the railing, staring at the floor. The woman takes out a book from her handbag and begins to flip through the pages noisily until she arrives at where she wants to be. She makes a small noise of satisfaction, then holds the book up inches from her face and begins to read. But only a few minutes later she places the open book on her knees and looks up at the boy. Do you remember, she says, where we need to get off for this thing? The boy gives a small shrug of his heavyset shoulders. It's *your* thing, the woman says. How can you not remember the stop? I mean, it's *your* thing. Do you remember anything? Or is your mind constantly a total blank?

It's strange, Nora thinks, but she too cannot remember the specifics of what had happened in those moments in the bathroom that day, not beyond a certain point – how it had felt, how it had made her feel, all that personal, emotionally significant stuff. She doesn't know about the boy, but her mind, definitely, is blank and perhaps *this* is the prayer that had been answered. Even now, even after time has passed and the terror has waned, her brain has mercifully chosen to block things out. Not everything. There are flashes – smells, tastes, sounds – that come back to her randomly, unexpectedly, out of sequence and without warning, when she is doing other things, innocuous things like waiting for the bus or buying bread or lying in bed, waiting for sleep to come. But other things, the truly vile things, she cannot remember, almost as if they never happened. Like a time-log that has been singled out and erased. Self-preservation, she thinks, one of the most powerful tools of the human mind, Darwinian in its purpose. Necessary in order to carry on.

Extraordinary too, because *after* it was over, she remembers everything that followed with all the clarity of cool, polished glass. How matter-of-factly he had zipped up his trousers. How he had rubbed his chin with the back of his wrist. How he had held open the bathroom door and indicated for her to leave. I'm going to pop into the shower now, he had said. She had obeyed silently, walked through the open door, collected her trolley from the far side of the room by the windows where the sun was streaming in. She had just about exited the suite, the trolley already outside the door, when he emerged from the bathroom, completely naked.

Won't you finish cleaning my room? he remarked in surprise. It's your job, isn't it?

She remembers that. She remembers going back in to finish cleaning the room. She remembers him whistling the theme song from *Chariots of Fire*. She remembers the rest of the day passing in a dreamlike state. She remembers changing out of her uniform at the end of her shift and dumping it in the staff laundry. She remembers praying it would come back smelling of detergent. She remembers the bus ride home. It had rained that evening, the first time in two weeks. The traffic had been chaotic. She remembers that. On a day when all she wanted was to get home and into bed with the covers pulled all the way up, the bus had crawled the whole way through, inching forward sluggishly like a gigantic animal unable to support its own weight. She remembers that she sat in the front row of the upper deck and watched the rhythmic sweep of those enormous black wipers on that huge window, that it calmed her in a strange way, the movement of the wipers, swish-swish-swish, the comfortable predictability of the action – more than one could say about the actions of humans.

Now she wonders how a man who had everything – money, class, education, family (perfect wife, perfect children) – could still want for something. And that too from a person like her who, by his own admission, was no one and had nothing. But maybe that was it, she thinks. Maybe that's what he had wanted ultimately, to make her feel what *he* felt she was, to make her believe what *he* believed she was: something truly worthless.

She had called in sick for the next three days. On the fourth day, when she came back to work, she came back knowing definitively that he'd be gone. The Head of Housekeeping called her into her office and handed her a sealed envelope. From the last guest at the Eisenhower Suite, Jane Macdonald said unsmilingly. I haven't opened it, but he seemed very impressed with you. Told me that he's never seen someone do such a thorough job and that you were a keeper. Of course, that's more my decision than his, she added perversely.

When Nora opened the envelope later, she found ten £50 bills and a handwritten note that said:

Buy yourself a frock. I recommend Harrods. It used to be my mother's favourite and now it is my wife's. The handwriting was so neat it looked like print.

She told no one.

She still has the money.

ELEVEN

At Lord's Cricket Ground bus stop, a great throng of people get off. A match is at play. England vs. New Zealand, as advertised by the brilliantly lit, larger-than-life scoreboard. Nora can hear the jubilant roar of crowds even from inside the bus. It seems strange to her how a single concrete wall separates one kind of performance from another kind. Runs and wickets on one side, the routine humdrum of daily life on the other. On that side, a game is being played at the end of which somebody will win and somebody else will lose. On this side, one can argue a different sort of game is being played at the end of which nobody wins, and everybody, eventually, loses. Like two parallel versions of reality happening at the same time.

Nora, who herself has no great interest in cricket, had once dated a pale-skinned ginger man called Graham who was obsessed with it to such an intolerable degree that he subsequently made her lose any small interest she might have once had. He would frequently give live commentary in his sleep, and on one occasion even interrupted a sexual act to check the score. She told herself many times that their break-up shortly afterwards had nothing to do with the incident itself. Especially, that is, given her private issues in that particular area, it wasn't something that should have materially bothered her. Now, with the benefit of hindsight, she's not so sure that she hasn't downplayed its significance in the eventual breakdown of their relationship, not so much because of the specific event, as much as the specific event being a sort of final culmination of a long series of warning signs. And also because of what it hinted at about the man himself in the larger and more philosophical scheme of things.

But imagine – she said to Elena once when she was relaying the story – imagine if I had stopped him mid-orgasm to check if Mary Berry served her carrot cake hot or cold?

Elena shook her pretty head in horror. *Patriarcado!* she concluded. This, what you just told me, is such a good example of the patriarchy. Same in Argentina, same in Spain, same in this country, same everywhere. London, New York, Buenos Aires. Everywhere. Unbelievable. Good for you, you dumped his lazy arse. Nora had chosen not to clarify that it hadn't played out that way, exactly. Meaning, it was true that they'd broken up, but she hadn't wanted to hurt his feelings by getting into arguments about gender dynamics. Instead, she had lied about not being able to have children. He had been horrified, given her a long monologue about his 'seed' and the importance to a man of the continual survival of said seed in bed that night. He was still talking when Nora fell asleep. When she woke the next morning, she found him gleefully devouring a full English, hash browns, black pudding and all. By the time she returned from work, there was no sign of him nor of his cricket paraphernalia. She never saw him again. In truth then, rather than her having dumped his lazy arse, it turned out that he had dumped her fictional infertile uter-arse. So to speak. Anyhow, as far as she was concerned, the intended result had been achieved, so in the end, how they got there, mattered little.

Right now, she's interested to note that there seems to be no dearth of cricket enthusiasts in the country, for it would appear that at least half the bus has left to watch the game. Perhaps it is this, the fact of the upper deck being suddenly emptied of its occupants, that makes her notice the hooded boy when he appears at the top of the stairs. Or maybe she would have noticed him even on a packed bus. There's a certain something-ness about him that makes him stand out in a crowd; it's not only his appearance, which is long and gazelle-like, it's the attitude, the deliberate swagger, almost a cockiness that emanates from him when he flicks his hoodie off with a brush of his fingers, then changes his mind and pulls it on again, lower this time, so low it almost completely covers his eyes. It is a way of being which would probably constitute whatever it is that people allude to when they talk about someone as 'having personality'.

He's wearing a black baseball cap under the hood. A pair of baggy jeans sit low on his hips, from which emerges a three-layered waist chain that hangs in concentric loops down one leg. The sweatshirt itself is black with white writing across the front in Japanese script. When he raises his arm to hold the pull as the bus jerks forward, he exposes the smooth dark skin of his stomach – it is enviably flat, a cloth stretched taut between two bones, rib and hip. It strikes Nora that while it might be hard to tell his exact age from his physique, his face in those few seconds without the hood on gave it away blatantly – he couldn't possibly be older than eighteen or nineteen, he's still got the round, guileless face of a baby.

Head bobbing rhythmically from side to side to the beat of his music, he swivels around to survey the back of the bus. It's the moment when Nora first notices the blue-eyed black boy in the front seat turn around. He's staring directly at this other boy, a shadow of familiarity passes over his face, his eyes widen with

228

some kind of unknowable emotion, giving him an animated, highly dramatised look.

The reunion that follows as soon as the hooded boy turns back around is almost touching. The hood comes off. Under it – Nora only notices now – he's wearing not one but two baseball caps. He reaches the front seat. Cheers and whoops. Back-thumping, fist-bumping, a complicated handshake. Great wide smiles. The glint of metal inside one mouth; inside the other, two rows of large, very white teeth. Alright, blud! says one. Long time, bruv! says the other.

The elderly white couple on the seats two rows behind them turn their heads around anxiously, eyes darting here and there. Two black youths fist-bumping directly in front of them with only one row in between. Empty too. An unlikely defence in case of potential trouble. Were they going to be safe? The woman, a large, pasty-faced thing with short sandy curls turns around and tries to catch Nora's eye. It is a plea of sorts, a plea, as Nora understands, seeking solidarity. Nora pointedly looks away. In these matters, her loyalty is unwavering. Living on the estate, where she sees little white kids playing with little black kids and little brown kids all day long happily, united by something much more fundamental than melanin, she has learnt to diagnose this particular brand of anxiety in people like this woman and has no time for it.

In the front seat, the two black boys are conversing vociferously. Nora has to admit they are a little loud. That, plus the fact that there aren't many other people present, means that if she cared to pay attention, she'd be able to eavesdrop with ease. But she isn't interested in their conversation, not really. She understands that the two are familiar with one another through other common acquaintances, and haven't seen one another for some time, and meeting on the bus like this has been an act of serendipity for both of them. One of them says something then, and the other bursts into a hysterical fit of childish giggles. Almost immediately, there's a loud shhh. The boys turn their heads. They look around. No one dares meet their eye. The hooded boy laughs. The blue-eyed boy brings a finger to his lips in a gesture of parody. It makes the hooded one laugh louder. The irony is not lost on either of them. But after a while they appear to quieten down, speaking in hushed tones, punctuated by the occasional loud guffaw. A few seconds later, the resonant human-not-human voice of Childish Gambino filters through the bus. 'This is America,' he declares, loud and clear, unambiguously scathing even in the ringtone of a mobile phone. The white woman claps both her ears dramatically. The hooded boy puts his feet up on the front ledge and answers his phone. Yo, he says, s'appnin', blud! You ain't gonna *believe* who I'm jammin' with, the hooded boy says into his phone, if it ain't the blue-eyed boy hisself! *Yeah*, blud! On the 13, fam! The blue-eyed boy throws back his head and laughs.

The bus stops at the next stop. The doors open with a series of short, staccato beeps.

The northbound St John's Wood station bus stop is just ahead of the Tube station, on the other side of the road. This part of Finchley Road is wide, almost Parisian in character, flanked on either side by a mix of art deco apartment blocks and luxury new builds made entirely of steel and glass. From where she is sitting, Nora can see the entrance to the station, currently crammed with people emerging up the escalator and out into the evening cool. This is a specific variety of people, well-heeled and sharp-elbowed, in suits and dresses, carrying briefcases and handbags, typing furiously into mobile phones as they exit the building. The type of people, Nora imagines, who work in windowless offices all day long and sink gratefully into their Le Corbusier's in the evenings with a glass of Merlot and a copy of Kafka; Mozart's symphony no. 36 playing tastefully in the background.

The sun is slipping away now, the evening light becoming dusky. An Indian woman in a black skirt suit with plush, strikingly glossy hair falling straight down below her shoulders, slips into the seat next to Nora. She edges her heels out of her black stilettoed shoes but leaves her toes in, grimacing as she does this, as if relieving some terrible and longstanding pain. Hi, she says to Nora, then takes her mobile phone out of her bag and begins talking into it.

Hello? she says, what? No, you *can't* have more screen time. Practise your piano please. Do you know how much I'm paying for those lessons? No. *Not* after dinner. *Now*. Shilpa, the screen is not going to get you into any decent senior schools, Grade 6 piano is, no I don't *care* what Vicky and the others are doing, I'm not Vicky's mother, thank goodness, I'm yours. Now, I've had a very stressful day at work so please don't add to my stress. Can I speak to Daddy? He's watching what? The cricket? Well, tell him I need to speak to him urgently. Oh, before you go, can you take the chicken out to defrost. And the pesto from the fridge please. What do you mean, again? I can't remember when we last made pesto chicken. No, you can't have an apple for dinner. Shilpa, you're making me very concerned about you. If you think eating apples for dinner will make you look like Vicky and those other girls, well, I can tell you it won't. Different genetics.

She recoils suddenly as if the person on the other end has said something unbearable. Alright Shilpy, she says, that's enough for now. I'm almost home, let's continue this later. No, I don't need to speak to Daddy anymore. What? He's standing right there? Well, tell him I'll speak to him when I'm home. No, no, it's not that urgent.

Ouch! she says, ending the call and placing the phone on her lap. She looks at Nora. Was I this mean to my mother when I was a teenager? Maybe I was, and I just don't remember it. I suppose it's hopeless, she says, shaking her head. Nothing's really changed, has it. Still starving ourselves, still running around half-naked to please boys, still trying to be the very thing we're not and can never be...

The lady is very attractive, Nora notices, even though her make-up has started to fade. Her lipstick which was probably bright red when freshly applied has dulled to a kind of insipid coral hue. Yet it does not detract from her natural good looks. In fact, Nora decides, it lends her a sort of ruined beauty, like that of an ancient monument that still retains the remnants of its former glory. Decayed, perhaps, but deflowered, never.

... she's clever, my daughter, top of her class, the woman is saying, but she doesn't care about all that. She wants to be thin and good at sports and wear no clothes – she thinks that's what will make her popular. She has curly hair, you know, and sometimes I see her looking at my hair with such burning envy, my heart goes out to her. If I could cut off all my hair and give it to her, if that would bring her any joy, I'd do it in a heartbeat, I'd shave my head like that Irish pop-singer woman. She pulls her hair forward then, letting it fall freely over one shoulder. It's so luxurious, Nora notes, it makes one want to reach out and run one's fingers through it. I mean, the lady continues, you're too young to have kids obviously, but one always hopes things will be better and brighter for your kids than they were for you. But no. I wear these bloody heels all day long because I think it makes me look professional and competent, and a woman who looks professional and competent is what pleases my all-male bosses. My daughter wants to go on an apple diet because she thinks it will make her thin and popular, and a girl who is thin and popular is what pleases the boys at school. I mean, what's the difference? By the way, are you in housekeeping or something?

I thought so. We're both in uniform, see, in our own way? You know, all I want is for our lives – my life and my daughter's life – to be simple and systematic, solvable by rational decision-making. Instead, it's turned out to be a continuous stream of oppositions, so that no matter what choice I make, it conflicts with something else that seems equally important. My mother says it's from a lack of religion in our lives; if we had God, she says, we wouldn't focus on all these vain pursuits. It's a dig at my husband of course, who's Jewish and openly an atheist. It's my second husband, you see. The first one was chosen by my mother. She knew this woman from the Punjab who moved to the UK after she lost her husband. She came here to live with her son, who happened to be of marriageable age, which apparently was about the only qualification he needed to get my mother excited. It's all she could talk about for nearly a year. So, I married him to please my mum and went all the way to Scotland where they lived in some kind of dilapidated castle miles from the nearest town. I stayed there for eight months before I realised I was in a marriage with a man and his mother. She shudders. Now, if *that* doesn't make you an atheist, tell me what does. I'm not an atheist myself, well not exactly, but the thing with religion is that it takes commitment. Who has time for all that? Easy for my mother to go around criticising her faithless daughter, when *she* sits around all day with nothing to do. I work ten hours a day, five days a week. I don't even have time for myself, how do I make time for God?

There's a sudden commotion in front of the bus. The two black boys are scrambling off their seats in a big rush, as if they've missed their stop or changed their minds about where they want to get off or something. They are literally climbing on top of each other to get out, attracting all sorts of attention. The white woman is clutching her heart and making little gasping sounds. The man is patting her arm in a bid to try and calm her down. The boys stop momentarily at the top of the stairs, then disappear down them, their footsteps clattering noisily on the metal treads. There's the sound of someone yelling. Then, laughter, loud and irreverent. Two seconds later, Nora sees the boys jog across the street immediately in front of the bus, expertly weaving in and out of the rows of jammed cars. Death wish, Nora thinks, rolling her eyes.

The driver swears expletives into the microphone then promptly apologises for it, explaining that he had wrongly assumed he had turned the thing off, and the reason – in case anyone wanted to know – for his unexpected burst of emotion was on account of the two 'miscreants' who had pressed the emergency button above the rear doors and exited on a red light, which was, as we were all aware, a reckless and illegal act that could endanger not only their own lives but those of others.

There is a loud gasp of disapproval from the white lady. The white man shakes his head sadly and adjusts his hat and scarf, which are both woollen, even though it's the middle of August.

But at least I don't have boys, the Indian lady next to Nora says. Especially black boys. Heart-breaking to be the mother of a black boy these days. Everyone's scared of them. Don't even have to do anything for everyone to be scared of them.

Nora looks out of the window to see if she can still spot the two, but they've already gone, melted into the twilight.

TWELVE

She hears the sound of running behind her, footsteps making loud thumping noises that echo into the darkness.

This part of Boundary Road is badly lit.

Instinctively she places her hand over the opening of her cross-body bag, itself a kind of defence, for a thief would need to uncross it from her body in order to steal it, a difficult manoeuvre surely when compared to say what little is needed to make off with a handbag that dangles carelessly from someone's shoulder, half slipping off already, unwittingly aiding its own theft. It had happened to so many of her friends on this particular road, this kind of practised bag-theft. Didn't take much. A runner, a motorcyclist, a kid on a bike, everything gone before you even realise, money gone, keys gone, ID gone, thief gone, sleight of hand, so easy.

Nora quickens her stride. She can see the straight lines of the tower blocks silhouetted ahead.

From there, it's only another few yards to the entrance of the estate, a wide opening between two rows of gorse bushes which are currently covered in tiny yellow blooms that fill the air with the smell of coconut and lime. The council had planted them six months ago. So far, they have not been destroyed. In a way,

Nora thinks, this – just the fact of them being intact – represents something, a leap of faith or something.

A lone streetlight marks the turn-in. Across the road are a few shops, already closed this time of evening. Framers, opticians, Bruno's Deli, Perfect Dry Cleaners, nail salon, chemist. There used to be more shops along this row – the store fronts still exist, only now they've been shuttered, family businesses once thriving, now dead, having fought and failed, no match for the might of London rent.

Apart from Nora, there is no one about, not unusual for this part of town at this time of night. She has been warned many times about being mugged, what to do when she's mugged, how to behave, just give them everything, don't be stupid, don't fight. Not *if*, but *when*. It's not happened so far. The footsteps are catching up to her; she wonders if this is when her luck finally runs out.

But she's wrong. It's not her bag, nor thankfully her, that he's after – *they* – it's two of them, she sees them from the corner of her eye, behind her now, next to her now, passing her now. Now. Now. And now, in the split second of geographical propinquity when all three find themselves positioned relative to one another in the shape of a scalene triangle, that it dawns on her that they are the two from the bus. Forming the top of the triangle is the blue-eyed boy, those showy Nikes glowing bright fluorescent orange in the darkness; in line with her on the part of the pavement closest to the road is the other one, the one with the baby face. He is wearing his hood all the way over his head, but she recognises him, the long legs, the low-waist baggy jeans, the concave dip of his stomach where his sweatshirt rises as he runs. She wonders how they've managed to run all this way so fast. They had jumped out of the bus ages ago, impatiently at the red light like two badly behaved kids, she remembers the consternation they had caused the driver.

She'd only just got off the bus herself, no more than a few minutes ago, and here they are, overtaken her already.

At roughly this same time, it strikes her that there is something unusual about the way these boys are running. Something not quite right about the body language, the urgency in the motion of their stride. This isn't just two people running. No, it doesn't look like that at all. It looks like one is being chased. The one with the blue eyes is running away from the one behind him. Running *away*. She finds herself strangely unnerved by this realisation. A sudden breeze passes overhead, a scrunched-up piece of silver foil rolls forward noisily on the pavement. Somewhere, a fox barks.

Nora watches as the hooded boy catches up to his friend, running those last few strides with his arm extended. He grabs his shoulder, swivels him around. Their bodies come together – are they embracing? They are right in front of the entrance to the estate now, their conjoined bodies illuminated by the murky glow of the streetlamp. Nora catches the glint of something metallic and then the hooded boy reaches for the waist of those baggy jeans. A glimpse of dark brown skin and then he's gone, running into the darkness, not looking back.

In front of her she sees the other boy falling to the ground. He's falling as if in slow motion, with his hand out, as if to break the fall, but the hand slides and the fall is not broken. Oh fuck, she says, and begins to run. He is lying sideways on the pavement when she reaches him, his body resting on one arm, the other hand is on his stomach. His shirt is bright red.

Oh my God, oh my God, oh my God! she says. Help! Somebody! Help! she screams into the empty street. She's frantic. She's jumping. She is jumping. She's holding her hands to her own stomach and she's jumping up and down. Why is she jumping?

Help! she screams again – screeches. It is a sound that's hers but that she's never heard before, so loud and so insanely high, she feels her throat is going to tear on the inside. But the only reply is the familiar rumble of the West Coast Main Line carrying across the still night from somewhere behind her.

Okay, she says to herself, okay, okay. Deep breaths. Calm down. She kneels down on the pavement next to him. Because of it maybe, or maybe because it has nothing to do with her at all, he turns his body slowly, so slowly, as if even the smallest movement is too much effort. She recoils instinctively. Now his back is flat on the ground. He is holding his stomach with both hands. There is a pool of blood on the road from where he's moved, already turned dark red. She tries not to focus on it too much. On how much of it there is. A small noise comes from him, like a low rumbling groan. Then, nothing. Tentatively, she shuffles closer and crouches over him, her palms flat on his shoulders on either side of his head. What's your name? she says, who did this to you? Jesus! Who would do such a thing!

He is looking up at her with wide open eyes. Those eyes. Bright blue. The colour of the Mediterranean Sea on a summer's morning. They blink. That terrifies her, that action, but she knows too that it is good. Movement is good. *Any* movement. Inexplicably, she touches his face with a finger, tracing a line from the high bones of his cheek to his jaw. Nothing. She doesn't know what she expects, but she gets nothing. No pushback, no reaction; there is no expression on that face at all. It reminds her of the faces of the mannequins that stare back at you through shop windows, frozen in postures of drama and determination. She's always been creeped out by those shop mannequins, ever since she was a little girl, something about their unfinished, empty beauty.

Nora stands up again as if it's suddenly hit her what she needs to do. She reaches into her bag, pulls out her phone, then drops it promptly. It falls to the ground, glass on concrete. Stupid, stupid, she says, as she reaches down to pick it up, stupid hands. The screen is a spider's web of shattered glass, but the phone seems to still be working. She knows what she needs to do, it is simple really, one digit, three times, that's all but her hand is shaking so badly, it's not the phone, it's her fingers that are not working. Come on, she says out loud, you need to do this. Amazingly then, her index finger is obeying, pushing down on the number 9. Once. Twice. A third time.

There's... there's been a stabbing, she whispers when they answer.

She hears instructions. The voice on the other side is perfectly composed. It is asking her some questions, but mostly it's telling her what to do. For this, she is grateful. She needs to be told what to do. Stay calm, the voice instructs. Miss, I can see that you are very upset, but it's important to stay calm. Then other things, more practical things; thank God, she thinks, for more practical things: Does she know how to administer first aid? Is there anyone else around? Any shops open? Passers-by? We need you to stay there please. We have your location. Don't move. Don't move the victim. Don't tamper with the crime scene.

At one point they ask her to check if there is a pulse.

She takes her right hand and places two fingers on the side of his neck. She has seen it done this way in the movies. She had felt it, she had felt it! The steady rhythmic beat of lifesong. Yes, she says, feeling relief. Yes, I feel his pulse.

That's good, they say. Well done. We will be right there, they say. As soon as possible.

She turns to the boy. They will be right here, she repeats. As soon as possible. That's what they said. As soon as possible, they'll be here. Can you hear me?

The boy is looking at her now, intently, with those astonishing blue eyes; she feels like they are talking to her, trying to say something, but she cannot understand what. He opens his mouth; it stays open like that.

She crouches over him again on all fours as if the mere proximity of their bodies will enable some of the life in hers to pass to his. Who did this? Who did this to you? she asks again, shaking his shoulders. She is touching him, her touch is not light, maybe she is even hurting him she thinks, so why isn't he screaming from that open mouth, why isn't he telling her to stop, why isn't he overpowering her with his superior strength and pushing her hands off his shoulders. She wants him to. She wants him to look at her with indignation, with anger. She wants him to throw her body off his own, forcefully, so she loses balance and falls to the ground. She wants him to yell at her: What the fuck you think you doing. Why you touching me in that way. Get your damn hands off me. Get off me, bitch.

But he doesn't do any of that no matter how much she tries to provoke him.

Their bodies are so close. She has never touched a stranger's body in this intimate way. But he isn't reacting, he isn't responding. He's just staring at her. How is this happening, she thinks in sudden horror. How is this even happening? Is this real? How is she in this place? How is he? How are they? For one bizarre moment she wonders if she should pray. Surely if there was any time it needed to work, this was that time. Surely. It's a prayer she learned in school, the school she went to when she lived with Claudia. She's never repeated it since, not once; she still remembers the words.

Our father who art in heaven, she prays, *hallowed be thy name… Why did you put me in this shit?*

Oh mate, she pleads. Stay with me. Just stay with me. Talk to me… Oh God, I don't even know your name! I'm Nora, look, I'm Nora. Who are you, who are you, what's your name?

Above them the streetlight flickers, but when she looks up, she realises it's not the lamp at all. A pair of giant moths hover around the light, dancing, casting shadows. Creating the illusion of a malfunctioning bulb.

But you're only a kid, she says out loud, as if the fact of this has just dawned on her.

She thinks she hears a sound then and looks up, across the street, but there's no one. On the shuttered storefront between the deli and the chemist, she sees the colourful manifestation of urban desolation – the words 'Leo loves Talia' spray-painted in neon green. 'Love' is represented by a bright pink heart. Below that, different words by a different hand, spray-painted in black: Fuck you! Nobody Cares!

Nobody cares. She mouths the words out under her breath. Does anybody care? she says aloud.

He moves suddenly, it is the only motion he has made since he turned on his back, as if the absurdity of the question has compelled him to respond to it. His torso heaves enormously, clearing off the ground as if it has been administered some kind of electric shock, then flops back down heavily at the same time as she hears the shriek of the siren.

She jerks her head back, turning around to see if she can spot them. She cannot and yet the absolute knowledge that the sound provides fills her with relief, a sound that even ten minutes ago would have been loud and loathsome, causing her to clap her hands over her ears, is now music, pure music – they're here, just like they promised, they're here.

They're here! she yells, still staring down the empty road. Look, they're here, they're here!

When she looks back down at him, she is confused by what she sees. But how can this be? She frowns. Why are you doing this? They're here! They're going to save you. Don't you believe me? Damn you, don't you believe me?

But Aron done believing.

His face is closed. His eyes are open. Bright blue and unspeakably beautiful. The ambulance arrives now, bathing the perimeter of Boundary Road in deep cobalt blue.

Acknowledgements

To Tom Dawson, for proposing I create a novel that ends in the middle.

To Aaron Goldberg, for that passing observation that Nora is Aron spelled backwards.

To the beautiful dark-skinned boy with the blue eyes on Oxford Street; I couldn't take my eyes off you. Nor, it seems, my mind.

To John Nutter, who taught me football in a classroom.

To the talented, young footballers of North London, who taught me football on the ground.

To the housekeeping staff at a certain London hotel, for giving me a tour of the guest bathrooms.

To Barbara Davis, for explaining the workings of the foster care system in this country. To Sandie Banks, foster parent, extraordinary human, for the incredible insight and experience.

To Denise, Conda and the fam in Antigua, for local knowledge.

To my usual gyaldem for reading, discussing, critiquing. So grateful.

To Geoff, for reading literally everything I write. Invaluable, irreplaceable, inexplicable.

To Laurence Cole for such conscientious editing. To Holly Ovenden for a creating a cover I love.

To my kids for riding the Number 13 up and down with me more times than I can remember. Also, for accompanying me to countless housing developments in North-West London. Always with a smile. Every mum should be so lucky.

To Mikka, for giving Aron and Nora the space to exist.

To Sid, for giving me the space to exist.

Thank you.

AMI RAO